In loving memory of Patricia (Na...

Acknowledgements:

A massive thank you to my husband Chris, and friends Chrissie Richardson, Vicky Husted, Charlotte Smith, Chloe Rosser, Kathy Murray and Gary and Peter Cooksley.

Not only for believing in me but also for giving me the constructive criticism I need.

Dedications:

To everyone who has supported me, believed in me and encouraged me throughout my attempts of becoming a self-published author.

To my mummy, Claire Attfield, who is the strongest and most inspirational woman I know. Without whom, I would not be half the person I am today.

To my biggest fan, Janet Finch. I promise to sign this copy for you.

Part 1

0

It's cold today. The wind is picking up and the sky is bright white. There's been mention of snow coming but then again, they always say this on the weather channels, and it never comes. It's definitely cold enough for it though. My arms are folded, and I pull them closer into my chest and peek down at my watch, twenty past three. I let out a sigh. School is meant to finish at quarter past, but his teacher always lets them out late. You would think after spending a whole day with thirty 5 to 6-year-olds that she would want to get rid of them as quickly as possible but apparently not. I always arrive early, something I pride myself on, but on days like today when it's so cold I wish I had spent a bit more time in my car with the heater on before braving the playground.

I look over to my right as I hear the word "dead" coming from one of the other mums to the side of me. There, huddled together, are three of the other mothers. Rachel, Alison and another mum who's name I've yet to learn, probably because I don't care enough. Rachel's the one speaking and I crane my neck slightly to get a better chance of hearing exactly what's being said.

"They found him just now in his shop, they don't know what's happened yet, but it definitely seems a bit suspicious doesn't it. I saw the ambulance driving away just before I parked up by the school a minute ago" Rachel is saying.

1

So, I should probably go back to the beginning. This is all new to me. Before all this started, I was just your average housewife. I work part time from home doing admin work, data entry and the like and my husband Tim works full time as a doctor at the local University hospital. He's a Pediatric surgeon so works long days and long hours and is frequently on call so he's not around much and we have a 6-year-old son called Sam. My life was the pretty standard routine-based day to day that I expect most women in their late 30's experience. Every morning is the battle of the school run, getting Sam up and out of bed and ready for school. I then come home to do some work, followed by the household chores, maybe a bit of yoga. Then it's back to the school run to then complete the nighttime routines of dinner, bath and bed. Day in and day out, nothing really changes, just the date on the calendar. Don't get me wrong, I don't have a bad life and I could never complain. I have a beautiful house, a loving hard-working husband, a well-behaved son, but where is my own identity? I'm mum, wife, admin clerk, but who is Chrissie? What can Chrissie do that no-one else can do? What's special about me? Not a lot really. I wonder if a lot of people feel this way or if most people are simply happy with the day-to-day grind? Sure, I can better myself, learn a new skill, get more fit, maybe run a marathon. I took up calligraphy for a bit, but as therapeutic as it was, it still just seemed somewhat pointless. That's not to say that killing

"How many is that now?" asks Alison. "I'm pretty sure that brings us up to three deaths now." Rachel responds.

The third mum gasps, "You don't think maybe they are all related in some way?"

I'm trying to not look too conspicuous, and I lean to the side even further to continue listening. I don't have the type of relationship with these women where I can just interject into their conversation, but I want to know more about what they are saying. How much do they know and how do they know so much so quickly? Two of the three deaths they are speaking about only happened within the last twenty-four hours. But then it's a small village, word does tend to travel fast around here, and this is the most exciting thing to have happened here since the new leisure center was opened two years ago.

I see Rachel look around the playground before locking eyes with me. "If they are all related, then we have a serial killer on the loose" she states to the woman beside her. I smile at Rachel and wave; she can't know that I've been listening to their conversation surely and even if she did, who wouldn't be considering the topic. I avert my gaze as Rachel goes back to speaking to the other mums and brings my focus to the classroom door which is just about to open to let the children out for the day. I need to maintain my composure; no-one would ever suspect me. I'm just another school mum, doing the school run, I'm certainly not a serial killer, well not in their eyes an people then became my new hobby as such. I kind of just fell into it really and then it may have spiraled a bit out of control. But I'm getting ahead of myself.

Maeve lived directly across the road from me in a small bungalow. She's lived there for years and years and was one of the first neighbours I ever met when we moved into our house five years ago. She's an amazing woman, or I guess I should say was an amazing woman. In her late eighties and sharp as a tack. I'd pop in to see her two to three times a week when Sam was still at school, and we would chat about the good old days. She'd tell me all about her ex-husband who ran off with her sister, leaving her to raise their children alone. She was a strong woman, had worked all her life as a seamstress and was physically fit until about a year ago when she was diagnosed with terminal lung cancer. She had known for a while that something was wrong, she was getting more and more breathless doing everyday things that she had previously had no issues doing and was so tired all the time. But Maeve, like many of her generation, was as stubborn as a mule and just put her symptoms down to the aging process, not getting checked out until it was too late. And this stubbornness was why I knew I couldn't say no to her when she asked me to help her to die.

Maeve had been suffering for a while. Her cancer had progressed very quickly, and she had reached the point of not being able to do very much for herself easily at all. She had been offered carers to come in and support her, but she had refused this help, being too proud, so I would help her with anything I could whenever I went round to see her. I'd help her get washed and dressed and do some housework for her, but she always hated that she couldn't do any of it herself. Towards the end she was on full-time oxygen therapy and was essentially bedbound, being unable to get up and about to care for herself at all.

"I've had enough Chrissie; you've got to help me put an end to this please." She said to me the other day. I laughed it off, like I always did, as this wasn't the first time she had said this to me, and I doubted it would be the last. "I mean it this time Chrissie, what life do I have now? I'm laid up here in bed, can barely breathe, hooked up to this oxygen tank all the time. I'm nothing but a burden on you, and my kids and grandkids barely visit."

"You're not a burden on me!" I exclaimed. "You know I love you and coming to see you and if the tables were turned you would be doing all this for me, I'm sure."

"But the tables aren't turned are they Chrissie. You come over here and see me and help me out so much but then you get to go back to whatever it is you want to do. I don't have that. I lay here, day in and day out, just waiting for visitors who sit and watch me struggle. I hate it. I've not got long left anyway and I've had a good life, I don't want it to end like this. I could be stuck like this for weeks or months, please let it just be over now." She paused for breath between every sentence.

"What are you saying?" I asked her, knowing full well what she was asking of me.

"You know what I'm saying Chrissie. It's time. I'm ready to go and I need your help to do it because I'm not strong enough to do it on my own. I need you to end this for me now." She pointed her hand towards the small fridge in the corner of her bedroom where she kept her insulin medication. "That's the way we should do it. Pump me full of my insulin, it will be quick and painless."

I looked over at the fridge and then back at Maeve. There was a pleading look of desperation in her eyes that I had never seen before. She had always been a strong woman to me, even in this state, unable to move around or breathe without oxygen, she was still the strongest person I'd ever met. But she didn't look strong anymore. She was done and I knew it. I thought for a second about how I would feel in this situation, if I would want to live like this and the answer was of course, no. No-one would want this life.

"You've done so much for me Chrissie, you've kept me sane the last few months, kept me clean and presentable, cooked for me, cleaned for me. You have been my guardian angel during the worst times of my life. But now I need you to be my angel in death. Help me this one last time."

I looked around the bedroom, taking in a lifetime of memories of this woman laid in front of me. Photographs on the walls of smiling children and babies, mementos from holidays and travels adorning the dresser. Maeve had lived her life and she had lived it well, working hard to provide for her family after being left by her husband. Never having contact with her sister again or having another relationship herself. When her children became adults themselves, she decided to live life to its fullest and she travelled to anywhere she could afford to go, spending time hiking across Europe and driving through the United States. She had found ways to afford almost anything on her shoestring budget. Having lived such a full life to then end up as this shell in front of me, I could understand why this is not how she wanted it to end. But sometimes these choices are not in our control. She may not be able to decide how she dies, but she has certainly decided when and she wants this to be now.

"Are you sure?" I murmured, not quite believing that I was contemplating her request.

"I've never been surer of anything in my life" she responded.

I slowly made my way over to the mini fridge and bent down to open the door. Inside were boxes of what I assumed were her insulin pens as well as a few cans of fizzy drink and a bar of chocolate. "You can have the chocolate if you make this quick" she laughed softly.

There were three boxes stacked on top of each other on one of the shelves and I pulled out the top one which was already open. Inside the box were two pens labelled Humulin U-500. I took one out and brought it over to Maeve's bedside, handing her the pen.

"There's some needles on the cabinet next to the fridge." She stated, pointing over to where a box of needles laid. I walked over to grab one, opened it up and handed this to Maeve also. I watched her expertly pull the lid off the pen before twisting the needle onto it. She then removed the cover of the lid and then a further inner thinner cap, revealing the shine of the needle.

"What do you need me to do." I asked, hoping that there wasn't much more than providing her with the implements that she needed. She slowly lifted her t-shirt, revealing her stomach.

"I need you to do the injection for me." She stated matter of fact. "I've tried to do it myself several times, but I've always lost my nerve. I need you to do it for me so I can't lose my nerve again."

"If you haven't been able to do it yourself, maybe it's because you don't really want me to do it" I responded, hoping that this could be my opportunity to change her mind.

"I know this is a big ask of you Chrissie, but I really need this. There's no going back now for me, I can't go on like this. I'm ready." She then began to twist the bottom dial of the pen, click, click, click, click. With every click I felt a pang of dread in my heart. I wasn't familiar with insulin, but I could tell by the look in her eyes that she was turning the dial much further than she normally would. Click, click, click. The clicking felt like it went on forever, but eventually it stopped. I looked down at the dial and read the number 300. "I need you to put this needle into my stomach and then press down on the end of the pen until you can't press down any further. There should be enough insulin in here now to kill me."

"Don't you take insulin everyday though? Are you sure there's enough there that you won't just become really ill?" I enquired, worry beginning to set in. What if it doesn't work and she ends up worse off than she is now? What if she survives and tells someone what I did?

"You don't need to worry Chrissie; I inject 10 units of this insulin a day and I've now set this to 300 units. There is no way I will survive this amount. Now, take this needle, do as I've said and then make sure you leave the pen with me so it looks like I did it to myself and there's no suspicion that anyone else could have been involved. Once you've done it, I will go to sleep and not wake up."

She handed me the pen, one hand securely holding onto her T-shirt that she was still holding up to reveal her stomach to me and then she took a deep breath. "I'm ready" she stated.

"Is there nothing else you want to do or say before I do this?" I asked, hoping for some type of delay for what I had somehow inadvertently agreed to without actually agreeing to it.

She sighed "This isn't a TV series, the longer we prolong this the worse this is getting for me. Please just do it and do it quickly. I've told you I'm ready. I'm sorry for this Chrissie, but I really appreciate you and I love you and I hope you have the best life; I really do." With that she put her head back further into her pillow and closed her eyes.

The time appeared to have come. I looked down at the pen in my hand which was shaking. I took a deep breath. This is it, I thought to myself, I either do this now or I let her down. Before I could overthink it further, I plunged the needle into her stomach, just below and to the right of her belly button. I pressed the button at the top of the pen, feeling minimal resistance against my thumb. I then removed the pen, seeing a small drop of blood trickle out from where the needle had been. I rubbed the blood away with a corner of her t-shirt, covering her stomach back over.

"Thank you, Chrissie," she whispered. I pulled her duvet cover over her, held her cheek in my hand and leant down to kiss her forehead. "Sleep well Maeve" I whispered back.

I could feel tears begin to roll down my cheeks as I stood there over her body, watching her chest rise and fall, knowing this was likely to stop at any point. The more I watched the more I realised that I couldn't be here to see her chest stop moving. I wasn't sure if she was still awake or not, but she looked peaceful, so I didn't want to disturb her either way.

I began to walk out of the room, turning round at the doorway to blow her a kiss before then leaving the bungalow and returning back to my own home, where I cried until I had to go pick Sam up from school. But then it was back to the routine, there was no more time for tears, no more time to think about what had just happened. A brave face was needed to be returned to, I couldn't show any upset now, I needed to pretend as if everything was normal. I have to pretend that I don't know that Maeve is probably dead now or that I had anything to do with that. So, I put on my coat, grabbed my car keys and took one last wipe of my eyes and as I locked the front door behind me and walked across the driveway to my car, I realised that I was getting back into the routine more quickly and easily than what I should be and that putting on the brave face was almost natural.

2

The next day I was surprised to still not feel too bad about what had occurred. I woke up with my alarm at 7am as usual, got myself up and dressed and then proceeded to get Sam washed, dressed and ready for school. I completed the usual mundane tasks that I do every morning, I brushed my teeth for two minutes without thinking about anything in particular, I made breakfast for Sam without having a second thought of the day before. It wasn't until I was completing the drive to do the school drop off, driving on autopilot, that I suddenly thought about Maeve and wondered if the insulin had done as she had wanted it to. I really hoped so. The idea of her still being alive but now maybe feeling very sick or in pain wasn't a nice thought, but she was confident that her plan would work so I had to believe that she was right.

I walked Sam to his classroom door after parking my car on a side street next to the school. When the teacher opened the door to let the children in, I leant down to give him a cuddle and wish him a good day. "Love you mum" he shouted as he ran into the classroom.- I waved to the back of his head as he ran through the door and turned to say hello to a familiar mum's face as I headed back to the car.

As I was about to get into the driver's side which was closest to the road, a car came speeding up, almost hitting a car parked a bit further down and causing me to jump back between my car and the car parked in front of me.

"Jesus Christ!" I screamed as I watched the car continue to careen down the road. What was this guy playing at?! This is a quiet side road in a small estate right next to a primary school, he could easily have killed someone the way he was driving. The more I thought about it, the more I saw red and before I knew it, I had jumped in my car and proceeded to follow the speeding silver BMW.

It didn't take long for me to catch up with him, he had needed to stop at some traffic lights just round the corner from where he had almost run me over. I leaned forward in my car seat trying to get a better look at the driver. I knew it was a male, but I wasn't sure if he was older or younger. As the traffic lights turned from red to orange, the BMW screeched off at top speed again. It couldn't get very far, it was nearly 9am at this point, the peak of rush hour, which even in our small village, did result in traffic. The BMW kept swerving onto the other side of the road, clearly in a rush and looking for opportunities to potentially overtake the cars in front of him that were preventing him from being able to put his foot down any further. No luck for him though, the traffic continued steadily all the way along the various roads he took and to which I followed. I kept a small distance between us so that he wasn't aware that I was following him, not that I think he would have noticed, even if I was right up behind his car, as he seemed completely focused on where he was going and getting there as quickly as he could.

After about ten minutes, he suddenly pulled into a secondary school car park and into a parking space. I pulled into the school car park behind him but went to park my car in a space further away, so as not to be noticeable. I watched him jump out of the car, grabbing a briefcase from his passenger seat and then walked quickly into the school building. I managed to get a good look at him as he paced past my car, but he didn't look at me, his eyes appeared fixed at the school building straight ahead of him. He was a plain looking man. Dark hair with wisps of grey and thinning at the top, round spectacles perching on his nose. He must have been in his forties, about 6 foot tall, relatively slim but with a pot belly protruding out from the checkered shirt he wore, one too many beers of an evening perhaps.

As I watched him enter the building and out of my eyesight, I came to the realisation of what I had just done. Why had I followed him? What had I achieved from this? If I had intended to confront him for his poor driving, I had missed my chance now as he's gone into what I'm assuming is his place of work. I could have gotten out of the car and confronted him before he went inside but I didn't. I also could have called the police whilst he was driving to report him, but again I didn't. I turned the engine of my car back on and drove home, thinking to myself the whole way back about the man in the checkered shirt with the pot belly and his need for speed.

Once home, it was time for me to start work. I set myself up in my office, fresh cup of coffee to the side of me and opened my laptop up. I had a string of emails to attend to as well as numerous data files that I knew needed organising this morning, but work didn't seem to be able to keep my attention. My mind was elsewhere, thinking about the events of the morning.

I opened a google search on my laptop and typed in the name of the secondary school I had parked up in this morning, "Semberton High School". I wasn't going to be able to focus on my work until I knew more about this man. I needed to scratch this itch before I could get on with my day. The school's home page opened up on my laptop screen, a large picture of a school crest with some smiling students underneath it. There was a menu bar at the top of the webpage which I clicked on and scrolled down to where it stated, "Meet the Team". Within this next page were numerous pictures of smiling faces, men and women of all different ages, with their names and roles within the school underneath. I scrolled down the page until I saw a picture of the face I had studied this morning. "Mr. Turner, Geography Teacher" was written underneath. Mr. Turner...... so now I know your surname, your profession, what car you drive and where you work. I still didn't know what I intended to do with this information or why this mattered so much to me, but I knew there was nothing more to be gained from Google at this point and therefore proceeded to close the webpage down and tried to get some work done.

Before long, work was completed. I had also done a 30-minute yoga session and I had walked the dog. Now it was time to pick Sam up from school. As I drove the familiar roads to the primary school, I thought about Mr. Turner again, who for the most part I had forgotten about for most of the afternoon whilst completing my usual day-to-day activities. I picked Sam up from his usual classroom door, said hello to the usual mums I say hello to with the odd bit of chit-chat here and there and got back in the car, ready to drive home with Sam in the back. It was then that I realised, if Mr. Turner was a teacher, he was likely to be finishing work soon and I can see how he drives home, when he's not in a rush.

I pulled away from the curb and proceeded to drive the way I had done this morning when following his speeding BMW. "Where are we going Mum" Sam asked from the back of the car, after having realised that we were not heading in the direction of home.

"I've just got a quick few errands to run before we head home buddy" I responded, whilst not taking my eyes off the road. "Ugh mum I want to go home and watch You-Tube" he groaned. "We won't be long" I quickly retorted and continued to make my way to the secondary school.

Just as I was coming up to the road the school was on, there he was, driving his BMW towards us on the opposite side of the road. He didn't appear to be in as much of a rush this afternoon and was sticking to the speed limit. As his car became parallel with mine, I looked across at him and he appeared to have a big smile on his face. I wonder what's gotten him so chipper after his road rage this morning. Must have had a good day at work.

I turned my car around in the nearest side street and proceeded to follow him back down the road we had come. Sam didn't appear to notice our U-turn or if he did, he didn't say anything. I looked into the back in my rear-view mirror, and he was looking down into his lap, fiddling with a toy he had found in the back of the car. I looked ahead, up the road, searching for his car but there were several cars in front of me now. I wondered if I had lost him. But as I continued along the road, I suddenly saw him turn into a side street a few cars ahead. Bingo. I followed along the side street and saw him pull over to the side of the road. I had stayed back again to be inconspicuous, so I too then pulled over, about 100 meters away from where he was parked. He didn't get out of the car, just sat there, the engine still running. I turned my engine off. I wasn't sure how long we would be sat here for, but I thought my car may be more easily spotted if the engine was on.

"Where are we?" Sam suddenly asked. "Oh, I'm just waiting for an important phone call for work, so I've pulled over. I can't answer the phone properly when I'm driving so, I thought I would be safe and just wait for the call." Sam huffed from the back of the car, but he seemed to accept my explanation.

We waited for what felt like forever, but in reality, was probably only about five minutes. I then saw a young girl in Semberton school uniform get into the front passenger seat of his car. That's odd, I thought. If that is his daughter and he teaches at her school, why didn't they both get the car together to go home from the school car park? Why would she want to walk all this way to get a lift home with her Dad? Something wasn't adding up. After a few more minutes his car pulled away from the side of the road and I quickly started my car back up and proceeded to follow again.

"What about your phone call Mum?" Sam asked as we continued down the road. "They've just sent me a text to say they are going to call in a little bit, so I'll keep driving for now." I replied.

We drove through several roads until we reached the motorway. I followed him on the slip road and onto the motorway, heading southbound. I continued to follow, leaving a few cars between us so as not to be noticed until he pulled off at a service station about 10 miles down the road.

It was quite a large service station and as well as there being the usual petrol station, small selection of shops, takeaways and a drive through Starbucks, there was also a Premier Inn hotel. He pulled his car into a parking space near the hotel, rather than near to the shops and I parked up in a space a bit further down, next to a bright yellow Mini. I leaned forward in my seat as far as I could to try and get a good look into his car. It was difficult to see much other than the shadows of the two people sitting in the car but even from where I was sat, I could see that they appeared to be kissing. I knew something was off, clearly this was not his daughter but instead likely a student of his that he is taking advantage of. I could feel the rage beginning to build up inside me as I watched him get out of the car, leaving the young girl sitting in the passenger seat. He proceeded to walk into the Premier Inn on his own and I didn't see him return to the car. I waited a further ten minutes before noticing the girl got out of the car and head towards the entrance of the hotel also. This time I was able to get a good look at her. She couldn't have been much older than thirteen. She was fresh-faced, no make-up on and her long blonde hair was tied up in a high ponytail on her head. She looked nervous as she walked towards the hotel entrance, her hands clasped tightly together in front of her. I felt sick imagining what was about to happen in that hotel room, but what could I do? I couldn't intervene without making myself known to them both and I didn't want to be involved, well not in any way that identifies me. I can make him stop in other ways I'm sure but what could I do right now?

"I've just got to run into the shops quick and get something", I said to Sam who was staring at me, clearly bewildered as to why we had parked up in a service station, not particularly close to home and then continued to sit in the car. "My phone is about to ring any second and I need some privacy so I will run into the shop and take the call outside, you wait here, and I will get you a treat whilst I'm at it for being so patient." At the mention of a treat Sam's eyes widened and he smiled at me. "Ok mum".

I got out of the car, picking my phone up from the center console where I stored it. I took a slow walk towards the shops, whilst googling the phone number for the premier inn and pressing the call button once found. "Hello there, I'm just calling because I wanted to raise a concern" I began to say to the receptionist who answered the call. "I've just seen a man go into your hotel and a young girl joined him shortly afterwards. It might be nothing, but they didn't look like father and daughter if you catch my drift so just wanted to make you aware incase anything untoward was happening." The receptionist appeared to take note of what I was saying before asking if I could provide any further details and asking for my name. "I wish to remain anonymous thank you, but the girl was wearing a school uniform and the gentleman only checked in about ten to fifteen minutes ago so hopefully you will have an idea from your system who I'm referring to, thank you for your help" I stated before hanging up the call.

I then walked quickly into the shop, grabbed a bar of dairy milk chocolate off the shelf and paid for it before returning to the car and handing it to Sam.

"Why are we here Mum?" he asked whilst tearing the wrapper off his treat.

"I've been told that this petrol station has the cheapest fuel at the moment, and I needed to fill the car up" I thought aloud quickly. If I had told this lie to any adult who drove a car, they would know immediately that what I had said was fishy; a service station having the cheapest fuel would never happen. But luckily, little white lies like this tend to go over the head of most 6-year-olds. I restarted the car and pulled into the petrol station where luckily, I only needed to put in quarter of a tank before it was back to full again and I didn't need to pay a fortune to fill the whole car up.

We then headed back home, all the while my mind being on Mr. Turner. So, he's not only a road racing menace that puts people at risk when he's running late for work, but he's also most likely a pedophile too. What a disgusting human this man is, the dregs of society. Taking a position in a school where he can gain easy access to vulnerable young girls. The more I thought about it, the angrier I became. My thoughts flitted back to Maeve again, poor Maeve having to get help to end her own life because cancer ravaged her body. Poor Maeve who had done nothing but work hard and care for her family and then you get people like Mr. Turner who are worse than the cancer that was killing Maeve, who probably has a clean bill of health. Life is so unfair sometimes. But then again, does it have to be? I know what Mr. Turner's big secret is now, I know what he's up to and I can do something about it. I just need to figure out what that something is going to be.

3

And that was all I thought about. What I could do to exact my revenge on Mr. Turner. To make sure that he was never a risk to any other young girl again. I had thought about it all night. I had thought about it whilst making breakfast, whilst getting Sam ready for school and whilst doing the school run. Work had suffered yet again as my thoughts remained on Mr. Turner. I'd best not make a pattern of this, or my boss will start to wonder why my productivity has suddenly dropped.

I went into the kitchen and flicked the kettle on. Whilst doing so my gaze lingered out the window in front of me and saw a large black van parked outside Maeve's house. Private Ambulance was written across the side of it. Oh god, she's been found and clearly her plan had worked. I stared out of the window at the van for what felt like hours, transfixed at what was happening outside, before my trance was interrupted by the kettle clicking off, indicating that it had boiled.

What am I supposed to do now? Do I go over there? Do I pretend like I've not noticed? I could see other neighbours looking out of their windows or standing in their doorways. Of course they are, nosey bastards. None of them had given Maeve the time of day before but now there's something for them to gossip about with their other halves over dinner later. I can't pretend like I've not noticed surely. Everyone in the cul-de-sac knows that I work from home and that I'm friends with Maeve, it would probably look more suspicious if I didn't go over.

I grabbed a pair of trainers and quickly shoved my feet into them before jogging gently over the road. Her front door was open. There was a car on the driveway that I knew belonged to one of her relatives, but I could never remember whose car was which, mostly because they so seldom came to visit, I rarely saw their cars. There was also a police car on the other side of the private ambulance, hidden behind where I hadn't been able to see from my kitchen window. My heart skipped a beat. Why are the police here? Do they know something is amiss? Do they suspect that Maeve didn't do this intentionally herself or that it wasn't her cancer that killed her? I took a deep breath before walking through the front door.

"Chrissie!" cried out a somewhat familiar voice. I looked across the living room to see Maeve's niece Kathy sat on the sofa, a male police officer sat beside her with a notepad in his hand. Kathy's hands were clinging onto a mug that was balanced on her knee, the police officer didn't seem to have been offered anything to drink, or if he had, he had declined.

"Kathy what's happened? Where's Maeve?" I asked, quickly walking straight into the living room, not daring to glance towards the bedroom at the opposite side of the bungalow.

"Can I ask who you are Madam?" The police office addressed me before Kathy could respond.

"I'm sorry officer, my name's Chrissie. I live across the road and saw the ambulance. I'm a friend of Maeve's." I responded. I looked around the living room, nothing was out of place from the last time I was here, but then it wouldn't be would it.

"She's my aunt's carer too." Kathy stated as she stood up and rushed over to give me a hug. "She's gone, Chrissie. I found her this morning in bed, pale as anything and stone cold to the touch." Her grasp around me tightened as she said the last part.

I let out a small gasp. I was going to have to play the part of my life now so as not to arouse any suspicions. "Oh my gosh!" I exclaimed and pulled away from Kathy to put my hands over my mouth as if in shock.

"You're her carer?" The police officer interjected. Of course he was going to focus on that. For goodness sake Kathy, why did you have to mention that I was caring for her. He's going to want to ask me more questions now, isn't he? "When did you last see her then?" He continued.

"Oh, erm, let me think." I stammered. I should have thought about this before I came over! Why didn't I? Now I'm well and truly on the spot. I can't say it was only two days ago because they can tell the exact time people die now, can't they? But then what if they decide to speak to the neighbours and someone saw me going into her house? "Oh gosh, I'm sorry, this is all very sudden I think I'm in shock."

"Take a seat and just take your time." The police officer said gently, beckoning towards the armchair across from the sofa where they were sat. I perched onto the edge of the chair and put my head into my hands. I took a few deep breaths, giving myself a few extra seconds to think.

"I didn't come in to see her yesterday so it must have been the day before." I said. "I usually pop in a few times a week to see her, usually in the mornings and then I can help her with getting dressed or doing some housework if she needs me to."

"Right, right" the police officer mumbled as he began scribbling into his notepad. "And how was she when you saw her the day before yesterday? Did you get her dressed?"

"Erm, no she said she wasn't feeling well and wanted to stay in bed. So, I did a few errands round the house for her and just let her sleep and then I went back home." I replied.

"Did she look more unwell than usual when you saw her? Or did she say anything to make you think that she may have required any additional medical help?" He enquired whilst maintaining direct eye contact with me.

"To be honest, I didn't really think much of it. She's been so unwell for so long now. She seems to have more days than not where she prefers to stay in bed and not want to do anything. She has lung cancer you see, so everything she did made her feel so unwell that she preferred not to do very much most of the time. I didn't see the point in pushing her to get washed or dressed when she would just end up back in bed anyway and feeling worse for it."

The police officer nodded and appeared to accept what I was saying to him.

"Where is Maeve?" I asked, looking between Kathy and the police officer.

"I found her in bed this morning. The coroners had just taken her into the van before you arrived. I believe they will be leaving shortly; I think there's something they said I had to sign first. Did you want to see her before they leave? I can ask if it's ok." She asked me.

"No, no" I retorted quickly before slowing my speech down so as not to be too abrupt. "I'd rather just remember her as she was thank you."

The police officer stood up from the sofa then and crossed over to the living room door. "There's not much more that is needed from us at present" he said, looking at Kathy. "It's routine for us to attend when someone dies at home and for us to support the coroners. I'm very sorry for your loss."

He took one last look at us both before letting himself out of the house. We both sat in silence for a few minutes, neither one of us knowing what to say to the other until the sound of the police car was heard driving away. I thought about how I would be able to make an excuse to leave without looking uncaring towards Kathy. What do you do in these situations? How long are we expected to stay here for? Surely Kathy won't be staying too long now, especially once the coroners leave. I could hear little sniffles coming from Kathy and the sound of what I assumed were van doors shutting. My mind thought back momentarily to Mr. Turner. Even in this current situation he hadn't fully left my thoughts. It's a shame he can't be as easy to dispose of as how easy it was for me to help Maeve end her life. A quick injection to end it all, probably a nicer way than Mr. Turner deserved, that's for sure.

My train of thought was suddenly interrupted by a man standing in the lounge doorway. He was a large man, must have been over six foot and was as wide as he was tall. "Sorry to bother you ladies" he spoke softly, not the voice that was expected to come out of this giant of a man, "we are pretty much ready to leave now, just need to go over some paperwork with the next of kin."

"I guess that would be me then" Kathy stated, getting up from the sofa and beckoning for the man to follow her into the kitchen.

I was left alone in the living room now, back to my thoughts of how I can escape this current situation but more so about Mr. Turner. What if it was as easy as it was with Maeve? It might not be that easy to get close to inject him, but if all I needed to do was get the insulin in him once I had figured out how to do it then it was an easy way to get rid of him. Wouldn't make any mess, wouldn't require needing to overpower him. It's the best solution.

I got up from the chair and began walking towards the bedroom. I knew Maeve still had insulin left because I had seen it all in her fridge. I passed the open kitchen doorway where the coroner and Kathy were both hunched over some paperwork on the kitchen countertop, neither one of them paying any attention in my direction as I sneaked past and went straight into the bedroom.

It was odd to see Maeve's bed empty. I couldn't remember the last time I had seen her properly out of bed without me physically assisting her to be. The sheets were strewn all over the place, clearly just thrown out of the way to be able to get her body out of the room. I could feel tears begin to stream down my cheeks and I swallowed them back quickly. Now isn't the time to mourn, I need to be quick before anyone sees me and wonders what I'm doing. I ran over to the mini fridge and grabbed the remaining pen from the open box and quickly shoved it in my pocket. I grabbed a handful of needles from the box on top of the cabinet next to it and chucked them into my pocket also.

"Thank you so much for everything" I heard Kathy say from the hallway. I quickly ran out of the bedroom which was just around the corner of the hall, as was the bathroom and joined Kathy and the man who were now stood outside the kitchen. Kathy looked at me with a questioning glance before shaking the man's hand. The man did a small bow before us and then headed out the front door, closing it behind him.

"What are you doing?" Kathy asked me, clearly curious as to where I had just come from considering she had left me sitting in the living room.

"Oh, I just went to the toilet to wash my face quickly, from the crying." I responded quickly, which she appeared to accept. "Well, I suppose I had better head back home; I'm meant to be working currently and I've not told anyone at work that I was going away from my desk."

"Oh, uh, yes of course." Kathy stuttered. "I had best start making some phone calls, let the relatives know anyway."

"You know where I am if you need me, Kathy. I'm so sorry for your loss." I gave her a quick hug before heading towards the door. I heard a big sigh from behind me. I wasn't sure if that was a sigh of relief that I was leaving or if she had started to cry again but I didn't turn back to see. The insulin pen was burning a hole in my pocket and all I wanted to do was get home as quickly as I could and hide it somewhere that no-one would accidentally find it. As I closed the front door behind me and walked towards my own house, I felt a wave of relief hit me. No-one seemed suspicious of me at all and if they were, they certainly didn't make it clear. I don't think anyone is going to think anything is amiss and they won't do an autopsy surely, considering she had terminal cancer. The only thing I needed to think about now was how I was going to be able to use this insulin on Mr. Turner, but first and foremost, where to hide it whilst I figured that out.

4

I spent the next few weeks on a secret mission to figure out how and when I could get to Mr. Turner without being detected. I had been secretly following him at every given opportunity that I had to find out as much information about the man as I could and to say that I had quickly become obsessed would have been an understatement. If my husband Tim was home to look after Sam, I would find an excuse to go out to continue my reconnaissance mission. I would tell him that I needed to pop to the shops to get some bits for dinner and would conveniently bump into a friend and end up chatting for a while or that I was going to drive to the local country park to go for a long run. Sometimes I'd take the dog in the car with me to pretend that I was taking him to the beach or the dog park. I had to be careful with some of these excuses though so as not to attract the attention of Sam and him want to accompany me.

Luckily, Sam also attended a Martial Arts class two nights a week, every Tuesday and Thursday. I would take him straight from school and drop him off and not have to pick him up for another hour and a half, so this was my best time to complete most of my sleuthing. After dropping him off at the class this gave me just enough time to drive to Semberton before Mr. Turner was leaving for the day and then I could follow him home. In doing so, I managed to learn exactly where he lives, which didn't happen to be too far from my own home at all, only about five or six streets away. It was a normal road with houses on either side of the street, nothing that would make you suspect a monster would live there. But then, monsters are known to be good at blending in with their surroundings or hiding in plain sight.

As well as learning where he lived, I also learnt that he had a wife and two young daughters of his own. His girls couldn't have been any older than 2 and 4 years old and always seemed to be home with his wife already whenever he got home from work. He didn't seem to go to many other places after work other than home, apart from two occasions where I had seen him pick up the same young girl I had seen him pick up before. The second time I witnessed this I attempted to follow him, but he managed to lose me in the traffic, so I wasn't able to see where he had gone with her and the last time I had seen them together was only last week. Unfortunately, on this occasion it was on a Tuesday when I had seen him driving off with her and he appeared to be taking her much further away than he had the first time when he had taken her to the Premier Inn. I wonder if my phone call had worked and they had been asked to leave before? Perhaps he won't intend to go back there again if it had. I followed him on the motorway for what seemed like hours, however we were getting further and further away from where I needed to pick Sam up from his Martial Arts class and I was running out of time to get back to him. I couldn't leave him stranded there. Tim was at work and there wasn't anyone else I could call to ask to pick him up, not without raising any suspicions as to why I wasn't able to do it myself. So, begrudgingly, I had been required to turn back around and wasn't able to see where they ended up going.

As the weeks passed, I begun to formulate a plan of action. I knew what days and times he was usually at home, and I knew where he lived. What I couldn't establish was when he was likely to be anywhere on his own where I would be able to get near to him. I began to realise that if I was going to do anything at all, it was going to have to be at his home. What I needed to do now was to get a closer look at his house without being spotted so I could figure out a plan of action as to how to get to him.

It was a Thursday afternoon and with it still being Winter, it was already dark when I picked Sam up from school. I handed him his Martial Arts bag and drove him to the Martial Arts studio, like we do every Tuesday and Thursday. I gave him a quick kiss and waved to him as I watched him walk into the studio. I then quickly pulled away, driving straight to Mr. Turners house rather than the school like I usually would.

I parked a little way down the road from his home so that my car was not obviously parked too close. A couple of weeks ago I had begun to panic about him noticing my car following him around so much so whenever Tim was working lates and was getting a lift from a co-worker, I would take his car instead so not to be as conspicuous. But today I was in my own car and luckily so, as I hadn't been super inventive with my hiding spot for the insulin. The only place I knew where no-one but myself would look for sure was in the back of the glovebox of my car, hidden under the car logbook. I sat in the car in anticipation, waiting to watch his car pull onto his driveway. It felt like it was taking ages, maybe because I had turned the engine off and the car had quickly become freezing due to the heater no longer being on. As soon as I saw his car pull up, I quickly got out the car, wrapped myself up in my large duffle coat and then proceeded to walk as casually as I could in his direction. A few steps away from the car I stopped, turned around and opened the passenger door, leant in and grabbed the insulin pen from the glovebox as well as a needle. I wasn't planning to do anything just yet, I still hadn't figured out what exactly I was going to do, but it's always best to be prepared right? Leaning forward beside the open car door I quickly unscrewed the top, screwed the needle onto the injection and then hastily put it into my pocket. I casually walked towards the house again, both hands in my pocket, the left hand clutching the insulin pen like my life depended on it.

From the direction I was heading towards the house I couldn't likely be seen from the inside. There was a large hedgerow blocking the view of the house and the driveway, which I used to my advantage. As I reached the entrance to the drive, I took a quick scan of the road up and down to check that there was no-one else around who had seen me and then ducked down between the car and the hedge. I squatted and made my way slowly towards the house, keeping my head low so as not to be seen from the windows of the house, the car keeping me covered. Once I reached the end of the car I could see the house in more detail, something that I had been unable to do up until now due to keeping my distance. The house was detached with a large bay window at the front and a big black front door. The driveway led down to the side of the house where another car was also parked, likely belonging to his wife and there was also a back door that looked like it led to the kitchen. At the end of the driveway was a large wooden gate and fence, which I assumed may have led to the back garden. I made my way slowly behind the second car, a red and white Smart car, and was going to attempt to take a quick peak into the window of the side door to get an idea of the layout of the house. However, just as I was able to raise myself into a standing position, I heard voices coming from the other side of the door.

I froze, did they know I was here? The voices were muffled, the benefits of double glazing I guess, but I could tell they were adult voices so it must have been Mr. Turner and his wife speaking. I crouched down next to the door, below the window where I couldn't be seen and strained my neck to see if I could make out what was being said, but I couldn't. What was I going to do now? I really hadn't thought this through properly. I crouched back behind the Smart car and begun to make my way back alongside the cars, next to the hedges, to head back to my own vehicle. At least I had some indication as to what the layout of the house was now so maybe I could think of some way in which this information could benefit me.

I was just about to reach the end of the driveway when I heard the creak of a door opening behind me. I quickly turned around and threw myself to the floor, into a commando crawl position. Mr. Turner had just come out of the side door carrying two large black sacks. I watched him carefully, not daring to breathe, scared that he would hear me. He walked with intention towards the end of the driveway, the other side of the car than I was, to where there were two large black wheely bins. Of course, it's bin day tomorrow. He lifted the lid of the bin closest to me, throwing both black sacks into it and then turned to walk back towards the open side door of the house. I readied myself to dart out onto the street away from the car and the drive but then stopped myself. He's only put the black sacks out so far. He is likely to have to make another trip out with recycling yet. This could be my one and only chance. It's now or never.

I peek out over the car to see that the side door is still open, but I can't see him. He must have gone inside to get more rubbish and if my thought process is correct, is planning to bring more stuff out and therefore hasn't shut the door yet. "Yes okay", I heard him shout back to his wife as he walked back out of the side door, carrying two large white recycling bags in each hand this time. I moved my way around to the front of the car, still crouched down low and watched him getting closer and closer. Time seemed to suddenly go in slow motion, every step he took getting closer to me seemed to take five times longer than it should have. My left hand was gripped so tightly onto the insulin needle, I pulled it out slowly, turned the dial at the bottom all the way around to 300 and pulled the safety cap off the top, exposing the needle to the elements. I watched as he bent down to place the recycling bags next to the wheely bins and as he raised back up and turned back to walk towards the house, it was as if someone had suddenly pressed fast forward and I jumped up from my crouching position, leapt forward and stabbed the needle into his thigh, pushing the plunger into it before withdrawing it back again.

He let out a scream of surprise and turned himself around quickly. We locked eyes for a moment, and it was clear that he was confused as to what was happening and who I was. In a panic, I then pushed him over, turned and ran. I kept running and I didn't look back. I kept running until I was several streets away, leaving my car where it was for the time being. I found an alleyway and leant against the cold brick wall catching my breath. I'd done it. Had it worked? I've no idea. I took a quick look at my watch and realised I didn't have much time left before I needed to pick Sam up from his Martial Arts class. As calmly as I could, I began walking back to Mr. Turners street and to where my car was parked. I nodded at a dog walker but otherwise kept my head low with my hands in my pockets, still clutching the insulin pen tightly. Once back to my car, I got in as quick as I could and drove off, not daring to look in the direction of his house, but there didn't appear to be anything untoward happening on the street so I'm not sure if that is a good sign or not. I guess now it's playing the waiting game, either waiting to hear if my spontaneous unthought out plan was worth the risk or waiting for the police to knock on my door to ask why I had randomly decided to stab a man in the leg in his own driveway and then run away. Luckily, a few days later I had my answer.

5

There it was, all over the local village Facebook sites, tributes to the beloved Secondary School teacher who had passed away unexpectedly. I scrolled down further to see numerous different local online news articles, as well as different people posting their condolences and commenting on the posts. Sam was at school, Tim was at work, and I was also meant to be at work, but instead I sent a quick message to my manager to let her know that I had a dentist appointment that morning and would be logging on late. I needed time to go through all of this information to find out what everyone knew.

I opened up a few of the different news articles which all appeared to have the same information, just with different wording. Paragraphs about how much he had done for the local community, what a great teacher he was, how he had inspired the next generation blah blah blah. Funny how when someone dies, they suddenly become the best and nicest person in the world isn't it? Can't be speaking ill of the dead now, can we? Even if he was an adulterer and pedophile, not that anyone other than me and the girl he was abusing likely knew that information though, to be fair. But every news article all said the same thing in regard to his death, that the cause was yet to be determined.

I then began to take a look at some of the comments under the posts. Again, most of these were the same things over and over again. Ex pupils of his commenting on what a great teacher he had been, friends and family mourning for him, each commenter wanting to make their point that they had known the deceased. With the number of comments on these posts you would expect his funeral to be heaving considering so many people apparently knew and liked the man.

Suddenly one comment in particular caught my eye, as did all the responses that followed beneath it. Someone by the name of Claire Seeker had commented only two minutes ago to say that he had clearly been murdered and that the police needed to start looking for the crazy woman who had attacked him. My breath caught short. Less than one minute after this comment, a reply beneath by someone called Renee stated "how do you know that? What happened?". I could see the small blue bubbles coming up at the bottom of the comment thread. Someone was typing a response to it and less than a few seconds later, a response from Claire popped up.

"Shelly is a friend of mine and she told me what happened. Dave came into the kitchen after taking out the bins looking really shook up and told her that he had just been attacked by a crazy woman."

Bubbles appearing again underneath. How fast does the insulin work before it takes effect? Clearly, it's done the job because the man is dead, but how long was he alive before it kicked in and how much information was, he able to tell his wife. I felt sick to the pit of my stomach, waiting for the bubbles to reveal the next piece of information that could potentially incriminate me.

Renee – "OMG what crazy woman? When did this happen? Did he tell you who it was? What did she do?"

Crazy woman? If only they knew how I'd saved a vulnerable teenager from being abused. Saved his wife who I now knew was called Shelly, from discovering that the man that she had loved, the father to her children, her two young girls who may have become victims if they weren't already, was a sex offender. I know it's bad to victim blame, but on this occasion, there was no victim and there certainly wasn't a crazy woman roaming the streets attacking innocent men. But I was just going to have to accept this narrative if I didn't want to get caught.

Claire – "She said that he started having seizures as soon as he said about the crazy woman and didn't get to say anything else. She called an ambulance, but they couldn't save him. No idea what happened to him yet, gotta wait for the coroner's report. Poor Shelly is in bits and the police don't seem to be taking it seriously yet."

If this Claire is telling the truth, then it sounds like he wasn't able to say anything to his wife about me before he passed away. I could be in the clear. I let out a loud breath of air which I had been holding the entire time waiting for these messages to pop up. More bubbles were coming up, indicating another response. However, all of a sudden, the messages appeared to be deleted and the post had turned off further comments. That was odd. I wonder if someone asked her to delete what she had written or if maybe the police don't want any speculation? Either way, this information being removed from the public eye can only be of benefit to me. I just need to make sure I play it cool, there's no reason I would be suspected. As far as anyone knows I shouldn't even know Mr. Turner, I have no links to him whatsoever. And I'm not a crazy woman. I'm a god damn hero, but I guess that's just something I'll have to keep to myself.

6

A few weeks pass and there's nothing more on Facebook about Mr. Turner's death, nor does there seem to be much in the news either. Apart from the occasional hushed conversations I overhear from the school mums at pick up and drop off, I've barely heard anything about what has happened. The curiosity is killing me, I've constant feelings of a mixture of fear and anticipation. Part of me just wants to know what's going on to make sure that I've not been suspected at all, but I know I can't risk being overly curious in case I end up accidentally incriminating myself as a result. But as they say, no news is good news right, so surely the fact that I've not had the police knocking on my door must be a good sign. The problem is, I need a distraction from this. Something to take my mind off Mr. Turner. It was Maeve's funeral last week, which was a good temporary interruption for a while. It was a somber affair as you can imagine, sadly not as many people turned up for it as you would have expected, but it was nice to be able to say a proper goodbye. It was also nice to know that there didn't appear to be any concerns from anyone in relation to how she passed. Mostly people were saying about how death was likely a welcome release from the cancer for her.

As it happens, my new distraction that I was so desperately seeking came sooner than expected. Tim arrived home from work last night in an absolutely foul mood. It took me ages to coax out of him what the matter was but as soon as he started to speak to me about it, it was as if the floodgates opened and weeks and weeks of inner turmoil and frustration, he had been silently experiencing came pouring out of him.

Tim was well known in the hospital that he worked in for being the "go to" doctor. He was one of those men that knew almost everything there was to know about his profession and if he didn't know, he knew exactly how to find out and would make it his mission to find the answer and ensure that the next time he was asked, he would know. As a result of this, as well as his hard-working nature and willingness to drop everything else at the drop of a hat to accommodate whatever the hospital needed, Tim had earnt himself a good reputation at work and therefore he, and almost everyone else at the hospital, were anticipating him to get the latest promotion on offer, Head of Pediatric Surgery. And this is where Tim's frustration lay, as yesterday the announcement was made as to who was being given this promotion that he had worked so hard for, and it wasn't him.

The promotion had been given to a woman by the name of Kelly Stimpson, a woman who my husband informed me was not only exceedingly incompetent but also just so happened to be the daughter of one of the Hospital Board of Directors. Nepotism at its finest. I listened to my husband recall numerous different stories of times where Kelly has been incompetent and he has had to pick up the pieces, incidents of mislaid paperwork, inaccurate prescriptions and even one occasion where a patient became incredibly unwell after Kelly had performed surgery but the reason for this had been kept under wraps. Word around the ward from some of the theatre nurses was that she had left a piece of gauze inside a child who had then developed Sepsis as a result, the sort of incident that would result in significant disciplinary action for most people, but not for the daughter of a member of the medical board, no, then you get a promotion.

According to Tim, Kelly wasn't even in the remotest bit nice as a person either. Clearly having been brought up with a silver spoon in her mouth, the woman had an air of superiority about her that she cast down upon those who she felt were beneath her, which appeared to be almost everyone she worked with. No-one at work liked her and it was a running joke especially with the nursing team that they would make sure to book annual leave or try to swap shifts whenever they were put onto her rotation.

No amount of comfort from me appeared to help ease Tim's disappointment during this conversation and all I could do was let him rant, whilst taking stock of all the little details he was telling me about this person. After about an hour of this, Tim decided to take himself off to bed, not before grabbing a bottle of whiskey from the drinks cupboard to take up with him. Luckily, he had a few days off from work now, so he had the time to mourn the loss of his promotion.

Once he was safely upstairs, I got my laptop out, poured myself a large glass of wine and opened Facebook. I had recently learnt of something called a VPN which I had downloaded to my laptop. My understanding of this was that when I turned it on, my IP address couldn't be tracked. I turned it on in the hopes that this would therefore help to hide my identity and proceeded to open a fake profile I had made on Facebook years before. Once logged onto this, I then searched for Kelly. She was easy enough to find, as well as there only being a few Kelly Stimpson's on Facebook, she was the only one with a profile picture of herself in a pair of scrubs. I clicked on the picture to load up her profile. She had already changed her Bio to support her new job promotion title, I wonder how quickly she had done that after Daddy told her what he had done for her.

Scrolling through, I would have almost felt sorry for this woman had I not known what she was really like. Her whole life, or at least that which I could see on Facebook, appeared to be quite solitary in nature. Her friends list appeared minimal and almost all her posts were of pictures of her cats or the odd post about going out with her parents. There was nothing on there to show any good friends or partners. Her relationship status was set to single, interested in men, and the further I scrolled down the more it was apparent that this woman likely hadn't had a partner in some time. The one thing I did notice though, was that she had liked a page dedicated to a dating app specifically for finding love for professionals.

I searched the dating app and loaded it up on my screen, "Pro-Love – Dating for Professionals". I hovered my mouse over the sign-up button of the page before clicking quickly and finding myself creating a false profile. "Ben Fisher" was the name I came up with. According to my profile I was 6ft tall, worked as a lawyer and enjoyed playing tennis as a hobby. I also made sure that I made it clear that I was a cat person, as this was predominant throughout Kelly's Facebook profile. Her love for her cats, which looked like she had several of, was plastered across most of her Facebook posts, making more appearances than any person, or even herself. I then loaded up some family photos in my phone and found one of my cousin Greg. He would be the perfect person to be the face of Ben. He was tall, good looking and had a strong dislike of social media so he wouldn't be likely to be found online anywhere else easily. He was also married, so fingers crossed, wouldn't crop up on any dating sites either. Greg was a similar age to myself and growing up he had always been a hit with the ladies, so the combination of his face and the profile I had made, tailored specifically to what I knew of Kelly's likes, would hopefully be a hit.

Once my profile was created, I began to narrow my searches down to specifically try to find Kelly. I was able to get her date of birth from Facebook, so I knew her age, although I gave a window around this as we all know how ladies aren't always the most honest in this area. I was able to narrow it down by location also, as although I didn't know where she lived, she was bound to be within a reasonable distance of the hospital that she worked at so that was where I put my address as.

It didn't take long to find her once I had narrowed the search fields down. Her profile picture was the same as the one on Facebook. I clicked onto her profile and scrolled down to her bio:

"Short, sassy, sexy, surgeon, searching for love. Looking for my Mr. Right to spank me when I'm wrong."

I felt bile rise up in my throat. Surely men don't respond well to that? Probably not actually, that's likely why she is single. I flicked through some of her pictures she had put up, mostly of her in positions that I'm assuming she believed made her look provocative, but actually just made her look like she was nursing a bad back. I chuckled to myself at the desperation that oozed from the dating profile. Underneath her Bio was a large red button stating, "Send Kelly a message". I clicked on the button which brought up a chat box and I also noted at the top of the box it gave an indication of when she was last online, which appeared to be 4 hours ago.

"Hi there, I'm Ben. I came across your profile and thought you looked like a really interesting woman. Hope we can chat soon" I typed into the chat box before hitting send.

The bait had been set, now it was time to see if she responded to me. I drained the last of my wine from the bottom of the glass before beginning to shut down my laptop for the night. I wasn't exactly sure what my intended purpose was for trying to catfish her on a dating site yet, but after the heartache that her incompetence and nepotism had caused Tim, I just knew I wanted her to suffer, and I could have some fun whilst doing so.

7

The following morning whilst Tim was taking Sam to school and I was getting ready to complete some admin work, I pulled up the dating site to check for any messages and low and behold, there she was. Kelly had responded to my message only minutes after I had turned the laptop off last night. Clearly an eager beaver.

"Hi Ben, thanks for reaching out. Are you new to the site, I've not seen your profile on here before?" The message read.

I responded back "I am new to the site yes; I've never been on a dating site before but with my work it's hard to meet people."

She responded back pretty quickly after this, and it wasn't long before we were involved in an in-depth conversation. She told me all about her 5 cats, her recent job promotion and how she loves to crochet in her spare time. We were chatting through the online chat box for about two hours before she informed me that she needed to head to work for an important meeting. It had been a very one-sided conversation luckily, Kelly clearly enjoyed talking about herself and she had asked "Ben" minimal questions which was good for me. The less I had to tell her, the less I had to remember telling her. Before signing off, she sent her mobile number across, requesting that I text her instead so that we can keep our conversation going outside of the website. I felt a small pang of panic, I can't text her from my number just in case she somehow manages to trace the number back to me.

How would I explain that to her, or even Tim? I jotted her mobile number down on a piece of paper next to me on the desk, logged out of the dating site and then proceeded to finish my admin work for the morning.

Before I knew it, it was lunchtime. Tim came into the office with a fresh cup of coffee and a chicken sandwich he had made me. He was so thoughtful. He sat down in a chair next to me and proceeded to apologise for his ranting the night before.

"I don't know why I got my hopes up to be honest, I should have known this would happen. I should have seen it a mile away." He said matter of factly, clearly still feeling down about the situation.

"You deserved that promotion, none of what has happened is fair and you need to fight back" I responded. "Isn't there anyone you can speak to about it? Surely everyone can see that you were the right choice for the job?"

"It's not as easy as that though is it. Even if everyone wanted me to get it, no one is going to overrule the board of directors. What's done is done, I guess I'm just going to have to learn to accept it." With that, he got up from the chair, leant down to give me a small peck on my forehead and then proceeded to leave the office, sighing as he walked out.

I hastily finished my sandwich and coffee, shut down my laptop and grabbed my coat and bag. "I'm just popping out to the shop" I shouted to Tim as I grabbed my car keys from the kitchen counter. I jumped in my car and proceeded to drive to the mall. I headed towards a small phone and gadget stall in the middle of the walkway and began to scan the mobile phones they had on offer. An older gentleman approached me and asked if I required any assistance. I told him I was looking for a cheap handset and a pay as you go sim card which he located for me on his stall and advised me of the price. I told him I would be back shortly with the cash and headed to the nearest ATM so as not to pay by card. I withdrew the money that was needed as well as some extra to buy myself some top-up credit vouchers also.

Once I had bought everything that I needed, I hurried back to the car and plugged the charging cable that came with the phone into the USB slot under the radio to boot the phone up ready. Once the new phone was all set up, I used the credit vouchers to top it up with some credit and then proceeded to add Kelly's phone number to the contacts list before sending her a quick text message, "Hi, it's Ben."

I drove home, thinking about what my end game was going to be with this. Seeing Tim so upset was a driving factor in me wanting to get the best possible revenge on Kelly, but not only that, I wanted Tim to be able to get what he deserved, what he had worked so hard for.

As the days went on, Tim continued to look dejected. He was clearly feeling depressed by what had happened, no longer wanting to speak about it but instead had resolved himself to this sad acceptance of the situation. After his days off he returned to work, but seemingly lost the spark he had previously felt when going into the hospital. I continued my text conversations with Kelly, finding out more and more about her likes and dislikes, listening to her moaning about how incompetent the nurses are she works with or how the hospital couldn't run without her. The woman was obviously deluded and this recent unearnt promotion had undoubtedly just further ignited her ego. I had never spoken to someone so self-centered before. Clearly all she wanted to talk about and cared about was herself and she was loving the attention she was getting from "Ben". I made sure to continue to stroke her ego, giving her compliments at every opportunity and telling her what an inspiration she must be to those who work with her. She was lapping it up. But then the inevitable happened, she asked to meet up. I knew it was coming, she had hinted a few times about us meeting and I had been able to skirt around the topic before, but now she had directly asked me and there was no getting away from it. If I wanted to keep her talking to me, I was going to have to arrange a meet, now was the time to figure out where this was all going to lead to. Time to shit or get off the pot. The more I had spoken to her, the more my dislike of her had turned to pure hatred, there were no redeeming factors of this woman, no-one would miss her surely if she were gone? I'd probably be doing the world a favor, definitely the hospital. I began typing back to her:

"I would love to meet up with you. Let me plan the perfect date for me to wine and dine you, the way in which you deserve. Just let me know when you are free, and I will make all the arrangements."

Within minutes she had responded back, "I'm free on Friday, can't wait."

Well then, Friday it is.

8

The days leading up to Friday appeared to drag. I was so excited about my upcoming date with Kelly that it was all I could think about. I'd selected a relatively busy Greek restaurant on the outskirts of town and set a time to meet for 7pm. I told Kelly I'd be holding a red rose for her so she would know for sure it was me at the table when she came in and she had told me that she would be wearing a red dress to match.

Friday evening came and I had told Tim that I was going out for a drink with one of the mums from school. I put on a pair of black skinny jeans and a smart black top and tied my hair up into a ponytail. I didn't want to look out of place at the restaurant or raise any suspicions to Tim that I wasn't going where I said I was, but also, I needed to make sure that I was inconspicuous looking and that I could easily blend in with the crowd. As much as it's nice to be noticed sometimes, tonight was not one of those nights.

I left the house just after 6pm and made my way over to the restaurant, parking up towards the back of the car park, where I then sat and waited. The anticipation was killing me, I couldn't wait to see her sat waiting for "Ben", all excited and hopeful for this new budding relationship. "Ben" was her perfect man, she was going to be absolutely gutted when she realised that he wasn't real, well if we even get that far. I sent her a quick text message "running a bit late, got stuck at work in a meeting, I've booked the table under my name so just let them know when you go in. I've ordered your favourite wine to the table already for you."

I then made a quick call to the restaurant. "Hi there, my boss made a reservation under Ben this evening for 7pm but he is unfortunately running late. His friend whom he is meeting should still be arriving on time however, so he has asked that I call ahead to request that she be seated upon arrival and that a bottle of Chateauneuf du Pape be ready on the table for her." The lady on the phone was very accommodating and agreed that this would all be put in place as requested.

I watched as numerous cars entered the car park one by one and stared intently at the occupants leaving their vehicles, waiting for the first glimpse of Kelly. I didn't have to wait too long luckily, she arrived at 6:45pm in a brand-new black land rover defender. I watched her getting out of the car, wearing a long red dress which hugged me in the waist and flowed down to her feet. She was also wearing a short black leather jacket and black heels. I could see her shivering in the frosty night air as she came round to the passenger side of her car to grab her purse. It was difficult to see in the darkness, but the purse looked like it was likely expensive. She was clearly benefiting from Daddy's money as well as his connections at work. I watched her walk unsteadily towards the entrance of the restaurant, clearly not used to wearing heels. Once she had disappeared inside, I gave it a few minutes before following in myself, but not before readying myself another insulin injection which I then slipped into the side pocket of my handbag for easy access.

As I entered, I made sure not to look around too much, although the urge to immediately seek her out was strong. I knew this was the time that I needed to be the most careful and ensure not to draw attention to myself. I was met with a young cheerful looking girl standing at the hostess podium just inside the front door.

"Good evening, madam, do you have a reservation?" she asked me brightly.

"Erm no sorry I'm just meeting a friend for a drink the bar tonight." I responded.

"Not to worry at all, the bar is just over there" she gestured over to the right-hand side of the restaurant. I followed her gaze to where she was pointing to see a large bar area tucked into the far corner of the room.

"Thank you very much" I replied and then I headed towards an open seat at the bar, tucked round the side a bit and out of the way enough that I wouldn't be too obvious to anyone but also in a good enough position to allow me to survey my surroundings. As I walked towards my seat, I cast my eyes around the restaurant quickly, locking onto my target who was already sat at the table which was about 20 feet away from the bar. I sat down onto the stool and picked up a drink's menu, casting my eyes over the top to fix my sights on Kelly, rather than truly looking at what beverages were on offer. She had clearly made herself comfortable at the table already and didn't appear to be feeling the need to wait for "Ben" before tucking into the bottle of wine I had ordered. Her jacket was laid across the back of her seat, purse sat on the table next to her cutlery and she was sipping from a largely poured glass of red.

"What can I get for you Miss?" the bartender asked. I gave a slight jump, startled as I had been so transfixed on what Kelly was doing that I had almost forgotten that I needed to order a drink so as not to draw attention to myself. "I'll have a glass of the house white please".

I gave a quick glance down at my watch, 7:05pm. I hadn't given any indication to Kelly as to how late "Ben" was likely to be, however clearly five minutes was late enough as I heard my phone ping from my bag just as the waiter placed a large glass of wine in front of me. I thanked him and quickly took my phone out. Best put that on silent, I don't want that going off every time she sends a text message. She probably wasn't close enough to hear it, but you could never be too careful. I opened the message she had sent me, "How far away are you?". "About 10-15 minutes, I'm very sorry, please enjoy the wine while you wait" I hastily replied.

I looked over to her table again, she was tapping the heel of one of her feet constantly on the floor, is she nervous or just impatient? The time seemed to go so slowly as I sat sipping at my wine and casually gazing over to her table every now and then. Another text pinged through; it was now 7:32pm. "Are you almost here? It's been half an hour." She was clearly starting to get annoyed; her heel tapping had begun to get more rapid, and she was onto her second glass of wine. I wonder how long I can keep this going before she realised that no-one was coming. As I began to type my response to her, a gentlemen sat down next to me, blocking my view somewhat and gave a loud sigh.

"What a long week it's been" he said to me, as he signaled over the bartender. "I'll have a jack and coke and whatever the lady is having" he stated to him.

"Oh no thank you I'm fine really" I began to protest however he was having none of it. "Nonsense, I've had a long week, and it would be nice to treat someone other than myself for once."

The bartender nodded and began to make the drinks up, including the glass of wine that I had declined. I had a feeling this was not a man who was willing to be ignored and I can't be causing a scene or doing anything likely to draw attention to myself at this point. So, I smiled instead and thanked him and when the bartender handed me my drink, I made sure to hold it in my left hand, positioning it so my wedding ring was clearly on show.

The man begun to attempt small talk with me, asking what I was doing there that evening. I told him that I was waiting for a friend to meet up with before going into town and he informed me that he had just finished work at the factory around the corner and that he often popped into the restaurant for a drink before heading home. The man was harmless but clearly lonely, so I indulged him in his small talk whilst continuing to attempt to peek around him every now and then to check on Kelly.

After about ten minutes I checked my phone, remembering that I hadn't actually sent the last message that I had been planning to send to her before being interrupted by the man sat next to me. There were two more messages from Kelly, clearly, she was beginning to get annoyed. The first text stated, "I'm not going to wait here all night for you" and the second was just numerous question marks. It was now 7:46pm.

I was just about to respond to her when I saw her moving out of the corner of my eye. She picked up her purse, leaving her jacket sat on the back of the chair and appeared to be heading in my direction. She couldn't have figured out what was going on surely? Does she know who I am? Panic began to set in, maybe Tim had a picture of me on his desk at work and she has recognised me? The man beside me was droning on about something but I hadn't been paying any attention. He began to laugh, and I instinctively gave a small laugh with him, not that I knew what we were laughing at, but I didn't want him to be aware that I wasn't listening. As she got closer, I could feel the hairs on the back of my neck standing on end. She appeared to be walking with purpose, well as purposeful as she could when tottering on her too high heels that she clearly wasn't practiced in walking in.

Just then she breezed straight past me, not even casting a glance in my direction at all and walked straight through the door just to the side of me, the toilets. I felt relief wash over me, she hadn't pegged me at all, but this was clearly my chance. I excused myself to the gentlemen next to me, informing him that I needed to use the restroom and then headed through the door beside me.

I scanned the toilets as I entered, getting a quick summary of what the room was like. There were three toilet stalls on one side of the room with three sinks and mirrors directly opposite them. No-one else apart from me and Kelly appeared to be in here. As I surveyed the room, I noticed that the third toilet stall was the only one with the door shut and I could hear quiet sniffling coming from inside. I made my way to the stall in the middle, next to where Kelly was locked in beside me and positioned myself ready, close to the door of Kelly's stall but also able to close to my own stall door, quick enough to hide myself if required.

The sniffling continued next to me, and I heard her blowing her nose. I put my hand into the side pocket of my handbag and took out the readied needle in preparation. I wondered if she could feel the tension I did at this moment, the anticipation of what was about to come, not that she was aware of it. I labored my breathing as much as possible, not to make it known that I was next to her, with just this flimsy wooden wall divider between us. She let out a big sigh and then I heard the toilet flush. This was it, I quickly cast my glance to the sink area of the bathroom to make sure there was no-one else around, although I knew I would have heard someone enter if there had been, the silence had been deafening to me whilst I had been waiting for her to leave the bathroom stall. I heard the click of her door unlock, the tap of her heels on the linoleum flooring as she pushed her way through the door. This was it, time to shine.

I burst out of my toilet stall and just as she was emerging from hers, I pushed her back in, causing her to fall backwards onto the toilet behind her. I quickly locked the stall door behind me, trapping us both in the small cubicle. As she began to scream, I leant down onto her, holding my left forearm against her mouth to muffle the sounds and pressing my body weight against her, pinning her to the toilet. The needle was ready in my hand, and I quickly plunged it into her thigh, pushing down the button at the top, before extracting it. I continued to pin her down, stifling the sounds as she kept attempting to scream. She looked deep into my eyes, maintaining contact with me with a look of pure desperation and pleading. I smirked at her as I persisted to prevent her from moving. I then felt a hard bite onto my arm as she sunk her teeth into the flesh of my forearm, penetrating through my jacket and straight into my skin. I let out a shout which I tried to catch mid yelp so as not to make too much noise.

"You little bitch" I snarled at her, seeing red. I hastily grabbed as much toilet roll from the dispenser as I could and began stuffing it down her throat, to prevent her from biting me again, but also likely choking her at the same time too. I could feel the power of her struggle begin to decline. "You deserved this Kelly, you're a shit person, doing a shit job and getting rewarded for it just because of who your Daddy is."

Tears begun streaming down her cheeks as she begun to accept her inevitable fate. I could feel beads of sweat begin to form on my forehead, this had been harder work than I had anticipated. Just then I began to feel her body start to seize underneath mine. I continued to try and pin her down with my body weight, but the seizing was making this much more difficult, and I was beginning to struggle. Just as I thought I wasn't going to be able to carry on holding her down, the seizing stopped and her whole body appeared to slump to the side, half on and half off the toilet. I looked down at her eyes which had glassed over and were now fixed, staring in one position. I think I've done it.

I slowly lifted myself up and off her, brushed myself off and rearranged my clothing which had gotten twisted up in the process. I looked down at the lifeless body in front of me, her dress halfway up legs just above her knees, one of her heels hanging off her foot, the sodden toilet roll still bunched up in her mouth. I leant down and felt for a pulse to the side of her neck, nothing. A felt a small smile creep across my face as I heard the main bathroom door opening and the tapping of heels as someone entered the toilet stall next to us. I froze in place. No-one knew we were in here surely. I pinned myself against the wall, the other side of the stall and held my breath. I listened intently as I heard the familiar noises of urine hitting the toilet bowl, toilet roll being taken out of the dispenser and the toilet being flushed. I continued to hold my breath as I listened to the sound of the water running at the sink and the hand dryer being used, letting out a sigh of relief once I heard the door closing behind them as they left.

I looked down at the corpse of Kelly beside me. Now I needed to make this not look like what it is. I removed the toilet roll stuffing from her mouth and attempted to prop her up onto the toilet to make it look like she was using the facilities. I hiked her dress up over her hips and pulled her knickers down to her ankles. Repositioning her heels properly onto her feet. I gave her a quick once over to check that she did indeed look as if she was toileting and then stuffed the toilet roll down into the toilet bowl between her legs. Now I had to figure out how to get out of this stall whilst keeping it locked. I couldn't just walk out with it unlocked because that may raise suspicions. I looked above me, the wall dividers between the stalls had a large gap between the floor and the wall but also between the wall and the ceiling. The gap on the floor didn't seem big enough for me to crawl through but I should be able to fit over the top. I allowed myself a small laugh at the situation I was in as I took my shoes off and threw them over into the next stall alongside my purse which I had thrown the needle back into, it wouldn't do to be leaving marks on her legs as I use her to climb over now would it. Bare foot, I then stepped up onto her lap, holding onto the top of the divider wall and hoisted myself over. I landed onto the toilet with a thud, knocking my head slightly on the porcelain. That's going to hurt in the morning. I then put my shoes back on, dusted myself off, picked up my handbag and proceeded to walk out of the restroom as casually as I could.

I looked over to where I had been sitting at the bar and noticed that the gentleman I had been speaking to was no longer there. He must have left. Thank heavens, I can just leave myself now rather than having to keep up appearances with him. I made my way to the entrance, thanking the hostess as I walked out and proceeded to my car.

The time now was 8:36pm, too early for me to go home, I'd only been out for about two hours and Tim knows that when I go out for a drink I'm never home before 10pm. I pulled my car out of the driveway and proceeded to drive on autopilot. I found myself cruising down the motorway, thinking about everything that had just occurred, the rush I had felt, the euphoria of the pure adrenaline pulsing through my veins as I watched the life drain from her face. The way in which her eyes went from scared, to pleading, to lifeless. Should I be concerned by how exciting I find killing people now? It's not like I'm killing people that don't deserve it though. I'm sure the joy I'm feeling has more to do with the fact that I'm making the world a better place, by ridding it of those who don't deserve to share the same oxygen as the rest of us.

I carried on driving for a while longer, pulling into a service station and grabbing myself a takeaway coffee. I began to retrace the events of the evening in my head, making sure that I had covered all of my tracks. No-one knew I was going to that restaurant this evening; I didn't see anyone there that could have recognised me, and I had positioned the body well enough to not make it look like foul play. I reached into my handbag, pulling out the phone I had purchased to speak to Kelly to specifically. I deleted everything I could on the phone and then completed a factory reset. I then took the sim card out, chucking it into the leftover coffee at the bottom of the paper takeaway cup. I had a quick look around me as I stood next to my car, there didn't appear to be anyone around. So, I dropped the phone onto the floor, giving it a few quick stamps to ensure it was fully broken. I scooped up the pieces from the floor, chucking them all into the coffee remnants alongside the sim card, placing the plastic lid back on top before proceeding to throw the cup and its contents into a large bin. I then got back into my car, and before driving off I pulled up the sleeve of my jacket to inspect my left forearm where Kelly had bitten. There were deep looking red marks, looking clearly like a bite mark, etched into the skin. I'd need to keep my arms covered until that has healed for sure. I checked the time which was now 10:31pm and then drove home.

9

I awoke late the next morning and stretched my arms and legs out, star fishing in the bed. Tim had taken Sam to school on his way into work this morning so had afforded me a lie in after my night out the evening before. I got up and started my usual morning routine, brushed my teeth and combed my hair, pulling on some workout gear ready to have a yoga session in the living room before continuing with my day. I wasn't working today which was a bonus. I always enjoyed my days off; everything seems to go at a much nicer and slower pace, and I can really enjoy the time I get to myself.

I filled up my water bottle and headed into the living room to lay down on my yoga mat. I had been following a series on YouTube that was a combination of yoga, Pilates and guided meditation which I had found had not only been loosening my joints but had also helped me with relaxation, and I had noticed that my ability to keep myself calm and collected in situations of stress was definitely improving too, which considering some of the situations I had found myself in recently, was a requirement for sure.

I inhaled a deep breath as I positioned myself into a Sun Salutation pose, just as my mobile phone began to ring. How's a girl supposed to relax and breathe when there's interruptions like this? I glanced down at my phone which I had thrown onto the sofa prior to starting the workout and could see my husband's name lit up on the screen. Why is

Tim ringing me from work, he never rings me when he's working, only when he is on his way home and that wouldn't be for hours yet. I hit pause on the television and sat down on the sofa, answering the call quickly.

"You won't believe what's going on at work today." Tim said hurriedly over the line. It was hard to tell if his voice was laced with excitement, fear or stress.

"What's going on?" I asked innocently.

"Something's happened to Kelly." He paused "She was found dead last night."

"Oh my gosh! What happened?" I exclaimed, trying to force sincerity into my voice as best I could, but realising I sounded more sarcastic than sincere. Luckily, Tim didn't seem to notice.

"She was found in a restaurant restroom last night. Someone killed her!" The last three words took me by surprise. It wasn't supposed to be known that she had been murdered. I cast my thoughts back over the night before and the way in which I had staged her body. Why would anyone think that was a murder scene? When I left her, she looked like she had had a heart attack or something.

"Oh wow, that's awful!" I responded. "Do you know what happened to her exactly?" I asked, hoping to be able to garner some more details as I could feel the fear beginning to set in.

"No, not yet. All we know at the moment is that she was found last night by a waitress and that the police are investigating what they have determined as being a suspicious death."

"So, it may not be murder then" I asked hopefully, "If they are just saying suspicious then it could be anything couldn't it? Like a natural death?"

"Well, that's what I thought initially but apparently April in accounting has spoken to the police this morning about some guy that Kelly was seeing. She had a date at the restaurant with him last night, but the wait staff have said that they don't remember seeing her with anyone and it's a bit odd that if she was with someone, that they didn't raise the alarm to something being wrong when she disappeared."

I felt like I had been punched so hard in the stomach at hearing Tim's account of what was being discussed at work. I hadn't considered that Kelly might tell someone about "Ben". She had seemed like such a loner that it hadn't occurred to me that she might have work acquaintances she may be speaking to. Of course she was though, she had found the man of her dreams online, of course she was going to be telling anyone about it that would listen. I'm so glad I got rid of that phone, what I need to do now though is log back onto the dating site and delete the "Ben" profile. I rushed into the office where my laptop was sat on the desk and began booting it up. My mind was racing, all these thoughts going through my head a mile a minute, thinking about any clue I may have left behind to lead the trail to me. Had anyone seen me follow her into the bathroom last night? I had told the hostess that I was meeting a friend for drinks, I wonder if she had noticed that I never actually met up with anyone. Who was that man I was speaking to last night; would he likely have any suspicions of me? He had told me that he goes to drink there after work a lot, so he was bound to hear about what happened, what if he connects the dots to the woman he had never seen there before who had suddenly gone to the toilet and not returned? I could feel sick rising up into my throat as the panic began to overwhelm me.

"Chrissie, you still there?" I heard Tim saying through the phone I had laid down onto the desk next to me.

"Sorry, I'm still here" I replied, "I was just getting myself ready to complete some errands when you rang so I was a little bit distracted. How are you feeling about all this?"

I heard Tim give out a loud sigh. "I'm not sure to be honest. You know me and Kelly never really saw eye to eye, and I've obviously been upset about her getting the promotion over me….." There was a long pause. "But this…… I'd never wish this on anyone. Everyone here is really upset; it's rocked the whole hospital."

"I wonder if the promotion will be up for grabs again though now." I responded without thinking.

"Chrissie for heaven's sake how can you think about that, the woman has just died. No-one is going to be considering that now." Tim snapped, clearly angered by my suggestion of it.

"I'm sorry babe, that was inconsiderate of me." I quickly backtracked.

"Anyway, I've got to get back to work, just wanted to hear your voice after the shock of the news this morning." With that Tim said his goodbyes and terminated the call.

With that, I turned my attention back to the laptop which was now fully loaded up and presenting me with my home screen. I clicked onto the VPN app I had previously downloaded and turned it on before logging onto the dating site and deleting the profile. I then cleared my browser history as well as deleted the VPN software also, so as not to raise any questions if my laptop is looked at by anyone as to why I would feel the need for it.

I then just sat and stared into space for a brief period of time, unsure with what to do with myself. Profile deleted, second phone destroyed, no-one knew I was going to that restaurant, and I shouldn't have any connections to Kelly other than my association with Tim. In fact, he would likely have more of a motive than I would, not that I want to incriminate my husband, but at least I will know where the trail of the investigation is going if they start asking him questions.

I got up from the office seat. I can't just keep sitting here thinking about this over and over, I'm going to drive myself crazy. No, I need to keep myself occupied and I've officially gone off yoga for the time being. I went into the living room, tidied up my yoga equipment and turned the television off and then proceeded to grab my bag and shoes. I may as well complete some of those errands I needed to run like I said I was going to do. I checked my watch, I had about three hours before I needed to pick Sam up from school, which would be plenty of time to go into town, get my nails done, grab a few bits of shopping and send a parcel off.

10

I strolled through the high street of town, heading back towards my car that I had left in the multi-story car park. In one hand I had a bag for life with some items I had bought in the market for dinner. I had popped over to the butchers stand and to the grocer and picked up a lovely piece of Pork loin and some fresh vegetables to prepare for dinner later. After the shock Tim had had at work this morning, I'm sure he would appreciate a nice dinner to come home to. I brought my other hand up to take another good look at my fresh manicure I had just had done. I've always loved getting my nails done and it was a welcome distraction from the running thoughts in my head, especially as the girls at the nail salon always want to talk about the hot gossip around town, which luckily didn't involve anyone dying today.

A cold gust of wind came sweeping through the high street and I shivered. I put my remaining hand into my jacket pocket to warm up and felt a discarded needle cap. I flicked it casually out of my pocket and onto the ground as I continued walking towards the car. That's something I'm going to have to be more careful about in future, I must remember to discard the needles and packaging properly and not just remember to hide the actual insulin pen. I had yet to put the injection back into the glove box of the car, in fact the old needle was still on it from when I used it last night, so I need to remember to sort that out in a bit also and get rid of it. My handbag was hanging over my shoulder and I clutched it closer to my body with the top of my arm.

Before long I reached the car park and was just getting into the car when I heard a ping from my mobile phone in my handbag. I threw my handbag across onto the passenger seat, got myself settled into my driving position and then grabbed my phone out the bag to check the message before heading off. There was a text in a group message chain for all the mums at school from one of the mums called Coleen. She had a son called Max who had a birthday coming up.

"Hi Gang, still waiting on a few RSVPs for Max's birthday party this weekend. Please can you let me know if you are coming or not, so I know numbers for food."

I started scouring my brain for any recollection of an upcoming birthday party. I'm usually really on top of these things. I always make sure to RSVP as soon Sam comes home from school with an invite and then I put it straight onto the Calander hanging in the kitchen so that we don't forget. But for the life of me I could not remember there being a party coming up, especially not as soon as this weekend. Whilst I was thinking my phone continued to ping with responses coming in thick and fast from numerous other mums, all confirming that their child would be in attendance and the odd one saying thank you for the invite but so and so couldn't come for whatever reason. I started to type a response out myself, perhaps Sam forgot to give me the invite or he lost it at school.

"Hi Coleen, so sorry but I've not seen an invite for Max's party, not sure if Sam may have lost it. Can you let me know the details and then I can confirm whether or not we can come."

After I typed the message, I took a quick glance at the time displayed on the car dashboard. I had an hour until Sam finished school, plenty of time to pop into the post office shop round the corner from the school and then maybe just wait around a bit before picking Sam up as there wasn't enough time to go home in-between. I started up the car and slowly backed out of the parking space, driving with intent to my next destination.

About ten minutes later I was parked up outside the local post office shop. I reached into my bag again to check my phone as it had pinged numerous times whilst I had been driving, but not one to break the law, I had waited until I had parked to check it. Not one to break the law, I chuckled to myself. There were numerous other messages from mums all confirming attendance at the party this weekend but then I also noticed a separate message from Coleen sent directly to me only. I opened the private chat to see what it said.

"Hi Chrissie, I'm really sorry but Sam wasn't actually invited to Max's party this weekend as there was only a certain number of kids allowed at the venue. I had to ask Max to just invite his close friends this time. I hope you understand." Is she kidding me? I could feel anger bubbling up inside me from reading the message. There's only a certain number of kids allowed?! It's clearly a high number based on the amount of people replying to her messages. In fact, the more I looked at the group chat, the more I started to realise that almost every mum in the group had replied to say whether or not they were coming, which meant almost all of the kids must have been invited. Well, all of them except Sam clearly. Why wasn't Sam invited? As far as I knew he had always gotten along with Max and Sam was well behaved in school so there shouldn't be any concerns of him misbehaving at the party.

I started to respond to the message and then stopped myself. I had typed about three different responses, all getting more aggressive each time I started typing and then deleting it, typing and then deleting. I took a deep breath and leaned back against the seat of the car. I'll have a word with Coleen face to face, I think. She's always early for the school pick up and today I'm super early too so I should have plenty of time to give her a piece of my mind before picking up Sam.

I grabbed my handbag and leant behind me to also grab the parcel from the backseat that had been sat there waiting to be sent off for several days now. My mother's birthday was coming up and I had bought her a new wax melt holder and some different flavoured wax melts. I had packaged them up ready to send off to her but then kept forgetting to swing by the post office, so the parcel had been sat in the back of my car for a while now. I got out of the car, parcel in one hand, handbag slung over my shoulder and slammed the car door behind me. I was so angry at Coleen. No-one and I mean no-one will get away with excluding my child. Who does she think she is?

I strolled into the post office shop and over to the counter ready to send off my parcel, still absolutely seething to myself. The post office shop was family owned and everyone in town knew them. The owners were elderly and had been running the shop since their early adulthood, but they were getting too old to manage it as much now and were therefore relying on their adult children to run it on their behalf. Two out of the three children were known to be nice and pleasant, always wanting to go the extra mile to help you out with whatever you need and would always ask about your day. However, the youngest son was not so nice. In his early forties, he was an obese and unhappy man who clearly didn't enjoy working in his parents' shop. Unlike his siblings he had never married, never seemed to have a partner and was always miserable whenever you had to deal with him. Unfortunately for me, or maybe more so for him, it was the youngest son Craig who was working in the shop today when I walked in.

I was the only customer in the shop at this time so as I headed towards the post office counter, I was expecting pretty rapid service. Craig seemed to have other ideas. He barely looked up from his phone that he was sat watching videos on behind the counter. I cleared my throat in an attempt to get his attention, but he continued to ignore me. I was not in the mood for this level of rudeness. I slammed the parcel down hard on the counter, my fingers gripping the sides of the box so hard that they had turned white.

"Excuse me" I shouted across the counter to him. "I'd like to send this parcel first class please."

Craig looked up at me and huffed. Without saying a word, he took the parcel from my hands and placed it on the weighing scales. He then proceeded to start pressing some buttons on a screen and a postage label began to print off.

"£6.79" he barked at me.

I grabbed my purse out of my bag and looked inside. I only had about £4 something in change, otherwise I had a twenty-pound note. I handed the note over which he took, again without saying a word, and proceeded to put it into the till before then handing me back £3.21 in change. I stood there for a second, still looking at him with my hand outstretched, waiting to receive the rest of my change. I had given him a twenty-pound note, he had short-changed me by ten pounds. Craig ignored my outstretched hand, turning his body away from me and proceeded to go back to watching videos on his phone.

"You still owe me a tenna" I stated matter of factly to him.

"You what?" He retorted with a smirk on his face.

"You heard me, you owe me ten pounds." I could feel rage building up inside me again, furious at the audacity of this fat little man.

"I don't owe you anything, now off you go." He gestured towards the exit of the shop in a shooing fashion.

"I'm not going anywhere without my money" I snarled. Today was not the day to be messing with me. I was already wound up about Coleen and stressed out about how quickly they had decided that Kelly's death was likely foul play and now this horrible gremlin was really starting to poke the bear.

Craig leant over the counter, bringing his face up close to mine. I could smell a combination of onion and garlic on his breath and see the tobacco stains on his teeth. "You aren't getting a penny out of me, now get the fuck out of my shop before I make you." He threatened.

Any level of self-control I thought I had was lost in that moment. All the annoyances and frustrations of the afternoon boiled up inside of me and came steaming out like an overfilled kettle. I thrust my hand into my handbag, quickly locating the insulin needle in the side pocket and quickly turned the dial at the bottom, click, click, click, until it wouldn't turn any further. I started to make my way around the counter, there was a hatched doorway allowing entrance to the staff but was clearly not meant for customers to go through. I put my hand over to the lock of the hatch, opening it up and letting the door swing open.

"What do you think you're doing? You aren't allowed back here." He looked startled but also bemused. He clearly didn't know what I was planning to do but also must not have seen me as much of a threat. I watched as he slowly put his phone down on the counter and came towards me, his considerable girth taking up most of the space between the counter and the tobacco stand beside him.

He put his arms out in front of him as if to tell me to stop moving but I didn't. I carried on advancing towards him until I was close enough to reach him, my hand still firmly grasping the injection pen in my bag. He pushed forward with his hands, but I was too quick for him and managed to spryly dart to the side. When his hands didn't make contact with me, the force he had put behind the push caused him to topple forward. He grabbed at the counter as he started to fall to the floor, knocking off a selection of gift cards and parcel tape.

I chuckled at him, lying there on the floor, surrounded by gift cards. He looked ridiculous. I could have left it then. I should have. I had made my point. I had humiliated him enough. He was clearly embarrassed as he lay there struggling to get up, partly because of the lack of room behind the counter and partly because of his considerable size. I could have easily have just stepped over him and gone about my day. Everyone knew what he was like so I probably would have been applauded if anyone found out about our altercation, not that I'm sure he would want to tell anyone that is. But something was triggered in me the moment he was rude to me, almost from the moment that I had walked into the shop.

I pulled the injection out of my bag, leant down and whispered into his ear "This is what you get, you fat prick" before charging the tip of the needle into the top of his arm, feeling more resistance than usual when pressing the button at the top, likely because of the amount of excess tissue it was having to travel through.

"Wait, what was that? What are you doing?" He started shouting frantically to me as I got up, slipping the needle back into my bag and headed towards the door. As I made my way round the counter back round to the front of the shop, I picked up my parcel again. Can't be leaving this here now can I. With that I strolled out of the shop and back to my car, throwing the parcel backwards onto the backseat where it was likely going to stay for another few days before I got round to trying to post it again.

11

    I drove the car swiftly round the bend and along the few side streets to where I usually park at the back of the school, ready for pick up. I parked up on the street, beside a row of houses, where I would usually park, turned the car engine off and just sat for a moment in silence. What had I done? I may have gone too far now. It was one thing killing Mr. Turner, he deserved it. Even Kelly, although she may not have done anything specifically to Tim, her nepotism, shoddy work ethic and poor attitude were enough to warrant the world being a better place without her. But Craig, I didn't really know enough about Craig to be able to reliably say that he had what was coming to him. Other than knowing he was miserable in general and clearly didn't like his job, but I'm not sure that's enough to say that someone deserved to die. I started second guessing myself and my decision making, forming a back-and-forth argument in my head with the 'for' and 'against' my recent actions. The 'for' argument seemed to be winning though, sure I didn't know much about him, but if that's how he speaks to people and clearly tries to rob people, then perhaps all of this was done for a good reason.

As I pondered these thoughts, I caught sight of a blue Suzuki Vitara driving slowly past me and pulling over to the side of the road to park up. I knew that car, it belonged to Coleen. I was still seething from her messages earlier, and realistically, she was more to blame for Craig's death at this point than I was, because she had been the one to rile me up in the first place. I glanced around up and down the street, no one else was here for the school pick up yet. Only me and Coleen. I never understood why Coleen came so early, it was like she wanted to make sure she always got the best parking space.

I could feel the call of the needle from my handbag on the passenger seat next to me. I'd never really liked Coleen. She was one of those mums who always seemed to be looking down on you. Her children were perfect, her house was perfect, she always completed the school run with her hair and makeup done. She was a proper Stepford wife and loved to make others feel insignificant in comparison to her. I did another double check of my surroundings, taking note of the time also, it was only 2:40pm, plenty of time before people would start parking up for the school run. Fuck it, I've already done 3 if you don't count Maeve, what's one more?

With that, I grabbed the injection, slipped out of my car and headed in the direction of her parked vehicle. Without a word, I opened her passenger door, climbed into the seat and closed the door behind me.

"Chrissie, what are you doing in my car?" Coleen asked. She didn't look afraid, she didn't even look surprised, in fact, she looked more annoyed. Like me being in her space was inconvenient for her. The look she gave me was all the fuel I needed. Without responding I leant across, slamming the injection that I had prepared whilst walking across to her car, into her stomach and pushed down on the plunger.

She began to scream, just like Kelly did, and just like I did with Kelly, I forced my weight on top of her to stop her from moving and jammed my arm across her mouth to muffle the sounds. Luckily, unlike Kelly, she didn't try to bite me which was a relief. I could feel her struggling against me but the force in which she struggled seemed so much weaker than Kelly had last night. Coleen was a much smaller woman than I, she was very slim and likely didn't have much strength in her. Her seatbelt was also still on, further restricting her from being able to move. I could feel her begin to buck her hips, trying to throw me off her but she wasn't able to muster up the force to move my weight off from her.

It didn't seem to take long before the bucking stopped and the top half of her body began to shake, which is when I noticed that she wasn't fighting against me anymore, she was seizing now. I moved back into the passenger seat and watched as her body writhed about, before coming to a stop shortly after. There was no more movement now from Coleen. I leant over and pulled the lever of her seat to recline her backwards and then grabbed a blanket she had on the backseat and covered it over her. From the outside looking in it would now look like she was perhaps having a nap in her car before picking up her son.

I slid out of the car quietly and walked quickly back to my own car, sitting down in the driver's seat. Less than five minutes later more cars started pulling up alongside mine and Coleen's cars, parents and guardians ready to complete the school pick up. I stayed sat in the car, watching people parking up and getting out to walk through the school gates, keeping a close eye on whether anyone walked too close to Coleen's car or happened to notice her, but no-one did. Everyone seemed to be so involved in their own worlds, or talking to other parents they were coming across whilst walking along, that they didn't seem to notice anything else around them.

I waited until it was 3:10pm before I finally got back out of the car and headed up the path in the direction of Sam's classroom, blending in with all the other mums, almost as if it was like every other day.

12

I'm standing outside Sam's classroom in the playground, and I'm shivering. At this point I'm no longer sure if the shivering is from the cold or from fear. Fear following the realisation of what I have done within the last twenty-four hours. Three people I've killed, in such a short space of time and I had started to let my emotions get the better of me. As confident as I was in covering my tracks with Mr. Turner and Kelly, there had been no planning involved when it came to Craig and Coleen. I had acted in the heat of the moment and now I was likely to suffer the consequences from it. I had no way of knowing now if I had likely left any remnants of myself for someone to discover my identity. I still had one dosage of the insulin left in the pen, maybe I needed to just get rid of it so that I don't act on impulse again. But what if I need it?

My train of thought gets interrupted as I hear the word "dead" coming from one of the other mums to the side of me. It was Rachel and she was talking about Craig.

"They found him just now in his shop, they don't know what's happened yet, but it definitely seems a bit suspicious doesn't it. I saw the ambulance driving away just before I parked up by the school a minute ago" Rachel is saying.

"How many is that?" asks Alison. "I'm pretty sure that brings us up to three deaths now." Rachel responds.

A third mum gasps, "you don't think maybe they are all related in some way?"

I can't believe Craig was found so quickly! And if they are talking about three deaths, then they must have already heard about what happened to Kelly too. Three deaths they are talking about, but I bet tomorrow they will be talking about four, maybe even on the way home from school, because they didn't know about Coleen yet.

I see Rachel look around the playground before locking eyes with me. "If they are all related, then we have a serial killer on the loose" she states to the woman beside her.

I smile at Rachel and wave; she can't know that I've been listening to their conversation surely and even if she did, who wouldn't be considering the topic. I avert my gaze as Rachel goes back to speaking to the other mums and brings my focus to the classroom door which is just about to open to let the children out for the day. I need to maintain my composure; no-one would be suspecting me yet surely. I'm just another school mum, doing the school run, I'm certainly not a serial killer, well not in their eyes anyway, not at the moment.

"Where's Coleen?" Alison suddenly asked. "She's usually here by now and they are just about to let the kids out." All three of the mums started looking around the playground in an effort to spot her.

"Her husband's not here either, how strange." Rachel replied but was then quickly distracted by the opening of the classroom door and the thundering footsteps of children running out to greet their parents.

I kept my eyes facing straight ahead at the door, waiting for Sam to make an appearance. I wanted to grab him and go. The more I stood here, listening to the hushed conversations around me, the concerned voices of the community, fearing what was likely to happen next, the more I shivered. As Sam came running out of the classroom, I heard the sound of sirens, getting louder and louder, closer and closer. Coleen must have been found.

Sam came running out of the classroom and enveloped me in a giant bear hug. The warmth of his small body pressed up against mine was enough to stifle my shivers for just a moment. The guilt of what I had done to Coleen began to seep away as I looked down at the face of the child I had brought into this world, the child that I would do anything to protect. Sam started telling me about his day at school, talking about all the little details of what he had learnt and who he had played with. But as much as I love him, my attention was snatched away, and I was unable to hear a single word of what he was saying to me. Because walking directly towards me, across the playground, were two police officers.

Part 2

13

Sam, my six-year-old son, came running out of the classroom and enveloped me in a giant bear hug. The warmth of his small body pressed up against mine was enough to stifle my shivers for just a moment in the cold winter air. Sam started telling me about his day at school, talking about all the little details of what he had learnt and who he had played with. But as much as I love him, my attention was snatched away, and I was unable to hear a single word of what he was saying to me. Because walking directly towards me, across the playground, were two police officers.

It felt like someone had punched me hard in the stomach as I watched them walking far too casually across the asphalt. What am I going to say to them? How much do they know already? I need to make sure my story is straight in my head, that I have an alibi for everything that has happened. Not just over the last twenty-four hours, but the last few weeks also.

Because just a short few weeks ago, I was just boring school mum Chrissie, working part-time from home, looking after my son and husband and completing the usual day-to-day chores of school runs, dog walks and housework. But all of that changed when my elderly neighbour asked me for the ultimate favour, to help end her life. Maeve had been a good friend and neighbour for years and I had to slowly watch her decline physically following her lung cancer diagnosis, to the point where the once strong and independent woman was essentially bedbound and unable to care for herself anymore. When she asked me to help her end her suffering, I felt like I couldn't say no. I'm not quite 'Dignitas' but what are friends for if they don't show up during your hour of need? But something about that act had ignited a flame of justice in me, which had now overtaken my whole life. The unfairness of seeing the way in which Maeve had to suffer in her final days, whilst evil walk amongst us, has made me act in a manner I never thought I would. And that was why I did what I did to Mr. Turner, and to Kelly.

Mr. Turner was a secondary school teacher that I had discovered was having an illicit affair with an underage schoolgirl, and Kelly was a doctor that worked with my husband who had all but stolen his hard-earned promotion, purely with her nepotism. Her board of director Daddy had given her the job instead of my husband Tim, even though she was well known for having a poor work ethic and her clinical skills were considered undesirable at best. Neither of these two people deserved to be breathing the same air as us, and although perhaps their fate shouldn't have been in my hands, if I didn't act who would have?

Craig and Coleen may have been a bit of a different story though. Don't get me wrong, neither of them were great people but their deaths weren't planned like the other two had been. I needed to get these impulse kills under control because if I'm getting caught now, it's not going to be because of Mr. Turner and Kelly, it's going to be because of those other two, who I clearly got sloppy with. Craig was well known in the community, not in a good way by any means but still, his death was discovered all too quickly considering it had only occurred about an hour or so ago. And now that I'm seeing these police officers making their way over to me, I'm assuming Coleen must have also been found. Coleen, the arrogant school mum who tried to prevent my son from attending her son's birthday party, excluding him and what seemed like only him, for no good reason whatsoever. She might not have been as bad a person as the others, but I'll be damned if I'm going to let anyone hurt my baby. Craig wouldn't have had any ties to the school surely. I'm pretty sure he doesn't have any children and if he does, they don't go to this school. So, the only rational explanation for their attendance is Coleen.

My heart began beating harder and faster and I struggled to catch my breath as the anxiety and panic began to sink in. I was succumbing to the realisation of what was likely about to happen, do I run? Where do I say I've been and what do I say I've been doing? I wasn't prepared for this. But as these thoughts raced through my mind, the police officers continued walking on past me, with not even a glance in my direction and headed straight to the classroom door. A wave of relief washed over me as I saw them speaking to Sam's teacher Mrs. Edgeware, whose face soon became twisted in a mask of horror when no doubt the police had whispered the reason for their visit to her. Within a further few seconds, Mrs. Edgeware hastily ushered the police officers into the classroom, closing the door behind her.

I looked around at some of the other parents' reactions, some appeared confused, some worried. I attempted to mimic their expressions as I quickly guided Sam out of the playground and towards the school gates. The quicker I can get home and make sure I can piece together a reasonable explanation for my whereabouts today, the better. I can't be caught off guard like this again.

14

As we walked out of the school grounds, I noticed that the street alongside the school where we had parked appeared to be busier than usual. The school had a system in place to try and help with the flow of traffic around it, which entailed the different year groups being let out from their classrooms at various times. This would usually mean that a lot of the cars had already left by the time that we got back to the car from pick up, however this did not appear to be the case today.

As we continued down the road it became apparent as to what the issue was. There were police cars stationed at either side of the road, blocking cars from going in or out of the street. Several different parents were huddled in groups, mostly divided by what class their children were in, all looking scared and holding tightly to their children's hands. As we got closer to where I had parked my car, I was able to see past a particularly large gathering of parents to see where Coleen's car had been parked. Where I had left her lifeless body, laid back in the driver's seat. Where her car should have been, were now large, blue freestanding screens with police tape across them. My assumptions of Coleen having been found were correct, and they must now be reviewing the crime scene.

"What's going on mum?" Sam looked up at me, a hint of worry could be heard in the tone of his voice and the grip of his hand tightened in mine.

"I'm not sure darling" I replied, looking around, surveilling which of the parents were nearby and where these people's attention appeared to be focused.

"Why are there police everywhere? Can we not go home Mum?"

I continued to claim ignorance and told him that maybe we should go and wait in the car until we knew what was going on. I wanted to keep as low a profile as possible at this time and at least keep warm too, but just as I reached for the keys in my pocket to unlock the car, a familiar mum voice called over to me.

"Chrissie, do you know what's happened?" The shout came from a group of parents just off to the right-hand side of me.

I walked over to join the group, keeping my hand tightly around my keys and the other holding firmly onto Sams. There were four parents huddled together in a circle, with their children in an inner circle between them. Sam made his way into the throng of kids and began chatting to some of the children in his class.

"What's going on?" I asked, trying to look as nonchalant as possible.

"No-one is quite sure yet" one of the mums whispered back, clearly not wanting the children to be privy to the information being discussed. "We are worried about Coleen though."

"Coleen? Why's that? I don't think I saw her in the playground at pick up just now" I responded back, in an equally hushed tone.

"She wasn't at pick-up" One of the dad's chipped in. "But I definitely saw her car parked up when I was walking up to the gates, so why wasn't she there?"

"You don't think that's her car behind the screen, do you?" the first mum asked.

I allowed my glance to follow the gaze of the other parents, over to the blue screen and police tape across the road. There weren't any gaps to be able to see what was behind the screen at present, but the speculation definitely appeared rife.

"I wonder if this has anything to do with Craig" a mum with dark brown hair and an excessively long fringe, whispered.

"Who's Craig?" the dad enquired.

"You know Craig, the guy who works in the post office shop" fringe mum responded. "I heard a group of mums talking on the playground just now saying that he had been found dead in the shop not long ago."

"But that doesn't explain why there is a screen, and this road being blocked off here if he was found dead in the shop..." the first mum responded.

"Oh my god" I exclaimed, a little bit too loudly in my attempt to sound shocked, alerting the children between us to our conversation.

"What's up mum?" Sam asked, having piqued his interest.

"Nothing, nothing darling, I just remembered I forgot to buy milk earlier, go back to playing" I replied quickly.

A silence fell between the adults, whilst the kids chattered away about their toys and PlayStation games.

After a short while, the fourth mum who I hadn't heard speak up until this point whispered, "I'm really scared guys, I honestly think there's a serial killer going around, and we don't know who is going to be next."

"Don't worry Julie, they say nearly all murders are committed by people that the victim knows right? So, if we don't upset anyone too much, there's no reason for us to worry just yet" the dad responded, in what I can only assume was an attempt to be reassuring to the mum who I had now learnt was called Julie and had silent tears running down her cheeks.

"What worries me" fringe mum interjected "is that there doesn't appear to be any link to the murders other than the victims being local to the area. So how do we know what the motive for the killings are?"

"To be fair, do we even know how they died yet? I know there was some rumors going around about that teacher that died having been attacked by someone beforehand, but other than that, we don't really know much else, do we?" I added, in an attempt to steer the conversation away from murder.

"Craig was a big guy, maybe he had a heart attack." The first mum reasoned.

"Still doesn't explain the roadblocks and screen here though, does it?" Julie said shakily.

"Has anyone asked the police what's going on?" I asked.

"I asked when I first noticed the road was blocked" fringe mum responded, "they wouldn't tell me anything other than I just needed to wait for further instructions."

Almost as if summoned, a female police officer then approached the group.

"Excuse me all" she began "a series of serious incidents have occurred within the last twenty-four hours, and we need to ask all of you for your full co-operation at this time."

"Twenty-four hours?" the dad cried out, "I thought you said Craig was only just found?" He said looking over at fringe mum.

The police office cleared her throat before continuing. "We ask that there be no more speculation or discussion regarding what has transpired currently whilst we have an active investigation underway. However, what we do require is for you all to return to the school and head to the assembly hall."

"What, now?" squeaked Julie, "I have to get home and get ready for my night shift."

"I'm afraid your night shift is going to have to wait, right now our main priority is the safety of the community and to maintain that safety, we require everyone to attend the assembly hall, where you will receive further instructions. I suggest if you have any commitments coming up within the next hour or two that you call ahead and cancel as we cannot give an estimated time as to when the road will reopen." With that, the police office turned and headed towards the next group of parents that were chatting a bit further up the road.

"Come along then children" the dad commanded "back to school it is then". He began to pace back up the street, with the children and the rest of the mums hurrying behind him, like an anxiety driven Pied Piper.

15

    I sat in the assembly hall, where rows and rows of chairs had been put out for the parents to sit on. Julie was sitting to my left and fringe mum to my right. I looked around, trying to see which other parents I could identify and to try and guess how many parents were there. The hall was jam packed with more parents still filtering in through the open double doors at the back of the room. There were police officers stationed at the doors and by the stage in front of us, where some teachers were also sat, alongside the headteacher Mrs. Ivory. The children had been redirected to classrooms, away from the assembly hall with the teaching assistants so that the parents full focus could be on the stage and clearly there were going to be topics of discussion that would not have been suitable for the ears of primary school children.

I looked over to the right-hand side of the stage, sitting near the front were some of the mums I knew from Sam's class. I caught a glance of one of the mums called Alison and gave a small wave. She appeared to avert her gaze, but I wasn't sure if that was intentional or if perhaps, she hadn't seen me. She was sitting with her best friend Rachel, another one of the mums from Sams class, and a few other faces that I recognised but wasn't friendly enough to know their names. There were few parent names I did know, thinking about it. The school mum social scene had never really appealed to me.

Before long, the doors at the back of the hall were shut and I glanced round to see that the hall was so busy that there was a considerable number of parents having to stand at the back, with not enough chairs for everyone. Normally I would think myself lucky to have gotten a seat at all, but on this occasion, all I could think about was how difficult it would be for me to make a swift exit if I needed to. Surely there was a limit as to how many people were allowed in the hall at one time. Wasn't there a fire safety issue with this? I guess with what was going on, that probably wasn't their top priority.

My thoughts were interrupted by the sound of a chair scraping back against the hardwood flooring of the stage as Mrs. Ivory, the headteacher, stood up to address the sea of parents in front of her.

"Thank you all for your co-operation and attending the hall as requested." She began, as silence spread across the hall, no further mummering's between people, as she immediately captured the attention of everyone in the room. "As I'm sure most of you are now aware, a serious incident has occurred directly outside the school this afternoon which has caused considerable concern for the welfare of the children, as well as ourselves."

Hushed whispers could be heard, speculation as to what was going on, eager to be discussed by all. Mrs. Ivory cleared her throat, immediately commanding silence.

"I would like you all to pass your attention to Detective Inspector Wills who will be keeping us informed with as much information as he can, and what we all need to do moving forward." With that she stepped backwards towards her seat but continued to stand as a tall, blonde-haired gentleman in a tailored black suit stepped forward.

"Good afternoon, it is with great sadness that I have to inform you that there has been a suspected homicide having occurred on Crest Street this afternoon" he stated. He allowed a brief period of shocked gasps, and some further whispered voices before continuing. "A parent of one of the children within this school has been found deceased in her car, parked outside on the street, and at this time, this has been ruled as a suspicious death."

"Oh my gosh, Coleen" Julie gasped beside me.

"We don't know that it's her Julie" whispered the dad from earlier who was sitting beside her.

"If I could keep your full attention, please." DI Wills voice echoed out across the hall. "The death in particular has led our investigation to conclude that there is a potential link between this death and that of recent other deaths within the local area and therefore it is imperative that an action plan be put in place to maintain safety within the community."

"I knew it was a serial killer" I heard from a voice a few rows behind me.

"How many deaths have there been?" shouted a parent to DI Wills.

The detective waited patiently for everyone to look in his direction again. He clearly didn't want to have to keep repeating himself and must have been anticipating this question coming up.

"At present" he began, "there have been four deaths in the community within the last few weeks, all of which are being treated as being under suspicious circumstances."

"Four!" began echoing around the hall as a multitude of parents began to realise the severity of the situation and how little they had been aware of, up until this moment.

Questions began firing at DI Wills, who just held his hands up and awaited silence to fall again before responding. "We will not be disclosing the names of the victims or the current known circumstances around their deaths at this time so as not to potentially cause any disruption to the investigation. However, we do urge that anyone that may have any information in relation to any of the incidents having occurred within the last few weeks to come and speak to one of the officers or myself, who will be stationed outside the assembly hall."

My hands felt clammy, and I looked down to see that I had been gripping my hands together so tightly in my lap that my nails had sunk deep enough into the skin to cause an abrasion. I hastily wiped my hands on my jeans and attempted to slow my breathing down which I had also noticed had been going faster than usual. Julie's legs were bouncing up and down next to me, clearly in a nervous state following the information she had just heard.

"Four deaths, I wonder who the fourth is." Fringe mum whispered to me.

"Who's the third?" I asked, my mind rapidly trying to keep track of what I was supposed to know and what I wasn't supposed to know.

"Well Coleen must be the parent found dead. Ian said he had seen her car outside but none of us saw her in the playground at pick up and I've been trying to see if I can see her in the hall too, but she's nowhere to be found. Her husband doesn't seem to be here either. There's no way Coleen would be missing out on all this action if she could help it." She whispered back, almost sounding excited by the whole prospect of what was unfolding before us. If only she knew who she was really talking to.

Mrs. Ivory stepped forward again on the stage and cleared her throat to get everyone's focus once more. "Detective Wills has kindly asked that we all remain in the assembly hall for the time being, until they complete their investigations in the street outside. They will keep us informed as to when we can leave." She addressed the crowd. "The children will be kept entertained by the staff in the classrooms, videos have been put on for them and the kitchen staff are making up snacks and drinks. We want to keep them away from any talk of this matter, as much as possible."

This appeared to be the end of the information being given for now as Mrs. Ivory was seen sitting back down at her seat on the stage and the detective began walking down the steps and heading for outside the hall where numerous officers were now stationed.

As soon as the doors were heard to close behind him, the hall erupted into noise as all the parents began talking to each other. Julie appeared to be having a full-blown meltdown next to me, monopolising the dad from outside Ian's attention who was trying to calm her down. Numerous other cries could be heard around the hall, as were the voices of numerous parents all talking over each other, wanting to know who the victims were and how they had died.

Fringe mum appeared to be trying to get my attention to discuss further what was going on, but my attention was elsewhere, scanning the hall specifically to track who was going out to speak to the officers. A few parents went out, none of which I recognised so I wasn't overly concerned with whatever information they thought they knew and wanted to share. Some of which were likely just people wanting to ask more questions or try and find out more information. I started to relax a bit until I spotted one of the mums from Sams class heading over to DI Wills. I watched as Rachel strode confidently over to him and proceeded to engage in quite a long conversation. I could see the detective nodding along through the window between them and the hall, and his right arm moving where he was likely taking notes. What could she possibly have to tell him? Did she know any of the victims other than Coleen? I know very little about Rachel, maybe she was friendly with the family that runs the post office shop or maybe she works at the hospital with Kelly? I saw Rachel turn and look over in my direction and our eyes met. She averts her gaze before I do but then DI Wills turns and looks in my direction as well. I look away, why are they both looking at me? Has she said something about me to them? Surely not, what could she know?

"Water?" I turned round panic stricken at the bemused face of one of the kitchen staff who was passing out bottles of water to the parents. I shook my head and turned to look at fringe mum who had been watching me without me having noticed.

"Are you okay?" she asked concerned.

"Yeah, sorry, it's just a scary thing all this. Not knowing what's happening and to who." I replied quickly.

"I'm sure we will find out what's going on soon enough. There are never any secrets in this village" fringe mum let out a small nervous laugh.

No secrets in this village, that's what I'm afraid of. I looked back round to where Rachel had been talking to the detective, but she was no longer with him, and he appeared to be speaking with one of the other officers instead. Looking back around the hall I spotted her standing with a group of mums chatting again. I excused myself to fringe mum, stating that I had seen someone I wanted to speak to quickly, and headed over to where Rachel stood.

The conversation between the group Rachel was in was rampant, various speculations around who had been killed and what had happened. Coleen's name was mentioned a few times, as was Craig's but no one seemed to mention Kelly at least, so that was good. I nodded along with the conversation for a bit, not giving too much input myself but making mental notes of what everyone seemed to be thinking had happened. Nothing said seemed at all incriminating to me though, which was a relief. As time went on, a few of the mums excused themselves to either attend the restroom or to speak to other parents, until it was just me and Rachel left, both looking awkwardly at each other.

"I saw you speaking to the detective" I inquired, "did you find anything out?" I didn't want her to think that I was asking directly what she could have been telling him, but I needed to know what she knew.

"Oh that, I was just telling him about Coleen not being at the pickup and how that was odd." She muttered unconvincingly.

"Oh really, a few of the mums have said that they think she's the victim you know." I replied, trying to wiggle out some further information from her.

"Do they now?" she replied evenly, clearly not wanting to maintain the conversation with me.

Before I could try and probe any further, the headmistress was seen to approach the stage again and Rachel quickly turned her back to me, to face Mrs. Ivory.

"Thank you everyone for your patience this afternoon. I know the news has come as a terrible shock to all of you and wish to extend our support in any way we can. If there are any parent or child that has been directly impacted as a result of what has occurred, we have pastoral staff on hand for anyone that needs any further support." Mrs. Ivory was an older teacher, likely in her early sixties, and the events of the day had clearly taken a toll on her. She seemed deflated and tired as she continued. "The officers have informed us that the road is now clear, and you can collect your children from their classrooms and return home. Unfortunately, we do regret to inform you that the school will be closed for the rest of the week, and it is unclear when it will reopen. Detective Wills has asked for our closure to allow for more thorough investigations to take place. Please ensure to keep an eye out in your emails for further updates as to when the school will reopen. We also ask that no or as little information as possible be told to the children to prevent any undue harm. Thank you." She then left.

Everyone in the room appeared to spring into action. Chairs scraped across the floor as people got up and started collecting their belongings and making a beeline for the exit. I checked my watch to see that it was now 6pm. We had been contained in the hall for the last two hours. There were still officers everywhere as everyone dispersed in different directions to collect their children and head home. Once Sam was released, he immediately began asking what was going on and I continued to evade his questions, saying that we weren't told very much but that I did know that there was nothing to worry about. Which of course was true, there would never be any harm coming to Sam.

We headed back out the school gates for the second time this afternoon and straight to the car. As Sam buckled himself into his booster seat in the back, I noticed that the road appeared the same as every other day. The screens and police tape were gone and other than the odd police car still parked up along the street, there was no other indication of what had occurred earlier on. Not that there would have been much mess left for them to clear up, as a mum and housewife I always ensure to prevent making as much mess as possible.

I turned the ignition on, put the car into first gear and pulled away from the parking space, ready to return home and for this incredibly long day to be over.

16

A few days passed and the constant feeling of paranoia in the pit of my stomach hasn't changed. I've been able to keep myself distracted with having Sam home at least, but every car I hear outside or every knock at the door brings me instantly back to the police walking towards me on the playground. I can't stop thinking about Rachel either. I'm sure she knows more than she is letting on and she seemed off with me when I was trying to talk to her about it. Could she possibly have an indication that I'm involved?

My mother-in-law Diane was coming to visit today, in fact, now that I'm looking at the time she is due at any moment. Sam is really excited to see her. He hasn't seen her in a while as she lives about three hours' drive away, so it's hard to get visits in, especially with how much Tim, my husband works. I try to avoid visiting her without Tim. Diane and I have never really seen eye to eye. She's one of those mothers-in-law who blame the woman for taking away their son, rather than welcoming them into the family. She's also exceedingly condescending towards me. She never felt like I was good enough for Tim, her beloved doctor son. The whole family comes from money and are all doing well in their respective careers. Tim has a younger brother who is a lawyer and an older sister who does something in finance that I can never remember, despite her having told me numerous times. Diane always likes to ensure that it's known to anyone around that she doesn't approve of my lack of career. She's usually slightly better with Tim around and he was meant to be off work today, but just as my luck would have it, he got called in for an emergency surgery for a young girl who had been in a car accident.

I jumped with a start, as a loud knock on the front door rang through the downstairs hallway and into the kitchen where I was making a coffee. I knew she was coming; I knew it would be any time from now, but with me being constantly on edge now, I still couldn't stop my heart from racing and my body involuntarily shaking when the knock at the door came.

I heard Sam running to the front door, getting there before I could, to welcome his grandmother into the home.

"Gran!!" shouted Sam with clear excitement. "Gran, come look and see what I've been doing." He pulled her through the hallway and into the living room to show her his collection of dinosaur models he had been sat meticulously painting for the last thirty minutes.

Diane followed him, not that she was being given a choice, without taking the time to acknowledge me in the kitchen doorway or to take her shoes off before walking across the plush beige carpet. Time to bite my tongue, I guess.

"Diane, how are you?" I asked with a fake cheerful note to my voice.

"Clearly doing better than you Chrissie" she stated matter of fact whilst looking me up and down. It was only 10am and we hadn't needed to go out anywhere yet, so I hadn't bothered getting dressed out of my Pajamas or done anything with my hair. "You do realise it's the middle of the day."

I never quite understood why the women of her generation felt the need to get washed, dressed and put on a full face of make-up as soon as they wake up in the morning, even when not going out anywhere. Firstly, what a waste of make-up to wear it when no-one but yourself is going to see it, secondly, surely it just generates more washing to get changed into clean clothes every day when you're not going out and thirdly, all that makeup on your skin all the time can't be good for it. Wouldn't it be better to let it breathe occasionally?

"Oh, you know me, Diane. No need for all the razzle dazzle when I'm not leaving the house." I replied, trying not to let her spiteful undertone get to me.

"Well, I'm guessing you know why I've come to visit?" She asked.

"I'm assuming it's to see Sam whilst he is not in school?"

"It's about all this nasty business going on in this village of yours. Tim's told me everything". She looked over at Sam before lowering her voice so as not for him to hear, "all the m u r d e r s'" she spelt.

"Why would that bring you here? Looking for an early end to it all?" I joked, not that Diane had ever been a fan of my dark humour.

"Don't be ridiculous, I've come to protect my grandson." She scoffed. "I want to take him home with me for a while."

"I'm sorry you want to do what?" I asked incredulously. Had she already spoken to Tim about this? Was this already agreed upon without my knowledge? It wouldn't surprise me if she had planned this in advance. "Well, you can't, just because the school is closed at the moment doesn't mean it won't reopen at any time."

"I've already spoken to his school Chrissie, and they have informed me that there are no current plans to reopen." She retorted, clearly happy that I was put out by her request.

I walked into the kitchen, indicating for her to follow so that we could continue the conversation, out of hearing range of Sam.

"Why would you think it is your place to speak to the school? He's not your son Diane, he's mine." I shot back.

"Well then act like a responsible parent and let him come and stay with me until the school reopens. For heaven's sake Chrissie, there is a mad man running around out there, he could be anywhere at any time and there's nothing to make us think that the police are any closer to catching him. What do you intend to do? Keep Sam at home in hiding when he could come and stay with me, away from all this nonsense and be able to go out to the park without fear of a homicidal maniac coming after him?!"

She had a point, and I didn't know how to argue against it without revealing too much. Funny how she said mad man instead of mad woman though. I appreciate that female killers are of a lesser percentage than men, but in this day and age, you would think she could be a bit more progressive in terms of her stereotyping.

Of course, I knew that Sam was safe, but no one else could know that. I may have to just go along with her proposal. Then when the school reopens, I would have a good excuse to demand he comes back home and they can't keep it closed for too long, especially considering the last death didn't even occur in the school, just outside it.

"Okay Diane, fine." I let out a sigh. "I'll go pack up a bag for him."

"Fabulous" she smirked. "I'll just help myself to a cup of coffee whilst I wait then shall I." She then turned her back to me and proceeded to finish off making the cup of coffee for herself that I had started to make before she knocked on the door.

I muttered some not so 'PG' remarks under my breath as I stormed up the stairs and headed to Sam's bedroom to start packing up some clothes and toys for him.

Why could I never seem to win against Diane? Honestly, the woman has always known exactly how to get under my skin and wind me up. If it wasn't for the fact that I was trying to stem my murderous impulses and stop acting on emotions, as well as the impact it would have on Tim and Sam, I would have been reaching for the last insulin injection without a second thought. Instead, I allowed myself to daydream for a few minutes, sat on Sam's bed, thinking about the wonderful sight of Diane's shocked expression as I stuck the needle in her and her lifeless body lying on my kitchen floor. Shame it's not worth the childhood trauma that would have caused Sam.

I threw some items into a large duffel bag and came back down to the living room where Diane was sitting sipping at her coffee and Sam was starting to pack up his paints.

"Gran says I'm going to have a sleepover at her house" Sam beamed up at me.

"That's right darling, you get to go and stay a few days with Gran and maybe see some of your cousins whilst the school is shut."

Sam started chattering on about all the fun things he was planning to do once he reached his Gran's house and which family members he wanted to see and play with. I handed the duffel bag over to Diane and squatted down to envelope Sam into a big bear hug.

"I'm going to miss you so much buddy" I said to him, snuggling my head into his neck and kissing his cheek. "You be a good boy for your Granny, and I will see you in a few days."

Sam eagerly held hands with Diane and walked out to her car, not even looking back as he went. I felt the sting of tears hitting my cheeks as I stood at the front door and watched the car pull away. There goes my boy, my whole world and sadly, also my distraction.

As I closed the front door and returned to the living room, sinking into my usual space on the sofa, I was instantly brought back to the worries of my current predicament. I picked up my phone and started scrolling through Facebook, looking in particular at the local village and the school pages in the hopes that some new information had been put up to give me some hint as to what the police may or may not know, but there was nothing I hadn't already seen. Not surprising really considering how often I had been checking these pages over the last few days. The mums WhatsApp group had been exceptionally quiet recently too. I know there wasn't likely much to discuss in relation to school with it being closed, but there hadn't even been the odd meme shared, or any mention of what had been going on. Is everyone keeping their thoughts to themselves on the matter? Or are they only speaking to select people instead of the group as a whole? It's times like this I now regret my decision to not get involved in playground politics. If I had been one of the insider mums, then I would have had more information by now for sure.

I started flicking through some of the mums' Facebook profiles directly instead, to see if I could tell who was likely speaking to who. Sometimes you can get an indication as to how close people are to each other by how often they comment or like each other's posts. I needed to find something out soon or I was going to go stir crazy and now with Sam gone, there was nothing to distract me from the obsessional thoughts and paranoia starting to take hold.

Rachel was going to be the most important person to try and get some intel on. I loaded up her profile and started scrolling down to see what I could find. Her page seemed to be mostly focused on her business which I hadn't been aware of up until now, that she even had. Apparently, she runs her own nail salon out of an outbuilding in her garden. There were pictures plastered across to advertise her workspace, certifications and qualifications she had gained etc. Numerous before and after photos of nails. At the top of her page was also a link to, what I discovered upon clicking, was a business website. On the website, alongside most of the same advertisements that I had seen on Facebook, was also a booking page, to make an appointment with her. I looked down at my own hands, the rough cuticles, nails bitten down to the quick. Might be time for me to get my nails done.

I opened the booking link to see what information was required to be able to make an appointment. The information needed was surprisingly minimal. All that was necessary was to provide my name and select the date and time on a calendar based on her availability that I wanted to book into. There was no requirement for any further information to be given, no contact details needed or a deposit to be made. This couldn't be more perfect, I thought to myself. If Rachel has any suspicions about me, she's probably not going to want to spend an hour or two in a small outdoor office space alone with me, so a pseudonym was going to be needed.

The next available appointment was for tomorrow at 3pm. Her calendar didn't appear to be too busy, by the looks of the number of available slots that could be booked. I clicked onto the 3pm slot and a small box popped up requesting my name for the booking.

"Kelly Turner" I typed in, allowing a small giggle to myself. As I hit enter, a message flashed up to state that my booking had been confirmed and her business/home address was also then displayed for me, which I made a quick note of.

Let's see what Rachel has to say when it's just me and her together without the safety net of police officers nearby or other mums being able to overhear. Hopefully, it will turn out to all be in my head and she won't have any suspicions of me, but if I can't find out I don't know what I will do with myself. Best case scenario, me and Rachel become best friends and I leave with a nice new set of acrylics. Worst case scenario, I can ensure I have my trusty injection to hand, but that would have to be a very last resort.

17

I'm not quite sure if I'm more nervous or excited as I walk the few streets to Rachels house, ready for my appointment. Or should I say Kelly Turner's appointment. Once I had seen how close she lived I thought the best course of action would be to walk there so as not to have to leave my car anywhere too close by where it could be spotted. I've lived here for long enough now that I know all the back roads, so I didn't need to take any main roads where I could be seen either.

As I approach my destination, I can clearly see the outbuilding just to the side of the long driveway leading up to the main house. There are no cars on the drive so her husband must be out, hopefully with their children considering that Rachel is planning to be working. This is perfect, we should have total privacy. I approached the outbuilding and took a quick look inside through a window. I could see Rachel sat at a desk, eyes glued to her phone screen, so she had yet to notice my arrival. All along the back walls inside there were shelves with rows and rows of different nail polishes and framed certificates, clearly wanting to show off to her customer base just how many different nail skills she had. I give the door three strong knocks before hearing "come in" echo from inside.

I opened the door and walked in slowly, waiting to catch Rachels' attention which at present still seemed to be focused on her phone. Is this really how she is going to greet a customer? How rude. I cleared my throat, and she looked up at me for the first time.

"Chrissie!" she exclaimed, clearly surprised at my presence. "What are you doing here?"

"I'm your three o'clock" I replied coolly.

She was unable to hide the shock from her face as she quickly scrolled through her calendar on her phone. "No, no I've not got you booked in for any appointments. I'm expecting a new client. I'm really sorry but you will have to come back another time or you can book online if it's easier." She seemed to want rid of me, clearly uncomfortable being in my presence. I wonder why that was.

"Oh no, you've got me all wrong. I'm all booked in already. I just booked under a different name, that's all. Originally, I was booking the appointment for my friend Kelly, but she couldn't come so I decided that I would take the appointment instead. That's ok, isn't it? I responded, trying to hide my smirk.

"Why would you book under a fake name Chrissie?" she asked bluntly.

"It's not a fake name, I told you, I had booked for my friend." I retorted.

"Well considering how recent the booking was, I find that hard to believe." She started to get up from her chair and make her way towards where I was standing, the exit door behind me. She opened the door further and gestured for me to leave. "If it's all the same, I think I'd rather we just reschedule for another day. I've got a headache coming on."

"Come on now Rachel, why don't you want to do my nails? I'm a paying customer." I grinned at her, which seemed to make her even more uncomfortable than she already was.

"What do you want Chrissie?" she demanded.

"I want to know what you know Rachel, and what it was that you really told the police at the school the other day."

"I told you already" she stammered "I just told them that Coleen was running late for pick up."

"You never said she was running late when I asked you before" I probed "you just said that you had told them she wasn't at pick-up. So, what do you know about Coleen?"

Rachel was becoming evidently more scared by the turn of the conversation. She attempted to move towards the door herself, but I positioned myself to prevent her from leaving. Our eyes locked.

"You know Coleen didn't like you, right?" she stated, being the first to break the intense eye contact between us. "Why do you think that was?"

The question took me by surprise. Of course, I had an indication that there was an issue with Coleen, but I had assumed that the issue had been with Sam, not with me. When she purposefully excluded him from her son's birthday party, it hadn't occurred to me that it could have been anything I had done to have caused it.

"What are you talking about?" I asked.

"Don't play the innocent Chrissie" Rachel spat "You know exactly what I'm talking about."

"I'm not here to play games with you Rachel, tell me what you know now before you make me do something we both regret." I seethed.

"You really don't know?" she stated surprised "Coleen had found out about you and Greg. She told me all about it."

"Who the fuck is Greg?" I demanded, confused.

"Her husband, you were having an affair with him. Don't play dumb."

"What?!" I shouted incredulously "What bullshit is this? I'm not having an affair with anyone. How dare you make such a disgusting accusation against me."

Who did this woman think she was? She barely even knows me, so how could she conclude that I would cheat on my husband. Tim was the love of my life; I would never do anything that could jeopardise our marriage or destroy our family like that.

"Coleen had told me all about it. She had told a lot of the mums about it. Everyone knows what you're like Chrissie, that's why she didn't want to invite Sam to her son's birthday party and that's why a lot of the mums don't speak to you. No-one else wants you going after their husbands." Rachel seemed to be enjoying the confrontation now, almost as if she could see how taken off guard I was.

"Why would she think I was having an affair with her husband? I don't even know him. I barely know her." I muttered, my brain reeling at the revelation that there was a common misconception of me across the playground that I was a home wrecker. Here's me worrying about people thinking I'm a serial killer, when they already think of me as a whore.

"She had seen the messages on his phone Chrissie, you can't deny it. She took pictures of them and showed them to me. I've seen the dirty messages you were sending each other, the meetups you have arranged, the hotel you booked. I even saw some of the disgusting naked photos you sent him, but at least you were smart enough not to show your face in them otherwise I'm sure they would have made their way to the internet by now." Rachel was beginning to smirk, she clearly felt that she had bested me at this point.

"What would make you think those messages were from me though? I didn't even know the man's name until a minute ago when you said it. I couldn't pick him out in a line up. I've never met him. I've never been anywhere near him, and I certainly wouldn't be cheating on my husband. You need to set the record straight with people."

"He had your name saved in his phone, how many Chrissie's do you think there are running around this village? I only know of one, and that's you." Rachel began to raise her voice. "I won't be telling anyone anything, you're a disgusting slut! Now get out of my salon."

Before I knew it, I pushed Rachel backwards with force, causing her body to slam against the table behind her. She looked up at me, eyes wide, half stood, half laid back on the table.

"Oh my god. It was you wasn't it." Rachel muttered, her words coming out in barely a whisper. "You hurt Coleen didn't you."

This was not how this conversation was meant to go. Nothing about this had gone to plan. The information I had gained from confronting Rachel was definitely not what I was expecting and instantly my anger had raised her suspicions enough for her to realise that it was me that had killed Coleen. I wouldn't be able to let her live now. There was no way she wouldn't go straight to the police as soon as I left or tell the other mums what had happened. Everyone on the playground already thought I was a homewrecker; no-one would probably be surprised to discover I was a killer too after this. My innocent school mum persona had been tainted by Coleen's lies and now that everyone knew about this so-called affair that hadn't even happened, how many other people will think that I had a motive for killing Coleen?

I reached into my coat pocket and pulled out the insulin pen, which I had already prepared before leaving the home just in case the situation arose. I saw the fear flash in Rachel's eyes as I advanced towards her, injection at the ready.

"No, no, please" she pleaded as she tried to get herself up from the table. But I was too quick for her. In a flash I was on top of her, pressing my body up against hers and ramming the needle through her thin leggings and into her thigh.

"What are you doing" she screamed out in pain as she felt the sharp stab to her leg. "What was that?! What have you done!"

I smiled down at her as she struggled against my body weight. She was stronger than Coleen had been, but she still wasn't strong enough against me. She was already in a disadvantaged position from my push, so I had the upper hand from the jump. Tears began streaming down her cheeks, but she didn't scream out. It was almost as if she had succumbed to the inevitable and the fight from her seemed to go altogether. A few more minutes passed, neither of us saying anything to each other, her body just feeling weaker underneath mine with each passing moment, until she completely slid to the floor with a thud. I got up from the table that I was still half leant on and looked down at her as I dusted myself off. She didn't seize, isn't that supposed to happen? Her eyes appeared glassy and transfixed so regardless of the lesser dramatics of the kill, the job appeared to be complete.

I quietly left the outbuilding and made my way down the driveway as quickly as I could, whilst also trying to look casual in case anyone saw me. It wouldn't do to be raising suspicions now. Hopefully due to the nature of her business, an unfamiliar female face coming out of the outbuilding wouldn't raise any alarm bells. Once I was a bit further away from the house I broke into a light jog, with the plan to take the back roads and get home as quickly as possible.

18

    Halfway home and realisation hits me, I've not got the injection in my pocket. In my haste to leave I must have left it behind, likely lying on the floor next to Rachel's body. My footsteps halted, and I leant against a nearby lamppost to catch my breath. I'd have to go back and get it; I can't just leave it there for anyone to find. Although there's nothing linking me to insulin at the moment, what if they get my fingerprints from it? I've never had to provide fingerprints to the police before so it's not like they would get a match, but I do use the fingerprint sensor on my phone, what if that's somehow traceable? It's not a risk I can take. With a sigh, I turn around and start power walking back to Rachel's house.

There are still no cars on the drive when I arrive and I take a quick look around the neighbourhood, scanning to see if there's anyone out and about, but there's not. I quickly make my way back into the outbuilding where Rachels body remains laid out on the floor. I should feel bad about what I've done to her, she didn't really do anything to me or anyone else as far as I know, but I can't risk her telling everyone her suspicions.

I cast my eyes around the room, looking for something I can use to erase my presence here. I can't stop thinking about my fingerprints now. I swiftly collect the discarded insulin pen on the floor and shove it into my pocket and as I rise back up from the ground, through the corner of my eye I spot a bottle of acetone on the desk. Nail polish remover might not be quite the bleach I need but surely if it's strong enough to soak off acrylics then it has to be strong enough to remove fingerprints from surfaces. It certainly smells like it.

I removed the bottle from the desk and unscrewed the lid, letting the pungent smell hit me, bringing a smile to my lips. This would surely work. Now, what had I likely touched? In the far corner of the building was a sink with a paper towel dispenser situated above it. I grabbed some towels out and began pouring the acetone on to them before then rubbing down the door handles, the desk and any other surface I thought I could have potentially touched.

The whole room absolutely reeked, almost vinegar like, causing me to start coughing. The only other thing I would have touched now was Rachel, I can't rub her entire body down with this stuff though surely, and there's not very much left after I've used it on everything else. Alongside some of the nail varnishes there were a few more bottles of acetone lined up on one of the shelves. If there's one thing you can say about Rachel, is that she sure was organised.

I grabbed two more bottles, unscrewed the lids and then unceremoniously began dumping the contents onto Rachels motionless body beneath me. The smell of the acetone rising up, offending my nostrils. I felt like I was completing some sort of bizarre ritual, if I hadn't been the cause of her death, perhaps I would have felt inclined to have said a few words.

Once the bottles were empty, I scooped up all three empty ones I had used, alongside the paper towels and began to make my exit home again, using the paper to open the door handle to let me out. As I proceeded down the driveway and back onto the road, I saw the front door of a neighbour's house begin to open. I quickly stuffed the paper towels and empty bottles into the front of my coat, hugging my arms tightly against me in a folded manner to prevent them from slipping down my body and put my head down, staring at the floor in front of me in the hopes that I'm not seen, and if I am seen, that I'm not recognised.

I need to think of somewhere to stash all this rubbish before I get home. A few streets away was a large woodland area and I began making my way in that direction. I could feel the beginning of rain start coming down, gentle droplets hitting the top of my head as relief washed over me. If it's raining, there is definitely going to be less chance of anyone coming out for a walk and spotting me in the woods.

I made my way through a small alleyway between two houses, only a few streets away from Rachels and not too far from my own home either. At the end of the alley was a wooden stile, leading into the woods. I clambered over it, almost slipping on the wet wood in my rush. I caught myself against the alleyway wall beside me and continued onward. How deep do I have to go, I wonder. I need to make sure I find somewhere far enough that it's unlikely to be found, but also, I'm cold and getting wet and I'm just over it at this point. I push my lazy thoughts out of my head and instead begin to think about the repercussions of being caught, everything I would lose, my home, my husband, my son. This driving fact motivated me further and further into the woods.

I had been following the footpath for the majority of my trapse through the forest, but I knew I couldn't just leave it lying around in plain sight, no matter how deep into the woods I went. I began looking around me for small offshoots to be able to go deeper into some of the brushwood. The rain was coming down harder now. I could feel the mud squelching underfoot, slipping ever so slightly with every step. I had not been prepared for off roading, so my footwear was far from appropriate. I began pushing branches and leaves out of my way, to go as far in as I could, before coming to a very small clearing. This would have to do.

On the floor were various sticks and twigs and I picked a few up, weighing them in my hands to source out the strongest one. Once I had located one of a decent strength and weight, I began to use it like a shovel, digging into the wet earth between my feet. Down and down, I dug, mud splashing up at me, covering me from head to toe, but this was something I would have to worry about later. For now, it was imperative that I got this evidence hidden and got back home before anyone saw me milling around in this weather and covered in mud.

Once the hole was of a suitable size, I crammed the bottles, paper towels and the injection which was now empty and therefore no longer of any use to me, inside it. There was just enough space to fit it all in. The stick was next to useless now from all the digging, the wood having become so sodden that it was falling apart, so I used my hands to scope the mud back into the hole, stamping it down into place with my feet to even the ground level out. It wouldn't do to leave a big obvious lump to mark the spot of my buried treasure now, would it?

With the deed done, I began making my way back out of the woods, through the underbrush and back to the main walking trail, before heading back to the alleyway I had come in through. I heard a rumble of thunder overhead as I quick stepped through the path. I could never remember if being by trees was good or bad if there's lightning, but I wasn't planning to stay around long enough to find out. Once back onto the main roads, I broke out into a jog, still taking a few backroads to get back home.

I arrived at my front door, soaked through, freezing cold and absolutely covered in mud. I'm so glad Sam is with my mother-in-law and Tim is at work because I've no idea how I would have explained my current state to anyone. I must have looked like a mad woman. I unlocked the door, shook myself off and stepped inside. As soon as the door was closed behind me, I stripped off all of my sodden clothing. Standing naked in the hallway, I turned towards the large mirror to the right-hand side of me and caught a glimpse of my reflection. I couldn't help but chuckle at what was staring back at me. My hair, which was in a sleek, tidy ponytail when I had left the house, was now sticking up all over the place, half in and half out, of the once tight bobble. Mud was splattered all over my face and hair, with parts of my hair matted in placed. Imagine if anyone had seen me like this. I look like the wild woman of Borneo.

I picked up my bundled mess of clothing from the floor, leaving a large wet patch on the hardwood, which I would have to mop up later, and made my way into the kitchen. I threw my clothing into the washing machine, setting it to an intense wash and then made my way up to the ensuite bathroom to take a shower.

The heat of the water penetrated my skin. It almost felt euphoric, like the water was washing away everything that I had just done, not just the mud, but my actions as well. I reveled in the warmth of the water and the smell of my shower gel and shampoo as I began scrubbing every inch of me clean. I watched as the water by my feet went from brown to clear, a good indication that I had been successful in my cleaning frenzy. I turned off the shower and grabbed a large towel to wrap myself up in.

As I walked out of the ensuite bathroom and into my bedroom to dry myself off I was stopped in my tracks at the sight of my husband Tim standing by the bedroom door.

"What are you doing home?" I yelped out in surprise.

Tim gave me a big grin as he came towards me. "Shame I wasn't home a few minutes earlier; I could have joined you in that shower."

"Oh, if only Doctor" I giggled back, "I've been overdue for a physical this year."

Tim came towards me, wrapping one arm around my waist whilst pulling the towel from my naked body with the other. His lips met mine and we kissed passionately before he picked me up and threw me onto our bed. I looked up at him as he began undoing the buttons on his shirt. How did I get so lucky to have gotten a man like him? Strong, attentive, handsome, ambitious, the list could go on. Once his shirt was off, he leant down over me on the bed and began kissing me again, but this time not stopping at my lips. He worked his way down my neck, to my chest, sucking on my nipples one by one, causing a small moan to escape from me.

"Hurry" I gasped, as I could feel myself losing control. "I want you inside me now!"

Tim began pulling at his trousers and underwear, hastily dropping them to the floor, releasing his large swollen member. I moaned at the sight of it. After so many years of marriage, he could still take my breath away.

Before I could stare any longer, he entered me roughly, pinning me down to the bed with his hard body. I gave a brief thought as to if this is what my victims felt like when I had pinned them down with my bodyweight, although I suppose they were unlikely to feel as exultant as I am currently. The thoughts didn't remain in my mind long though, as I felt the orgasm building up inside of me like an orchestra meeting a crescendo. I screamed out in ecstasy as I felt the orgasm ripple through my body, helping Tim to reach his climax too as a few more pumps later, he also appeared to be finished.

Tim rolled over next to me, panting, with a large smile on his face. "It's been a while since we've done that" he chuckled.

"Well, you've been so busy at the hospital, I barely see you." I responded gently.

"Filling in as the head of Pediatrics since what happened to Kelly has definitely been more time consuming." Tim replied.

"Nice of you to find the time to fill me in too then" I giggled, resting my head on his bare chest.

"I'm sorry, I know I've barely been home."

"It's ok" I reassured him "This is what you've been working so hard for. You deserved that promotion from the get-go. Anyway, you never answered my earlier question."

"What question?" he asked confused.

"What are you doing home so early?" I reminded him.

"Oh yeah, I forgot to tell you." He laughed, "I've been sent home early to get ready for this evening."

"This evening?" I queried.

"Who's got the poor memory now?" He chided me.

"Oh my gosh, I had totally forgotten about it!" I jumped out of bed and checked my watch. It was 6pm and we had to be ready to leave at seven. I sprang into action, running into the dressing room to begin getting myself ready.

How had I forgotten about Kelly's memorial dinner this evening?! With everything else going on, it had completely slipped my mind. I know I've got to play the part but I'm really not up for pretending to be a happy go lucky boring housewife this evening.

I grabbed the hairdryer, switched it on and aimed it at my hair. My dress for the evening was hung up on the dressing room door, having been freshly dry cleaned for the occasion. A visual reminder that I had clearly missed. So, what else could I have been missing?

I had very little time now to get myself ready. Usually, I would spend hours preparing for a hospital event like this, especially one as important as a memorial dinner. Once my hair was dried, I expertly tied it into a loose chignon, leaving some strands dangling down at the front to frame my face. I then began concentrating on my make-up, when Tim walked into the room, currently wearing only a white shirt and boxer shorts. He must have just got out of the shower himself as I smelt a waft of men's fragrance follow him into the room.

"So, what did you get up to today?" he asked me curiously.

"What do you mean?" I asked, whilst applying mascara.

"Well, when I came in there was a load of water and mud all over the floor by the hallway that I had to clean up."

Fuck, I had totally forgotten about that. I had meant to go down and mop it up once I had gotten out of the shower but Tim's sudden arrival, or should I say arousal, had distracted me from the task.

"Oh that, I'm sorry honey. I was meant to clean that up after I had showered. I got caught out in that awful rainstorm when walking the pup earlier" I focused on applying the last of my lipstick, not daring to look at him in case he could sense I wasn't being entirely truthful. He didn't seem to be suspicious though, despite the fact that the dog was clean as a whistle. However, whilst maintaining my gaze at my lipstick application I noticed deep brown marks imbedded between my fingernails. I must not have scrubbed my hands thoroughly enough whilst in the shower.

He returned back to the bedroom to continue getting dressed and I let out a long breath. He must have bought my excuse, thankfully. I peered behind me to double check he was definitely gone before opening up the dresser drawer beside me and picking out a pair of tweezers. I dug the tweezers into each of my nail beds, digging out the incriminating mud left behind. My fingers were red raw by the time I was finished, but better to be red than brown. I gave my hands a quick wipe over with a make-up wipe before finishing off my lip liner.

Once my make-up was complete, I slipped on my long silk, emerald, green dress and admired my reflection in the mirror. I don't scrub up half bad for an ordinary school mum I thought to myself.

Tim returned into the dressing room, now fully dressed in a dark blue suit, looking as handsome as the day I met him.

"You look stunning" he said as he gave me a small peck on the cheek. He knew not to mess up my freshly completed make-up.

"As do you darling" I replied with a smile as I bent down to slip my feet into a pair of silver high heels.

"All ready to go?" he asked. I nodded and with that he led me down the stairs and towards the front door. "Let's do this."

19

We walked into the stunning venue hand in hand, the ultimate power couple. The dinner was being held in a nearby hotel and it was clear that no expense had been spared. Kelly's parents had organised the event and her father was a member of the board at the hospital in which Tim worked, and in which Kelly had used to work also. Her family were old money, no one really knew where the household had gained their money from all those years ago, but they were a prominent family in the village and had been for centuries.

As we walked into the big open-plan reception room there were numerous tables laid out with beautiful centerpieces, long white tablecloths and golden cutlery. Each table was set out in a circular shape with eight chairs around them. Each table setting had a placeholder with a name written in golden italic font and bottles of red and wine white, as well as champagne on ice.

At the end of the room there was a large stage, positioned on top was a giant projector screen, a long rectangular table also laid out like the others with a further eight seats facing out towards the rest of the room and a speaker's podium.

Tim led me through throngs of people, all standing around between the tables, making small talk with those who crossed our paths. Most of the conversations being held were medical in nature, not something I knew particularly much about, well other than the topic of insulin overdoses of course, but funnily enough that hadn't come up. I suppose the nature in which the victim had died probably isn't the best conversation starter at a memorial dinner in their honour. So, while Tim made small talk and charmed his bosses, I just nodded along with a smile on my face, being the picture-perfect wife, I knew so well how to be.

Before long, a tall and thin older gentleman in an impressive black tuxedo made his way to the podium. He tapped gently on the microphone to get people's attention and then smiled down at the crowd.

"My wife and I would like to thank you all for coming this evening. We so very much appreciate all of the time, care and effort that everyone has gone through for this evening, as well as all of the support we have received from you since Kelly's passing." He paused for a moment, appearing to be swallowing back tears. "She would have loved to see how many of you have come out this evening to celebrate her."

Stood slight behind and slightly to the right of him on the stage was a short plump woman wearing a navy dress that had clearly been tailored specifically for her. She stood stock still, eyes transfixed on who I assume was her husband, as he spoke at the podium, silent tears running down her cheeks. Despite these tears, her make-up remained impeccable, so I made a mental note to find out who her make-up artist was and what foundation and mascara she uses.

"We would like to invite you all to take your seats now, we have a presentation to show to you all before dinner is served." He continued.

Everyone started to mill around again, checking the name cards to see where their designated seats were.

"You're over here with us" a beautiful woman with long blonde hair and a cream fitted dress beckoned over to us.

We headed over to the table we were placed at, right beside the stage and the top table.

"I'm Delilah" the woman said to me "I'm Peter's wife, Dr Peter Stoneham, he works with Tim I believe."

"Oh yes, I've met Peter before I'm sure" I replied with a smile. "He specialises in pediatric orthopedics, doesn't he?"

"He sure does, for my sins!" she responded candidly "And oh, what a bore it is! Please do not ask me or him any questions about it because it will literally be all you hear about!"

I chuckled. I think I'm going to like this woman and as luck would have it, we were seated next to each other, with our respective husbands either side of us.

"Don't tell anyone, "She whispered to me as we took our seats, "but I actually moved some of the name cards around, so I didn't have to sit next to that one." She gave a small head nod towards a large woman sat across the table from us.

The table was big enough that we couldn't hear what the people across from us were talking about, but not so big that I couldn't hear the obnoxious snorting laugh of the larger woman, nor to not notice how yellow her teeth were.

"Looks like you've definitely saved yourself there" I giggled.

"Oh, you have no idea" she began, before being cut short by the tall thin gentleman back at the podium again, who was requesting everyone's attention.

I turned in my chair slightly to position myself to look up at the stage. The projector screen now had a large image of Kelly on it, whereas before it was blank.

"I hope you all enjoy the presentation. We have put together some memories of Kelly that various co-workers have sent in as well as friends and family. Please join us now in spending some time to look back at our dear Kelly, who was taken from us too soon."

With that the screen began to play a photo reel, somber music playing in the background as numerous photos appeared, one by one, of Kelly in various stages of her life. It started with Kelly as a baby and then through to childhood. It was clear that she had lived a privileged life. Most of her childhood photographs were of her on luxurious looking holidays, skiing in Aspen, riding an elephant in Africa, standing beside a pyramid. I think as a child the best holiday I ever got was a trip to Blackpool Pleasure Beach.

"Ugh, it's so hard to relate to someone who grew up with a silver spoon up their arse" muttered Delilah under her breath to me.

"I think the phrase is in their mouth" I whispered back with a giggle.

"No, I meant what I said" she responded bluntly.

Further photographs of Kelly in University, her graduation, her first job, a few of her with numerous cats. It became apparent as time went on in the photos that Kelly couldn't have had many friends. There weren't many photographs of her with other people, and if there were, they were clearly family members. I might have felt sorry for her, had I not known her.

"Did you ever meet Kelly?" Delilah asked quietly.

"No, never" I lied, my response in an equally as hushed tone. Well, as far as anyone else knows I didn't meet her anyway.

"Lucky you" she quipped, "I know it's not nice to speak ill of the dead, but the devil has gained a new playmate with her passing."

I knew Kelly wasn't well liked, but I was surprised to hear Delilah speaking in such a way about her, especially at her own memorial. "You weren't a fan then I take it?"

"You could say that", she slurred "we may have had a few choice words before at events like these. She always liked to think that Peter had a bit of a thing for her, and I liked to think that she was full of shit."

It was clear at this point that Delilah may have had more than a bit too much wine. Having only met her about twenty minutes prior, she had since finished off two glasses of red from the bottle on the table and was beginning to pour herself another. Peter leaned over and whispered something to her that I was unable to hear, but by her snappy response back to him, I imagine it was in relation to her drinking.

The video ended and Kelly's father returned to the podium, fresh tears still evident in his eyes.

"Thank you all for watching. I'm sure you all found that just as touching as we did. Now," he paused slightly "on to some slightly better news."

Everyone's attention appeared to have peaked at hearing that something else was about to be discussed other than Kelly. A quick glance around the room had shown most people's body language having been indifferent throughout the video reel, so it seemed that most people had attended the event out of obligation, more so than a want to celebrate and honour Kelly.

"As you all know, Dr. Timothy Grant has been filling in as the Head of Pediatrics since the incident and has been doing a spectacular job of it." Numerous people around the room cheered and I gave Tim a quick squeeze on his knee as he looked bashful at the applause he was receiving. "Well, as Dr. Grant had previously applied for the job in hand and has been completing the job role with success since Kelly's passing, the board has decided that further interviews and applications will not be required, and we would like to offer the position to him on a permanent basis."

Clapping erupted around us, and I felt Tim standing up from his seat next to me. I looked up at him, beaming with pride. This is it, not only has his hard work paid off, but mine has too. I just wish I could tell him how I had helped him to secure the position, but I'm not sure he would be overly happy about it if I did. Once the applause ended, Tim gave a quick thanks and acceptance, and hastily sat back down in his seat. He was never one for public speaking and as much as he had wanted this position, he was likely feeling somewhat overwhelmed at the amount of attention he was currently getting.

"Let us all raise a glass to Dr. Grant and of course also to my beautiful angel in the sky, Kelly." Her father lifted up a glass of champagne in the air.

I had been so caught up in Tim's promotion announcement that I hadn't noticed the waiters going around filling up glasses with champagne for everyone. I lifted up my glass with everyone else and shouted out "to Tim".

No-one other than Delilah appeared to notice that I didn't toast to Kelly, luckily, she was probably too drunk to remember this tomorrow, but either way, she hadn't toasted her either.

The rest of the night went along with an exquisite four course meal and after dinner coffees and mints. Whilst coffee was being served, we were encouraged to move to the sides of the rooms and some of the tables were moved out to make space for a small dance floor. Kelly's parents appeared to leave the event shortly after dinner had finished, perhaps not feeling in the partying mood, but all hospital events provided by the board were known to be late night affairs. There was an open bar, so the drinks were flowing, and a jazz band took to the stage.

I spent the rest of the night in a haze of tipsiness from one too many red wines and champagne cocktails and danced with a few of the other wives and an occasional slow dance with Tim, when I could get him to agree. It was a beautiful evening and despite the fact that I had not been looking forward to it, and the fact that it was meant to have been all about Kelly, she had barely entered my thoughts all night. Neither had anyone else for that matter, not even Rachel whose motionless body I had been staring at not even twelve hours before.

We ended the night canoodling in the back of a taxi like teenagers before heading home to bed for round two of our earlier exploits. Life was good.

20

It's been four days since the incident with Rachel, and Kelly's memorial dinner. I had received an email two days ago to announce that the children could return to school, but I hadn't heard or seen anything anywhere about what had happened to Rachel. There hadn't been any mention on the local news or online, not even on Facebook which I thought it would definitely come up on. My mother-in-law had brought Sam back home yesterday and luckily Tim wasn't working so I hadn't had to worry about her making any digs at me and she had only stayed for a coffee before heading back home.

It was so nice to have Sam back with us. It was Sunday yesterday, so we had taken Sam down to the local beach for a walk along the seafront before heading home for a roast dinner. It had been blustery cold down at the beach, but we had wrapped up warm and held hands as we walked, watching the tide crashing against the rocks. We had even stopped in a café for a hot chocolate. But today was back to the normal grind of the school run and getting ready for my work from home job, it was almost as if the last couple of weeks had never happened as I slid back into the routine with ease.

"Sam, go get your shoes on and grab your coat" I shouted up the stairs to him as I finished getting his school bag ready. I thought I'd have one more quick scroll through Facebook, to see if anything new had been posted but there was still nothing. In fact, apart from a few parents I didn't know commenting on the school page about it reopening, there was hardly anything posted on there over the last few days, nor had there been anything in the Mum's WhatsApp chat either.

Sam came bounding down the stairs, grabbing his coat off the coatrack and locating his shoes that were in the porch. "Have you brushed your teeth?" I asked him as he leant forward, blowing minty breath towards me. He giggled when I waved my hand over my nose and pretended the smell was unpleasant.

"Are you excited to go back to school?"

"I can't wait! I've not seen Charlie or Adam in forever!!" If only I could muster up his enthusiasm.

Once loaded up in the car, we drove our usual route to the school and parked up on the side street next to it. The last time we had been on this street we were sharing it with a dead body, I thought to myself, as I parked up in my usual space. Sam didn't seem to have been overly affected by what had happened the last time we had been here, all the police presence and the road being blocked. He just got out of the car and started walking up the street towards the school gates, just like he normally would. That's the marvel of a 6-year-old I guess, not old enough to fully understand what's happening around them.

As we walked onto the playground to wait outside the classroom door for school to begin, there was scarcely anyone around. I checked my watch, 08:40, normally at this time the playground was jam packed with children running around and parents having a chat. The classroom door opens at 08:45. I wonder if a lot of parents hadn't seen the email or if something had happened somewhere to cause many people to run late?

One of the mums caught me looking around and said to me "Gosh, it sure is quiet today isn't it. Where do you think everyone is?"

"I've no idea" I replied, "I was literally just thinking the same thing. It's almost time for class to start and there can only be about 7 or 8 children here."

Another mother, having heard our conversation, came over to join us. "I don't think we will be seeing many of the other children for a little while yet."

"Oh, what makes you say that?" The first mum asked.

"Are you not on that new Facebook group that was created?" She replied whilst getting her phone out of her pocket to show us.

Both mum number 1 and I shook our heads and leant forward to take a look at the Facebook page she had just loaded up on her phone screen. "This group was made a few days ago, it's all about what's been happening around here recently."

She scrolled down on the screen to show us numerous different posts. I couldn't get a good look at exactly what the posts were specifically, but I could get the gist. The group itself was called "Save our Schoolchildren" and the posts I caught a glimpse at whilst she scrolled through, appeared to be in relation to the local village serial killer and the events that have occurred over the last few weeks. She stopped scrolling at one post in particular and opened it up to show us in more detail.

"See, a lot of the parents have decided to boycott the school until the serial killer has been caught." She scrolled down the comment section of the post, where numerous different parents from all different school years had written on there to say that they would not be sending their children back to school and how much of a disgrace they felt it was that the school had even reopened.

"I never knew about this group at all" I replied stunned. This is why I hadn't seen any information online; a private group had been made and I hadn't been invited to it!

"Nor did I" the first mum chimed in. I felt some slight relief that it wasn't only me that hadn't been added. If it had, then maybe some people were becoming suspicious of me, but if there were other parents not invited then it could have just been an oversight.

"It's an invite only group, so a lot of the people have been invited into the group by other parents. I'll add you both now." she stated as she began furiously typing into her phone before hearing a PING from my own pocket. "There we are."

"Thanks so much" I smiled. Just as I went to take a look at my own phone, the classroom door opened and Mrs. Edgeware appeared, waving at the children to welcome them into the classroom. She didn't appear overly shocked that there were hardly any children running towards her, so I wonder if she's already in this group or at least knows about it. I blew Sam a kiss as he ran off into his classroom, thanked the mum again for the invitation to the group and made my way across the playground in the direction of my car.

Once home, I loaded my laptop up and made myself a coffee, ready to start trawling through the different posts and comments of the group. As soon as I loaded the Facebook page up, I could see that the group was very active. There were numerous different posts with streams of comments under each one. I needed to start looking at this properly and not just at what was catching my attention first, so I scrolled down to the very bottom of the page, to the very first comment thread, ready to work my way back to the latest one.

The page had been created the day after the school had been closed, when Coleen had died, and the creator of the group was Alison, one of the mums in Sam's class, and a friend of Rachels and Coleen's. The initial post read:

Hello all, I've started this group because there have been too many issues in this village recently and our children and ourselves are clearly not safe. There's a serial killer walking among us and we need to find them before they find us. The police don't want to tell us anything and neither do the school, so we need to start working together to try and work this out for ourselves. Please invite anyone that you know to the group that can help with this and let's keep our community safe. Alison.

The post had a multitude of comments underneath it, but nothing too concerning so far. Most of it was people tagging other people to let them know they had invited them to join the group, and there was the odd comment with people giving their theories. One person had said they suspected their neighbour, but it wasn't anyone I knew, and they referred to them as a "he" so no reason for me to be worried about it.

As I scrolled back up the page, the next few posts were about different theories people had. Some people referencing the "mad woman" who had attacked Mr. Turner, the secondary school teacher from Semberton School and only one reference I could see to Kelly's death likely being related. A lot of the theories felt that Mr. Turner, Craig and Coleen were all definitely related. No mention of Maeve anywhere, so that was also a relief at least. So, from what I could see so far, the general consensus was that there was definitely a serial killer, but the police would not reveal the cause of death to the public in case it interfered with their investigation, and no-one commenting seemed to be able to link any of the victims to each other to determine a pattern. I could feel my confidence increasing with each post, until I reached another post written by Alison, dated only three days ago, less than 24 hours after I had killed Rachel.

URGENT: Another death has been confirmed. The death is not currently being made public and my legal representative has advised me that I cannot reveal the identity of the latest victim at this time, for fear of potential legal repercussions against me. However, what I can tell you, is that it is another mother from the school, someone a lot of us know and loved and that I will not take this death lying down. Something needs to be done sooner rather than later. If you know the identity of the victim, please do not post it on here, but message me privately if you have any questions or if you know any information that we can take to the police.

So, Alison knew about Rachel. I shouldn't be surprised really; they are friends after all. Rachel's husband probably told her once he came home and found her. How fortunate that she can't post on the group who the victim is though, the less people that know who it is, the less people who can potentially link me to her. Most of the comments under this thread appeared to be people asking who it was and when it happened, none of which Alison had replied to.

I continued scrolling through the page, following the latest victim post there appeared to be numerous posts sprouting theories as to who they thought may be targeted next and who may be at risk. Alison appeared to have been commenting on most of the posts, encouraging their anger and fear, almost as if she was trying to rile people up. It appeared that Alison was a woman on a mission, which means she is a woman that is a risk to me.

Dated two days ago, there was another post by Alison, announcing her plans to Boycott the school now that it was being reopened and encouraging others to do the same. This post seemed to have more comments than a lot of the others, with a lot of parents jumping on the Boycott Bandwagon and agreeing that their children won't be going back to school, or anywhere else for that matter without constant supervision. I don't know how all of these people concluded that their children aren't safe? Not a single person that I've had to take care of has been a child and I would never harm children. It's so frustrating that I can't comment this, so much fearmongering for no reason, but I can't be seen as being sympathetic to the killer, or suspicious in anyway.

Alison appears to be on the warpath though, she clearly intends to stop at nothing to find me. At the moment she doesn't know who she is looking for, but if she keeps on digging who knows what she will find out? If she speaks to someone who had seen me near Rachel's house and she tells them that Rachel was the most recent victim, the dots could become connected. What if more people start mentioning Kelly and she discovers that my husband has just been given her job position? That could raise a few red flags for sure. No-one else seems to be as gung-ho for finding me and the police can't be too close to catching my scent either as I've not so much as seen a police car drive through the village recently, so Alison seems to be my main threat at the moment. A threat that I need to carefully consider how I am going to manage.

As I'm sat at my laptop, considering the possibilities of how I can get to Alison and what action I need to take next, a knock at the door startles me. I jump up from my desk, peering out my office window to try and a catch a glimpse at who it may be. I can't see the front door from where I am, but I can see the road and there's no unknown cars parked outside from what I can gather, and no police cars either. Maybe it's just a delivery and I'm getting myself all worked up for no reason.

I walk over to the front door, opening it slowly, not quite ready to see who is standing on the other side. But my fear quickly turns to confusion, when stood on my doorstep is Kathy, Maeve's niece whom I had met a few times over the years when she had come to visit her elderly aunt, albeit not frequently, but had also happened to be the person who had found Maeve's body.

"Kathy!" I exclaimed in surprise. "How nice to see you, how are you doing?"

"Oh, you know, as good as can be considering the circumstances." She didn't look too upset to be fair, at least nowhere near as upset as she had when I had seen her last, in Maeve's living room with a police officer.

"I can only imagine how difficult this has all been for you," I attempted to sound sincere, but it was difficult knowing that Kathy had barely spent any time with Maeve before her passing so likely wasn't all that cut up about it. "Did you want to come in for a coffee?" I suppose it would only be polite to invite her in.

"It's okay thanks, I can't stop. I just wanted to say thank you for everything you did for my aunt before she passed." Kathy replied. "I also wanted to let you know that I'm in the process of selling her house. I'm actually just about to meet with the estate agent and didn't want you to be surprised when you saw a for sale sign out front."

"Thanks for letting me know, it makes sense that you need to sell it though, none of the family live local enough to want to live here I guess." I didn't really know what else to say to this information, it didn't really impact on me what they did with the house, but I appreciated that she felt it polite to keep me in the loop. "Have you managed to sort out all of her belongings?" I enquired.

"Not yet, to be honest with you, this will be the first time I've actually come back to the house since I found her. I'm a bit nervous to go back inside." She stammered.

"That's understandable" I said reassuringly, "it must have been a fright to have seen her like that." I extended my arm out to give her a supportive pat on the shoulder. Shame she hadn't bothered more to see her when she was still alive, perhaps then she would have more memories of her aunt and her aunt's home, than just what happened recently.

"I'm just going to show the estate agent round today so that they can take some pictures and make a proper valuation for selling and then come back in a few days to start sorting through her belongings. Is there anything of hers that you would want?"

"That's very kind of you, but I don't think there was anything of sentimental value to me specifically. You should make sure everyone else in the family has anything they want first. Do let me know if you need any help with sorting or if there's anything you are looking for that you can't find though, I was there a lot, so I know where most of her things are."

Just then a small Ford Focus with "Cumming Estates" emblazoned across the side of it pulled into the road and parked up outside Maeve's bungalow. "That will be the estate agent" Kathy stated obviously. "I'd best get over there, thanks again for everything Chrissie."

I gave her a small wave as she headed across the road to meet the estate agent and then closed the door behind her. I'm not sure why the selling of Maeve's home feels a bit sad to me. I suppose with all the time I spent with Maeve and in that bungalow, it feels almost like the final ending to her story. I hadn't had much time to think about Maeve since her passing, what with everything that had been going on over the last few weeks, but I really did miss her. She wasn't just a neighbour; she was a good friend to me and someone that I spent a lot of time with over the last couple of years especially. I wonder what she would think of everything I had been up to recently. I had always told Maeve all of my secrets, she was my confidant, which is why she probably felt safe asking me to help her in the first place, but I'm not sure she would have fully approved of everything I had done, well maybe some of it. She understood the need for sacrifices sometimes for the greater good.

With a sigh, I returned to my office, sitting back down at the desk. As much as I wanted to spend some more time thinking about Maeve, I had more pressing matters at hand. I needed to figure out what I was going to do about Alison, I needed to stop her before it was too late. But how was I going to do that when she was keeping herself and her family in lockdown at home, and now that I had also run out of insulin.

21

    I spent the rest of the afternoon mulling over what I could do to mitigate the Alison risk, but I struggled to come up with much at all. How was I going to get to someone that is so on guard at the moment and is likely avoiding leaving the house at all costs. I couldn't follow her to find out where she lived like I did with Mr. Turner if she wasn't going to be at the school to follow, nor could I run the risk of hiding behind her bins to attack her either. Lightning doesn't strike twice. I continued to mull the thought over whilst completing the school pick-up. Stood in the playground waiting for Sam to come out of the classroom door, it took all of my willpower not to ask one of the other mums if they knew where Alison lived. What possible reason could I have to want to know that information without directly asking her myself?

Sam came running towards me, rushing over and throwing his arms around my waist, head buried in my stomach. "Missed you mum!" he shouted.

"Aww I missed you too Sam!! How was school?" I bent down to his level, wrapping him into a much tighter hug.

"It wasn't very good today" he said glumly, "hardly any of my friends were there. I didn't get to see Adam or Charlie."

"I know honey, some of the children haven't come back to school yet, but don't worry I'm sure they will be back soon." I attempted to reassure him.

He gave a small sniff and then took my hand in his to walk to the car. Within a few minutes he was back to his usual self, talking about his favourite Youtuber and what he had been given for lunch that day.

Once back home, he sat playing on his tablet and I started making dinner. Looking out of the kitchen window whilst washing some potatoes in the sink, I couldn't help but notice the new for sale sign stood up outside Maeve's bungalow. I knew it was coming, but I didn't realise they would put it up the same day as coming to value the house. That estate agent doesn't mess about, I must remember them if we plan to move in future. I looked across at my windowsill, where I had a large porcelain llama shaped mug in which I kept our spare keys. Inside the mug were keys for the radiators, the windows, spare keys for the back door and also, on a small heart key ring, was a key to Maeve's home.

Maeve had given me a key once she had become less mobile, so that I could come and go as needed and come to help her get out of bed in the mornings. It had been invaluable to both of us for me to have my own key so that she didn't need to worry about trying to get to the door and I wouldn't have to wait endlessly in the rain for her either. I wonder if Kathy knew I had a spare key. She certainly didn't ask for any keys when she came to tell me she was selling it. I guess the key isn't really worth much to me now that she's gone. Although, if I am going to do something about Alison, it might be useful to have some more insulin to hand just in case.

Most of my 'just in case' scenarios recently seemed to have warranted the need for a trusty injection in my possession and although I hadn't decided that I was going to kill Alison as such, I'm not really sure what other choice I have to keep her quiet and stop her sleuthing. Sometimes we just have to do what we have to do, I guess.

As I finished off washing and peeling the last potato at the sink and turned around from the view of Maeve's bungalow, I decided that my only option was to pop into her home one last time to grab some more insulin before the house was emptied out and sold. Once that happens, I won't have any more opportunities to get my hands on any and unless I discover I'm a natural at martial arts, or learn how to throw knives with precision, I can't imagine I would be able to overpower someone any other way.

I finished chopping up the potatoes into thin strips and threw them into the air fryer with some paprika seasoning and pressed the big red start button. I then friend up some sausages and onions to go with our home-made chips. Tim was going out after work for drinks this evening and wouldn't likely be home till late, he had told me not to wait up, so it was just me and Sam for dinner tonight. I could have made us our own separate dinners each but the idea of making two different meals didn't appeal, so sausage and chips will have to do for me as well.

We sat and ate dinner together at the dining table and Sam told me more about what he had been learning in school. They have been focusing on recycling a lot at the moment and Sam seemed particularly interested in telling me all about how most of the plastic we use isn't actually recyclable.

After dinner I gave Sam a bath and we snuggled down to watch a film together on the sofa before bed. Sam had wanted to watch a new superhero film that had recently come out, so I put it on for him and draped a blanket over us. I couldn't tell you what was happening in the film though, zero attention was paid to it as I thought about Alison and what I could do. I scrolled through the Facebook group again, there were no new posts and only a few new comments but nothing noteworthy. I kept looking at the same messages again and again, mostly from Alison and all negative in nature about the school, the police and of course the serial killer, until an idea struck me. If Rachel had thought that I was having an affair with Coleen's husband, because he had been receiving messages from someone with the same name as me, then the likelihood is, Alison thinks this also. They were all in the same friendship group and Alison had learnt so quickly about Rachels death, there's no way that she wouldn't have had the same information as what Rachel did.

I logged myself out of Facebook and began making up a new profile. I used my first name but created a different surname, typing in Jones instead of Grant. If I could convince Alison that I was the Chrissie that they had thought was sleeping with Coleen's husband, then maybe I can pretend that I know some information and get her to meet me somewhere.

I had a quick Google search of women in their late thirties and scrolled through several different pages before selecting a picture of a mousey-brown haired woman with a plain face. I chose her specifically because she had the sort of face that you could easily forget, so hopefully Alison wouldn't recongise this stranger. I added a few bits of information to my new profile but then set it as private, so that anyone who looked at the profile who wasn't a friend of mine on Facebook wouldn't be able to see any information other than where I lived, the profile picture I had chosen and a brief Bio that I had written, in which I had used a popular Maya Angelou quote. *'Try to be a rainbow in someone's cloud.'* Generic enough to not raise any concerns, but sufficient to make it seem like she was a real person, as close to *'Live, Laugh, Love'* as I could get. This way, when I messaged Alison and she checked the profile, she wouldn't be able to see that the profile had no mutual friends with her. I then proceeded to add as many random people as I could find to my friends list, just in case it displayed how many friends the profile had. I looked through a few different pages that came up under people you may know and added everyone and anyone I could. Now it was time to wait and see how many 'fake' friends I would end up with, to make my profile look as believable as possible.

Once the film was finished, Sam went upstairs to brush his teeth and I started helping him get ready for bed. I read a few chapters of his favourite Roald Dahl book and before I had finished the last few pages, Sam was fast asleep. Snoring softly beside me, cuddling his teddy bear. I leant down and gave him a kiss on his forehead, before creeping out of the bedroom and shutting the door carefully behind me.

I checked the time, it was 8pm and pitch-black outside. If I was going to try and get some more insulin from Maeve's, I was going to have to do it sooner rather than later, and this may be my only chance to do so. With Tim not home to question where I was going and Sam fast asleep in bed, I could run over under the cover of darkness, as quickly as possible and grab some insulin before anyone even realised that I had left the house.

I put on the long black coat I used for walking the dog. It had a thick quilt inside to ward off the cold and the colour of it would help me stay hidden just in case anyone did happen to look at Maeve's bungalow whilst I was entering. I put the hood up ready to cover my face, listened out to hear if there was any movement coming from Sam's room and once I felt comfortable enough that he would likely not wake, I slid out of the front door, locking it behind me just in case. I would never normally leave my 6-year-old son at home on his own, but needs must sometimes, and I was only across the road anyway.

Once the door was locked, I ran across the road, head down, mission impossible theme tune playing in my head. I had almost been tempted to commando crawl or dive dramatically through Maeve's bushes at the front of her home, but I maintained my composure as I reached her front door and without looking back, quickly slipped in the key and let myself in.

It was a good thing that I knew Maeve's home so well as it wouldn't be a good idea to be putting any of the lights on considering her home was known to be unoccupied now. So, I made my way across the hallway, feeling my way towards her bedroom, where I knew the mini fridge that kept her medication was located.

A wave of nostalgia hit me as I entered her bedroom, her last resting place, and where I had spent so much time sat beside her bed, putting the world to rights with her. I felt a small tear trickling down my cheek and brushed it away softly. It's funny how quickly your life can change. How one event can lead to a continuation of further occurrences, that can not only change your life, but your entire being. Never in a million years would I have thought myself capable of committing some of the recent acts that I had, not that I regretted any of them. I feel like my life has developed a new purpose recently, to rid the world of the evils that can harm others. It was just a shame that the world didn't have the same viewpoint as me yet. To everyone else in the local community, I was a 'serial killer' or a 'mad woman', this unknown entity that was a risk to their children. But in reality, if only they knew what Mr. Turner had been up to, how I had actually saved their children from harm. How I had restored fairness to my husband's workplace and created a nicer environment for shoppers at the local post office shop.

I opened up the minifridge and was surprised to notice that the light hadn't come on when I did so, nor did it feel cold inside. It must have been turned off. I suppose with no-one living here now, Kathy had likely gone round and turned all the electrics off before leaving. I felt blindly inside and could feel two boxes stacked up, the boxes which I knew contained the insulin pens I needed. I still had a few of the needle caps at home left over so I didn't need any more of them. Neither of the boxes had been opened yet so I was going to have to tear one of them open. I wasn't sure if anyone had checked the contents of the fridge before it was turned off to know how much insulin was inside here, but I couldn't risk taking a full box just in case. So, I made a small enough opening in the packaging to slide one more injection pen out and tucked it safely into my pocket, before putting the box back where it belonged. Maybe being limited to only five more kills would be a good thing.

I took one last look around the dark bedroom, barely able to see anything other than the outlines of the bedroom furniture and then left swiftly, returning home in the same manner I had when coming over here. Once I was safely back inside, I put my coat on the coatrack, transferring the injection pen into the inside pocket of the coat where it was unlikely to be seen or felt by Tim or Sam. I then crept back upstairs and put my head to Sam's bedroom door until I heard the familiar soft snorts of him sleeping. Mission accomplished.

22

I went down into the kitchen and poured myself a large glass of red wine, before picking my phone back up again and checking my new Facebook profile. My plan had worked, I had over 100 new friends on Facebook, none of which I knew and none of which knew me.

I typed Alison's name into the search bar at the top of the screen and scrolled down the options that came up for Alison Short, until I came across her profile. Once I clicked on it, I then selected the option to request to start a messenger chat with her.

I took a large gulp of wine, planning to head into the living room to put something on the television to distract myself whilst I waited, however the messenger pinged back almost immediately, showing that Alison had agreed to the messenger chat to be started.

'Hi Alison, I saw you had been asking for any information on the recent goings on and thought I might be able to help.' I typed into the message bar and hit sent.

'Hi Chrissie', she responded, *'Are you Sam's mum from school?'*

Clearly, she only knew one Chrissie like Rachel had mentioned too, so I needed to get that idea out of her head as soon as possible.

I began typing back to her, *'Sorry, I'm not sure who you are referring to. I don't have any children. But I do have some information about Coleen, if you are interested.'*

'Oh, I'm sorry, I thought you were someone that I knew. Who are you?' her responses were coming back fast. She was clearly intrigued as to who this mystery Chrissie was and what information I could potentially have for her.

'No, I don't think we've met before. I'm a friend of Coleen's husband Greg' I input quickly.

'I think I might have an idea of who you are actually,' her reply gave no further indication of what she had just pieced together, but it was clear that my plan was working.

'Do you think we can meet somewhere private to have a chat? I need to tell you something that I think is important in finding out what has been going on recently in the village.'

'Why do you want to meet, can you not just type it on here to me?' she responded.

'I don't trust that anything I tell you can't be traced over the phone or over the computer. If I'm going to tell you this information, it needs to be face-to-face and where no-one can overhear us.' I needed her to take the bait if I wanted to get her out of the house alone.

There was a long pause before she replied again. She was obviously having an internal battle with herself as to whether or not it would be safe to meet with me. Her heart likely telling her that if she wanted to help track down the killer then she needed any information she could get, whilst her head warning her of the dangers of meeting up with a stranger somewhere alone. After about ten minutes she finally replied.

'I understand. Where and when do you want to meet.'

'How about the car park behind the Old Railways Pub' I suggested. The Old Railways Pub had been closed down about three years ago and had just been left to rot. No-one had appeared to have bought it and it was never reopened as a pub or repurposed into anything else. It was situated on the outskirts of town, not far from a railway track that was no longer in service, hence the name of the pub. The pub was visible from the road that it was situated on, but the car park was behind it, completely hidden from any passersby. It would be the perfect location to meet up where privacy could be ensured.

'I know the one you mean' she replied back, *'when can you meet?'*

I thought for a moment. I guess the sooner the better in this instance. The longer time period I gave her to think about the meeting the more likely it could be that she would tell someone about it or decide against meeting altogether.

'I'm free tomorrow lunchtime if that works for you?' Tomorrow might seem soon to her, but considering she wasn't going to and from school at the moment and there was no evidence to indicate that she was employed on her Facebook profile, hopefully she won't already have any plans. Meeting during the daytime might also make her feel a bit more comfortable about the situation and the more

comfortable she feels, the more she will be likely to let her guard down.

'11:30 works for me. I will meet you there then. I'll be in a red Fiat Punto' the message read.

'That's great, please come alone though, the information I have to tell you could get me in a lot of trouble and I'm really frightened. I really hope you will be able to help me.' I couldn't believe she had fallen so well for the bait I had hooked for her.

'Don't worry, you can trust me. See you tomorrow.' I liked this last message she had sent, and then shut down the messenger chat.

I drained the last of my wine from the bottom of the glass and decided to head to bed for an early night. Tomorrow was going to be a big day.

23

I can't remember the last time I felt so exhilarated waking up in the morning. I got myself dressed and ready, carefully applying my make-up as if it were warpaint. I continued with my usual morning routine, getting Sam up and dressed and dropped off to school. I returned home and sent a quick email to my manager to advise that I wasn't feeling well and would try to log in to work a bit later, just in case I got caught up with time during my meeting with Alison. Everything was put into motion, now I just needed to wait for the meet-up time.

I felt like time was going so slowly as I waited to leave. I decided to get to the meeting place early, park up a few streets away so my car wouldn't be spotted and then hide somewhere in the car park to keep lookout for Alison's arrival.

I got myself ready to leave, putting on my coat and prepping my injection, just in case of course. I screwed a needle on to the pen top and turned the dial at the bottom of the pen, letting it click continuously until it wouldn't click anymore. I slipped the pen into my coat pocket and then put a pair of trainers on. I normally wear boots when I go out anywhere, but trainers seemed a better option today, again, just in case.

I got myself into the driving seat of my car and turned on the ignition. I could feel my hands shaking as I started driving towards my destination and I wasn't sure if I was more nervous or excited at this point. I made my way through the village, out to the outskirts where the pub was situated. I drove past it slowly, trying to look into the car park from the turning into it as I went past, but the view was completely blocked. This couldn't be more perfect for our meeting. I drove a few more streets away and checked the time on the car dashboard. It was 11:00, I had half an hour to walk back to the pub and find a good spot to scout out my prey.

I walked at a fast pace, head down and hands in my pockets. The fingers of my left hand held tightly around the injection pen. Before long I had made it to the car park of the pub. I surveyed my surroundings. The car park was relatively small, with only about 10 parking spaces in it, and was the length of the now closed pub. Behind the car park was woodland, the perfect place for me to hide initially to keep an eye out for her arrival. I made my way quickly across the tarmac and into the woods, squatting down behind a bush and in between two large trees.

I didn't have to wait too long, at 11:15, only minutes after I had secured my hiding space, the red Fiat Punto came slowly around the corner and into the car park. Reversing into a parking space almost directly in front of where I was hidden. I ducked down low for a moment in case she had noticed me between the leaves but after a few minutes of me hiding, I steeled myself to pop my head up and check to see if her car was still there. I had heard her turn the engine of the car off, not long after she had parked and from what I could see, she was sitting in the driver's seat of the car and there was no one else with her. I gave it another few minutes to ensure that no-one else arrived behind her and pushed my way out of the bushes.

I opened up her passenger door and sat down next to her. She yelped out in surprise.

"Chrissie! But" she started to say, her face contorted in confusion.

"Yes, yes, it's me" I interrupted her.

"What's going on?" she asked shakily.

"I needed to speak to you, and I knew you wouldn't come if you knew it was me."

"What makes you think that?" she responded.

"Let's not play dumb now Alison" I said sternly, "I know you, Rachel and Coleen all thought that I was having an affair with Coleen's husband."

Alison remained silent; her hands gripped the steering wheel in front of her so tightly, I could see that her knuckles were turning white.

"I wasn't though," I continued on, "I'd never met her husband, and I certainly wouldn't cheat on my own."

"Why does it matter what we think?" Alison responded quickly. "Is there another reason you wanted to meet me?"

"I just wanted you to understand how damaging it can be to someone to spread false accusations like that around. What if my husband had heard about it and for some reason didn't believe me? You could have ruined my life with your lies." I spat, beginning to become angered.

"It wasn't me spreading anything Chrissie," she stuttered, "I just knew about it from what Coleen and Rachel had told me, maybe you should speak to Rachel about it, she knows more than I do."

I laughed. She knew Rachel was dead, was she just baiting me to see if I revealed myself to her. I tried to maintain eye contact with her, to see if she would give away how much she knew, but she was staring directly in front of her, clearly too scared to look over in my direction.

"You know, I've not seen Rachel around lately, and she's not been commenting on your little Facebook group either has she." I started coolly, not quite ready to show all my cards.

"Has she not? I hadn't noticed." Alison squeaked.

"I find that hard to believe, considering how active you have been on that group. You respond to most of the comments on there, so you must have noticed that your best friend had very little to say on the matter."

It was clear that Alison was becoming more and more frightened, the more that the conversation progressed. I watched as she placed her hand slowly onto her car door handle, preparing herself for a quick exit if required. It was quite fun to watch her squirming to be honest. She had been so confident on the Facebook group, inciting the emotions of all the other parents, but not so much now that she was on her own and not hidden behind a computer screen.

"It's interesting what you've been posting online, you know," I continued. "You seem to be so set on finding the serial killer, but you've not taken any time to consider why these people are being killed."

She looked over at me in surprise for a moment. "What do you mean? It doesn't matter why people are murdered; no-one deserves to die."

"Of course it matters," I chuckled. "None of the people who have been killed have been good people. They all deserved it. Maybe the serial killer is doing the community a service."

This last comment appeared to have a hit a nerve with Alison. She turned her body round to face me, eyes glaring deep into mine and shouted "How dare you say such a thing! Coleen and Rachel never deserved to die; they weren't bad people! They were my friends and not only that, but they were also wives and mothers." Tears began streaming down her cheeks.

"So, Rachel's dead, is she?" I asked innocently.

"Oh, cut the crap Chrissie" she retorted, her anger now fueling her confidence and overtaking her fear, "you knew she was dead because you're the one who killed her, aren't you! The same way you killed Coleen! You were having an affair with Coleen's husband and Rachel and Coleen confronted you about it, so you killed them." She spat the words out as if they were venom.

"I've already told you that I didn't have an affair with Coleen's husband." I stated calmly.

"So, you're only going to deny the affair," she snapped back, "not the killings?"

I paused for a moment, my left hand steady on the injection pen still within my pocket. She clearly already knows far too much, and I definitely wouldn't be able to let her live after this conversation. So do I just get it over and done with now, or do I play with her a little bit first, see if I can get her to understand the good I've done, as well as the bad.

"We all do things that we may regret Alison, but sometimes we have to do these things for the greater good, and sometimes some people have to suffer as collateral."

"What do you mean?" she asked, her voice quivering.

"I didn't want to kill Rachel, but she didn't give me a choice. I thought she knew what had happened to Coleen and I needed to protect myself and my family."

Alison let out a small gasp but didn't say anything, so I resumed.

"I deeply regret what happened to Coleen, but it had nothing to do with her husband. I'm not an adulterer."

"No, just a murderer," Alison quipped, but I ignored her and continued on.

"My feelings had gotten the better of me with Coleen, I was upset about her deliberately excluding Sam from her son's birthday party and I didn't know why she would do that. Of course, I now know why she did it, even if it was for the wrong reason, but there's not much I can do about that now."

I could see Alison's hand reaching back for the door handle again, so I put my right hand onto her arm, wrapping my fingers tightly around her forearm to indicate to her that I wasn't going to let her go anywhere.

She looked resolved to her fate of staying in the car and didn't seem intent to fight back, well not yet at least. "So, what about the others? Why did you kill Craig in the shop and that schoolteacher?"

"That schoolteacher was a pedophile," I shot back at her, almost at a yell, "and Craig was a rude arsehole who gave that shop a bad reputation, and don't even get me started on Kelly."

"Kelly?" Alison whispered, clearly confused as to who I was referring to.

"Oh yes, Kelly. She was victim number 2 I believe." I replied nonchalantly.

"Oh my gosh, so there's more?" Alison's eyes widened in fear, and she attempted to move her arm away from me, causing me to tighten my grip further. "How many, Chrissie?"

I thought for a moment, I hadn't actually counted myself. Without considering Maeve, there would be five so far. I smiled at Alison, "Well I guess there is about to be six in total."

With that, I pulled out the injection from my pocket, raising it up above my head, ready to plummet it down into the shoulder of the arm I still had hold of in a vice like grip. Alison screamed, a loud high-pitched scream that echoed within the car.

I reeled my arm back slightly, still raised above my head, gathering the momentum to bring it down and inject her, but as I did so, I felt a hand clamp around my own arm and before I could figure out what was going on, I was being dragged out of the car.

"What the fuck" I screamed as I toppled out of the car and on to the floor. I could feel myself being pushed and pulled in all directions and then all of a sudden, I was lying face down, on the tarmacked car park, with something heavy leant on my back. I started thrashing about in an attempt to free myself from whatever was pinning me down, but it was no use. I felt both arms manipulated and twisted round to the small of my back and then the feel of cold metal touching both wrists. Handcuffs.

Within a few seconds I was then hoisted up into a standing position and for the first time I was able to take a look around and determine what was going on. Either side of me were two male police officers, now both holding a shoulder each to ensure I didn't attempt to run. I looked over to the exit of the car park to see a police van blocking the way, as well as numerous other police officers milling around. I hadn't seen the van turn up and I had no idea when it had arrived, but I must not have noticed it whilst being so focused on my conversation with Alison.

I looked over to Alison's car, which was now about 100 yards away. I couldn't believe how far the police had managed to move me throughout the scuffle. Alison was stood next to her car, talking to two police officers, tears streaming down her face. I strained to try and hear what she was saying but I couldn't hear anything other than the din of police chattering around me and the wind whistling through the trees to the side of us.

What had happened? How had they found me? Out of the corner of my eye I spotted a man in a sharp black suit walking towards me. It was DI Wills.

"Hello Chrissie. You're under arrest for five counts of suspected murder and another count of attempted murder." He stated to me, matter of factly.

"I don't know what you're talking about, let me go" I shouted.

"Now, now" he responded and then begun to recite my rights to me, "You do not have to say anything unless you wish to do so, but anything you do say will be taken down and may be given in evidence."

I wasn't listening to DI Wills. All I could think about was how this could possibly have happened. How did anyone work it out? How would they have known where I would be today? How did they link all the deaths together? As I pondered this, I caught sight of Alison handing something over to the police officer's she was speaking to. It was hard to tell what it was, other than it being a small black box with wiring attached to it. Had she been wearing a wire when we met? Had this all been a trap?

The police officers either side of me then began walking me towards the parked-up police van. DI Wills had already walked away, but I was unsure as to whether or not he knew that I wasn't listening to him. The officer on my left-hand side swung the doors open to the back of the van and the second officer then bent my head down and lightly pushed me towards the cage inside it. I climbed inside, not sure what else I could do at this point. I sat down on the cold metal bench inside the cage, my hands still cuffed behind my back and looked into the faces of the two police officers who were staring back at me from outside the van. Nothing more was said as the doors were slammed shut, leaving me alone and trapped, with no way out.

Part 3

24

Everything feels warm and fuzzy, my eye lids are heavy and I'm so tired. I'm laid down in bed and I can feel the warmth of the duvet around me, the pillow soft under my head, which is hurting quite a bit and difficult to lift up.

There's screaming coming from the room next door. Who is that? Where am I? I can feel fear start creeping in now. What's going on?

The last thing I can remember was getting arrested in the pub car park. Alison had been wearing a wire when I had met up with her. I knew she was a threat, but I still can't figure out how she worked it all out, how she had realised it was me.

I slowly start to open my eyes, it's difficult, but with some force I manage to open them sluggishly. I'm laid on my back, and above me is a singular light recessed into the ceiling. The light isn't on, but it's not dark in here so it must be daytime. I try to speak but nothing other than a groan comes out. My head is really starting to pound now. I feel a bit nauseous too.

I can hear what sounds like two people chatting beside me, but I can't quite decipher what they are saying. I don't think I recognise the voices either. My body feels like it is being pushed down into the mattress by some unseen force. I want to sit up, figure out where I am and who is sat next to me, but it's so difficult. Do these people next to me not realise I'm struggling here?

I let out another groan as I try to speak to them. What the fuck is going on?

"Are you okay Chrissie" one of the unfamiliar voices asks me?

Do I look okay? I'm laid here on my back like a plank of wood, unable to move, unable to speak. My confusion is slowly beginning to turn into a combination of fear and anger. Did Alison do something to me in that car park? Was that not the police that arrested me and put me in their van?

A face comes into focus, leaning over me, looking me straight in the eyes. It's the face of a young girl, can't be more than early twenties. Soft pale features and long ginger hair, tied back into a ponytail. "You've been out for some time." She said, her tone gentle and reassuring. "Don't worry, give it a few more minutes and you will start to feel a bit better."

With that, the face is gone again, and I'm left staring back at the ceiling above me. She continues chatting to whoever she is sat next to me with. I can start to understand their conversation now though. Whoever she is speaking to is male, and by the sound of his voice, seems to be quite a bit older than what she is.

"I'll radio through to the nursing station and let them know that she's starting to wake up. Katie will want to take her obs." The male voice said.

"How do you think she's going to be this time?" the girl replied, her voice sounding anxious.

"We've got a full team in today, so you don't need to worry" the man responded softly. "Room 2 to the nursing station, she's awake." There was a crackling sound, presumably from his radio.

"Understood" crackled back, distorted.

I can start to feel my extremities now. I begin moving my fingers and toes, wiggling them about. My arms and legs still feel heavy, but I think I can move them. I roll over to my side, to face the two voices beside me, and get a better view of my environment.

The two people are sat on beanbags by the door of the room I'm in, and I appear to be lying in a single bed. I take a quick glance around the sterile and plain looking room. There's nothing in it aside from the bed I'm lying on and some shelving sunken into the walls. The shelves appear empty though. There's a window with what looks like shutters built into it, inside of the glass though, with nothing but a small turning point at the bottom to open and close them. They are open at present, the sun shining in from outside. Between the wall with the window and the wall with the doorway where the two people are sat, there's a door. Well, half a door by the looks of it. It doesn't quite reach the floor, or the top of the door frame and the top of the door appears to be slanted. I'm so confused, where am I and what is going on?

The screaming in the room next to me seems to be getting louder and there's banging alongside it now. This is not conducive for my headache. If I didn't feel so groggy, I would maybe feel a bit more concerned for this individual, but I'm still not sure of what's going on yet.

"Steph is kicking off bad now" the girl's voice stated.

"Not much we can do about it to be fair" the man replies casually.

"Code Red" is heard shouting through the crackling radio, and I can hear footsteps running along the corridor outside the room.

The screaming continues to escalate, am I in danger here? What is this place and what are they doing to the woman next door? I push my hands down into the mattress and force myself to sit upright. The room starts spinning as I do so, and I take a few seconds to gather myself. I can feel the nausea washing over me, but I hold it in. Once the dizziness passes, I open my eyes and notice both people staring back at me. No-one says anything for a minute, it's as if they are waiting for me to speak first. I look down at my body, I'm wearing what appears to be a hospital gown but there's no ties on it, it's just loosely hanging so the back of me feels exposed. At least I'm wearing underwear, and is this a sports bra? This doesn't belong to me. Whose clothes am I wearing?

"Who are you?" I ask, directing my question to the young girl staring back at me.

"It's me, Sarah, we've met loads of times before." She replied to me with a smile.

Sarah? The name doesn't ring a bell and I don't recongise her either. I look over at the man sitting beside her on the bean bag. He's quite a bit older than she is, must be in his fifties. He's wearing black cargo trousers and a black t-shirt, the radio I heard clipped to his belt. He doesn't look comfortable on the bean bag, he's clearly quite tall and his legs are bent up, almost spiderlike, in his attempt to ensure ease with sitting.

"I'm Mark" he stated bluntly, no further exploration given.

"Where am I?" I wasn't sure if I was still asking this question in my head or if I had managed to say this out loud but as Mark started to reply, I got my answer.

"You're in Carting Hospital and you are safe" he responded, almost robotic like. Clearly, he had said this to people many times before. Hospital? Am I sick? I certainly don't feel very well, but what happened to me to get me here? I've never heard of 'Carting' either? Is this some sort of specialist hospital? I look around the room again, trying to get my bearings. This doesn't look like any kind of hospital I've ever been to.

A woman then arrived at the doorway, she had short curly brown hair and glasses and was dragging an observation trolley alongside her. She said a few things to Mark, but I couldn't hear their conversation over the sound of the screaming and banging next door. She then entered the room and smiled at me.

"Good morning, I'm just going to do some of your obs and let the doctor know that you're awake." She lifted my right arm and begun wrapping a blood pressure cuff around the upper part of it. The cuff was connected to a machine that sat on top of the trolley. I watched as she removed a small plastic sensor that she then placed on one of my fingers. She didn't say anything further to me as she began alternating her gaze between the rise and fall of my chest and the watch on her wrist. I could feel the blood pressure cuff squeezing the top of my arm, almost painfully, and the machine made a whirring noise next to me. Shouldn't she have asked for my consent before doing this? The thought clearly hadn't occurred to this woman. The whirring of the machine continued next to me before two loud beeps and the pressure of the cuff released. I let out a breath that I hadn't realised I had been keeping in. The noise from next door seemed to have stopped now.

"Obs all seem fine" the woman stated as she began jotting down on her hand the results from the machine with a pen she had appeared to materialise out of nowhere. It wasn't clear if she was telling me or the two people at my door that my obs were fine, but considering I wasn't sure exactly what she meant by that, I assumed it wasn't directed at me.

She took the sensor and the cuff from me and handed me a small plastic glass of water that the young girl had just handed to her. "You must be thirsty; you've been asleep for some time."

"What's going on?" I asked.

The woman looked at me and paused before answering. "Do you know where you are Chrissie?"

I nodded towards Mark who was still sat on the beanbag by the door, but now appeared to be writing something on a clipboard that I hadn't noticed he had before now. "He told me that I'm in Carting Hospital." The confusion could be heard in my voice.

The woman sat down on the edge of the bed, a look of surprise on her face that she appeared to be trying to conceal. "And do you know why you're here?" she asked gently.

What am I supposed to say to that? I still don't know what's going on or who these people are. Can I trust them? Do they know what I've done or what happened with Alison? I need to be sensible with this. I can't say anything until I know what they know. I shook my head side to side slowly.

"That's ok. Do you know how long you've been here?"

I shook my head again at her next question and she put her hand on my elbow in a reassuring manner. She was being too nice to me to know what I had done surely. Or was this a ruse to lull me into a false sense of security? I watched her look over to Mark and Sarah, who both seemed to look equally as surprised at my answers, which only further heightened my confusion.

The woman got up slowly from the bed. "She's lucid" she stated matter of factly, looking now at the two people on the bean bags rather than me. "I'm going to call Dr. Short" and with that she quickly left the room, taking her medical trolley with her.

25

I'm not sure how much time had passed whilst I waited for the doctor to arrive to see me. The two members of staff, Mark and Sarah, had introduced themselves as support workers on the ward and had explained to me that they had to always stay within eyesight of me, under the doctors' orders. I'd be sure to have a word with this doctor about that when I see them. Mark and Sarah had been reluctant to answer many of my questions, telling me consistently that I needed to wait and speak to the doctor, and that they would be here soon. They wouldn't tell me how long I had been here, why I was here or why I felt so groggy. All I knew was the name of the hospital and that I had to be watched by two staff members constantly, for safety, they said. I'm not sure if they were referring to my safety or their safety and I still didn't know how much they knew about me.

Eventually, after what seemed like an eternity, a woman in her mid to late thirties, dressed smartly in a tailored pinstripe navy skirt, matching navy heels and a white blouse walked into the room. She was carrying a manila-coloured folder which I could see had my name on it and like the staff members, also had a radio attached to the waistband of her skirt. She gave a small nod to Mark and Sarah who then proceeded to drag their bean bags out of the doorway, into the corridor and close the door behind them, leaving me and this woman alone in the room.

"I assume you're Dr. Short" I stated, to which she smiled.

"Do you remember me Chrissie, or are you making that assumption after being told that I was coming to see you?" She asked. She remained stood by the doorway, with the door closed behind her. Not that there would have been anywhere in the room for her to sit had she wished to, and she didn't seem the type to be willing to sit on a beanbag on the floor.

"Should I remember you?" I countered. Something about this woman did feel familiar, but I couldn't put my finger on why. Had I met her before? Is she someone that Tim, my doctor husband, has previously worked with perhaps?

"Well, you are correct. I am Dr. Short, and I am your consultant psychiatrist."

"My what?" I stuttered in disbelief. Since when did I have a psychiatrist. I'm not crazy, why would I need one. "What kind of hospital is this?"

"Chrissie," she started, her tone becoming softer, less authoritative, "You are currently being held in a high secure psychiatric unit under a Section 37/41 of the Mental Health Act. Do you understand what that means?"

I shook my head, words escaping me as she continued explaining my current situation to me.

"I'm not sure if you can recall at present, but there were numerous incidents that you were involved in that led to your arrest by the police. As a result, you were psychologically examined, deemed medically unfit and sent here for a more thorough assessment to determine if you are indeed mentally unwell and what treatment you require." She explained, "in laymen's terms, you have been sentenced to an indefinite period of time in hospital where you can be treated for your mental illness accordingly, rather than being sent to prison."

I couldn't believe what I was hearing. So, they did know who I was and what I had done, but I still didn't understand how and when I got here. The timeline wasn't adding up in my head.

"I don't understand" I began, pausing to try and gather my thoughts.

"What is the last thing that you remember before coming to hospital" she enquired.

"I was being arrested and being put into the back of a police van, and then I woke up here, in this bed, with someone else's clothes on" I looked down at my body again, feeling suddenly very conscious of the fact that I wasn't fully clothed.

"And when do you think that arrest happened?" She seemed to want to ask me a lot of questions, when really it was me that required answers, not her.

"I'm not sure how long I've been asleep, maybe a day or two ago." I was beginning to become concerned where this line of questioning was going, and the way in which she was phrasing some of these questions seemed a bit odd to me. I wish this headache would go away so I could think a bit more clearly.

"Chrissie, you've been in hospital with us now for the last six months." She paused, watching my face intently, which I'm sure showed nothing but horror and surprise.

Six months? I've been in this hospital for six months. There's no way that can be true. I racked my brain, desperately trying to remember how I got into hospital, but nothing was coming. She can't be serious; is this some sort of sick joke she is playing on me? Maybe she is gaslighting me, to make me think that I'm crazy, when I know I'm not. I could feel the nausea beginning to rise again, coming up into my throat from my stomach, like the crashing of a wave on the shore. I swallowed hard, trying to keep myself from being sick. I'm still not sure how mobile I am to be able to get to a toilet, never mind knowing where a toilet even is in this place.

Dr. Short stayed looking at me calmly from where she was stood. She gave no indication that what she was saying was a joke, or that she was playing a trick on me. "You've been very unwell since you arrived here Chrissie. There have been many incidents of aggression, harm to yourself and just generally putting yourself and others at risk, which is why you have spent a lot of time under sedation whilst in hospital here and likely, why you cannot remember very much at the moment."

"Is that why I feel so sick?" I swallowed back more bile that had risen up into my mouth. What have they been sedating me with? Is this even legal?

"Yes, unfortunately some of the side effects of Acuphase are dizziness, nausea, tiredness and generally feeling zoned out and groggy."

"Acuphase?" I queried. I had never heard of it. So, they were drugging me? Is this some sort of sick revenge? Injecting me with some horrific substance to make me ill because of how I was injecting people before. "What is that, and why have you been giving it to me?"

"Like I said before Chrissie, you've been very unwell and for the most part, actively psychotic and exhibiting delusional beliefs. As a result of these symptoms, you have been undertaking considerably risky behaviours which have resulted in us having to use necessary force at times to manage that risk." She paused, allowing some time to process what she was saying to me. "Acuphase is a medication given by injection which helps to control those symptoms, but with this symptom control, also comes these side effects."

"So, what you are telling me is, I have been here for the last six months, going crazy, not having any idea what is going on and you've just been continually drugging me?" My voice was beginning to rise as I begun to piece together what had been happening. "How is this allowed?!"

"Like I already mentioned, you are under a Section 37/41 of the Mental Health Act. This means that you are under my care as your responsible clinician and I am allowed, by law, to assess, treat and manage your illness." Dr. Short didn't appear in the least bit disturbed by my anger. I suppose she was probably used to people screaming and shouting at her if this is what she does to them.

"I'm not unwell" I spat at her, "the only illness I have is because of whatever chemicals you have been pumping into me."

"At the moment, you have a working diagnosis of Schizoaffective Personality Disorder, however as you have not been lucid enough to have a full discussion over the last six months, this could change with further assessment."

I slammed my fists down onto the bed beside me and screamed out loud. A long high-pitched scream that echoed around the empty, lifeless room. Dr. Short continued to remain statue still, she didn't even jump when the scream began. She was as cool as a cucumber. Mark and Sarah suddenly burst through the door, both appearing ready for action, clearly not sure what was currently happening. Dr. Short gave another small nod to Mark, and he beckoned for Sarah to follow him back out the door behind him, leaving the two of us alone again. Clearly this head nod was a well-known code between the doctor and her staff, because on two occasions now they had known to leave the room without so much as a word from her. She must not currently see me as a threat, which seemed odd considering she is trying to explain to me how I've had to be repeatedly sedated due to the danger I pose.

Once the scream had finished booming from my mouth, I felt somewhat better, a small amount of relief. But I still had more questions than answers and I didn't like what I had heard so far.

"Where's Tim?" I asked suddenly. Why isn't he doing something about this? "Does he know I'm here?"

"We can talk about Tim another time, Chrissie." She responded, evading the question. "For now, you need to get some rest and tomorrow we can have a more in-depth discussion regarding why you are here and what you can remember about what brought you here."

"That's not good enough, I need to speak to Tim. He must be worried sick about where I am".

Dr. Short gave a small sign, as if she had become weary of the conversation. "Everyone who needs to know that you are here have been made aware and they are all in support of you receiving the care that you need."

"So, what happens now then? Am I allowed to leave this room? Do I have to be followed everywhere? Am I even allowed to use the toilet in peace?" I was beginning to feel deflated. As much as I wanted to scream and shout at this woman standing before me, she had made it clear what will happen if I do, and if I want to figure out a way out of here, I need to keep my wits about me.

"Mark, Sarah" she shouted through the door, "you can come back in now."

She waited for the support staff to come back into the room, dragging their bean bags in with them, before continuing. "These are your support staff, and they will be staying with you until you have been deemed safe enough to have your observation level reduced. They need to always stay close by, to make sure that you and other people on the ward are safe."

I went to open my mouth to begin my protest against this blatant disrespect of my personal space and privacy, but Dr. Short merely lifted her hand up to signal for me not to speak.

"This is currently non-negotiable until such a time that you have been assessed to be safe on your own. You may leave your room as and when you like, and you can use the bathroom with a female member of staff observing and the other member of staff behind the door. Your primary nurse is called Katie, if you have any more questions or need anything you can ask her or any other member of staff on the ward." Dr. Short gave a quick glance at her watch. "It's almost lunch time, try to get something to eat if you feel up to it. I must head off now, I have a meeting."

She turned on her heel and left the room without a glance back, the sound of her shoes tapping down the corridor, getting quieter the further away she got.

I guess I will have to look around and get my bearings then. I swung my legs round to dangle off the side of the bed. Gently standing up, I clutched the back of my open hospital gown to cover myself.

"Can I get some real clothes?" I asked Sarah, who was watching me intently, clearly waiting to see what I was going to do and what my reaction was going to be, now that I was up and about.

She looked up at Mark, who then responded for her. "Your care plan states that you are not allowed any clothing that could be deemed as a risk currently, so the best I can do is get you another hospital gown to cover the back of you." Sarah seemed relieved that she hadn't had to break that bad news to me. Getting a good look at her now, she seemed so timid and scared. Did she know my history and feared me? Or had she been around during my apparent 'psychotic episodes' previously and was worried that it would happen again. That's if it had ever happened before, I wasn't sure I fully trusted anything that this Dr. Short had said so far.

I took a step forward, tentatively, like a toddler learning to walk for the first time. My legs felt like jelly. I must have been laid down for some time. My confidence began to grow with my movements, step after step, until the dizziness began to subside.

"Ok, let's get another hospital gown then, where can I get one." I asked.

"If you come out into the main lounge area, we have a linen cupboard, I can get one for you and then you can sit down for lunch." Mark replied, beckoning for me to follow him.

"Can you not just grab it for me before I leave the room?" I asked nervously, "I don't want to walk around with my arse on show."

Mark shook his head, "I'm sorry Chrissie, but you know the drill. We have to stay with you at all times, both of us. So, if one of us needs to go somewhere, then we all go together."

I clung tightly to the back of the gown, pulling it across as far as I could to try and cover up as much of my body as possible. I then pigeon stepped slowly beside Mark, who led me out of the room, through a corridor and into a large open space which must have been the main lounge. Sarah followed close behind me, watching me like a hawk, but I almost didn't mind at this point because she was acting like a human shield for my modesty.

I took a look at my surroundings; the whole room was open plan but had been segmented into separate areas. One part of the room had a large television behind a Perspex screen, so that the television itself wasn't accessible to the people on the ward. There were three large rubber-looking sofas, positioned in a C shape facing the television. In another part of the room were several tables and chairs, all of which appeared to be secured to the floor and all corners rounded off so there were no sharp edges. Everything seemed to be somewhat slanted at the top, all the doors and the chairs. I'm sure there was likely a reason for it, but I wasn't sure what it could be yet. Across one side of the room appeared to be an office, with large viewing windows leading out onto the ward. This must have been a staff office because it was the only room so far that seemed to have things in it that could be moved around or lifted up. I had a peek in as we walked past it. Inside were computers, filing cabinets and office chairs on wheels. There were two staff members sat at a desk, both typing furiously on their own separate computers, one of which was the women who had come into my room earlier to take my blood pressure. Neither of them appeared to look up from what they were doing to acknowledge me walking past.

Mark stopped in front of a door to the right-hand side of the office and pulled at a set of keys attached to his belt that came out on a pull string. There appeared to be a few different keys attached to the set, as well as a fob. He positioned one of the keys into the lock on the door and opened what appeared to be a small cupboard filled with towels, gowns and bedding. He took out a gown before handing it to me and locking the door shut again. I swiftly put the gown on to cover the back of me up.

I was just about to ask what we were supposed to be doing now, when a door opened up at the very far end of the room. A woman wearing an apron came in, pushing a large metal trolley. The wheels of the trolley squeaked on the hard flooring as she maneuvered it towards us, stopping at a door a few metres away before unlocking it and letting herself in.

"What's in there?" I asked.

"That's the kitchen area" Sarah replied, "It's lunch time now. Lunch will be served from there shortly."

"Can I go in the kitchen?" I queried.

"Only some patients are allowed in the kitchen, according to their care plan. You can't go in yet, people on constant observations aren't allowed in the kitchen." She responded.

"Well, that seems a bit silly, surely you would want more supervision in the kitchen then not." I retorted.

"It isn't a usual kitchen, it's a ward kitchen." Mark interjected. "There's only a fridge and some cupboards in there. Nothing you can hurt yourself with."

"So why can't I go in then?" I countered.

"Rules" was all he said back.

The door to the kitchen appeared to be cut in half and the top half of the door then opened, allowing a hatchway for the woman to give food out to the patients. There was already a line of people waiting for their food. Probably the highlight of their day, I thought, considering there didn't appear much else to do here, from what I had seen so far.

There were five people lined up so far, all woman and all seemed completely different to one another. There was an extremely large woman at the front of the queue and a very slim woman waiting beside her. The two stood next to each other looked like the number ten. Behind them were two woman who looked completely normal, just standing there, make-up on, nicely dressed, looking particularly out of place in their current environment, and at the end of the queue was a lady who seemed to be responding to something that no-one else could see. She was rocking back and forth on the balls of her bare feet, pointing at the floor beside her and muttering under her breath. She was also wearing hospital gowns like me and had two female members of staff standing close to her. I wonder if she had been medicated like I had. Is this how I am going to turn out if they keep pumping me full of poison?

Mark extended his arm in the direction of the queue, signaling for me to line up alongside the other women. I felt my belly rumble slightly. I was hungry, but can I trust the food that these people are going to give me? I may have to chance it, if I've been drugged and I've been sleeping a lot then I need to rebuild my strength somehow. At least not all the women seemed to be in bad shape, just me and Loopy Linda beside me.

As I got closer to the kitchen hatch, the smell of gravy and meat made my stomach grumble even more. I waited patiently until it was my turn and the woman in the kitchen gave me a big smile.

"Hi Chrissie, how are you feeling?" she asked brightly as she handed me a plastic plate with sausages, mash and peas on it. "You look really well today!"

"Erm, fine thank you" I mumbled, taking the plate. How did this woman know my name? No-one batted an eyelid at me walking around the room yet, either everyone already knew me and expected me to be there, or everyone is in on a joke that I'm the center of. Sarah took a plastic knife and fork out of the woman's hand and brought them along to an empty table where the three of us then sat down.

"You don't get to eat?" I asked Mark and Sarah.

"No, we can't eat with you, but we will get to eat on our breaks later." Mark replied.

We all sat in silence as I tucked into my food. I had always thought of hospital food as being disgusting, but this was actually pretty good. Not much different to what I would have made for my family at home. Before I knew it, all the food was gone, and my belly was full. I was starting to feel much better as a result too.

Once I had finished, another member of staff came over and collected my plate and plastic cutlery and returned it back to the kitchen, which was then swiftly locked back up again.

Katie, who I now knew to be my primary nurse, then came over to me at the table and asked how I was feeling and if I had spoken to Dr. Short. I nodded, not really feeling up to having any further conversation at this time, especially about why I'm here and why I'm being watched constantly. She seemed to sense that I wasn't in the talking mood. "It's been a long morning for you hasn't it." She said reassuringly. "Why don't you take some time to relax this afternoon, you can watch some television or have a nap. Dr. Short wants to see you again tomorrow to see how you are doing." I nodded again and she gave me a slight pat on the shoulder before walking away.

I looked over at the lounge area, all three sofas were occupied by the five woman who had also just finished their lunch. Little and large were sat in silence next to each other, eyes transfixed to the television screen where some sort of antiques show was being aired, the two normal looking women were chatting amicably to each other, and Loopy Linda was still mumbling to herself and pointing. I didn't really fancy joining the viewing party, maybe I would have a little nap, anything to speed up my time in this place. The quicker I could see the doctor again tomorrow, the quicker I could hopefully convince her that I didn't need to be watched constantly, or even better, than I didn't need to be here at all.

I returned to my room, followed closely, of course, by Mark and Sarah.

"I need the toilet" I stated and walked into the bathroom; Sarah close behind like a shadow. She shut the door behind her, and I could see the top of Marks tall head the other side of the not quite full door. At least I could see that it was the back of his head, so he wasn't trying to get a peek at me. Sarah on the other hand, stared directly at me the entire time. I pulled down my knickers and perched on the toilet, trying to position the gown to cover myself as much as possible. Sarah maintained constant eye contact with me, clearly trying to show that she wasn't looking anywhere private, but that she was also still going to be looking.

"Well, this isn't awkward at all" I muttered, as I then wiped myself and flushed the toilet. Once my knickers were back up, I then went over to the sink which seemingly had no taps on it, just a large button. I looked at Sarah briefly in confusion, before pressing the button, to which lukewarm water then came trickly out of a recessed hole that was barely visible at the top of the sink. I wet my hands and placed them under a small automatic soap dispenser which whirred and provided the smallest amount of soap going.

"It's an anti-ligature sink" Sarah advised; she must have become aware of my confusion as to why the sink was the way it was.

"Anti-ligature?" I asked, unfamiliar with the term.

"To stop people from trying to hang themselves" she said matter of fact.

"Oh" was all I could say to that. Is that why everything is curved and slanted then? So, you can't attach anything to them? This really was a secure unit.

I went back into the bedroom and sat back down on the bed. Mark and Sarah busied themselves repositioning the bean bags and getting themselves comfortable.

"Which one of those women out there was the one that was screaming earlier when I woke up" I wondered aloud.

"That was Rebecca", offered Mark, "She wasn't in the main lounge earlier though for lunch. She's been taken to seclusion."

"Seclusion?"

"It's a safe room, a bit like this, but even safer. You may not remember but you've been there a few times." Mark replied.

"Hmmm" What was I supposed to say to that? I don't remember being anywhere else in this hospital. I don't remember anything that these people have said had happened so far. "I'm going to try and sleep for a bit; I don't feel well still."

I laid down in the bed, turning to face away from Mark and Sarah so I didn't have to worry about them staring at me so much whilst I tried to sleep.

Just as I was beginning to fall asleep, I heard Mark and Sarah speaking to two other staff members, another male and female voice who I hadn't heard before. Mark appeared to be giving them a brief rundown of what I had been up to since waking up earlier and that I was now planning to sleep for the afternoon. The unfamiliar female voice thanked him for the hand over and the noise of the bean bags moving indicated to me that Mark and Sarah had been replaced by two new support staff. My eyes were so heavy though and I was exhausted from the events of the day so far, and all the information I was trying to process, that I couldn't bring myself to turn around and look at who was now likely staring at my back for the next couple of hours whilst I slept. Instead, as I drifted into sleep, I decided that I would just wait and see what awaited me when I get up again.

26

My awakening the next morning was considerably less surprising than the shocking realisation I had been faced with the day before. Mark was sat by the door in his hunched-up position on a bean bag, engrossed in a conversation with the woman sat on the other bean bag beside him. It wasn't Sarah this time, it was an older woman, must have been mid-sixties, with greying short curly hair and the facial expression of someone who had just been served gone off chicken at a restaurant.

The two of them were talking about another patient on the ward, but their voices were hushed so it was difficult to decipher exactly what it was they were saying. From what I could gather, something had happened during the night, which I had apparently completely slept through and had resulted in a member of staff being injured and taken to hospital. I hadn't been able to hear who the staff member or the patient was that they were talking about, but the stern looking woman clearly wasn't happy about the situation.

"This is what happens when they start letting the patients run riot." She whispered sharply, "She has been refusing her medication for weeks now and she's clearly manic, yet no-one has done anything about it."

"You know it's not that easy, with all of her drug allergies and reactions she has had previously to treatment, they can't risk sedating her again. Don't you remember last time? Three months she was in a coma for." Mark murmured back, in a much gentler tone than his colleague.

"Oh, I remember fondly" she remarked back, "three months of bliss that was."

I shuffled in the bed, trying to get myself in a more comfortable position and stretch out a bit after a long night of being still. The sound of the bedding moving was enough to halt the two staff's conversation and focus their attention on to me, where it should have been the whole time according to Dr. Short's care plan.

"Good morning" Mark said brightly. "How did you sleep?"

"Ok, I think" I mumbled, still feeling somewhat groggy and unsure if I was still on a significant medication comedown or just waking up. Who knows, maybe they drugged me again in my sleep and that's why I slept through whatever happened last night.

"I suppose you're going to want to use the toilet now aren't you" the woman said gruffly, clearly inconvenienced by the idea of having to move herself from her seated position.

Without responding, I got up out of bed, feeling much steadier on my feet than I was the day before when getting up, and padded into the bathroom to start my usual morning routine of wee, face wash and teeth brushing.

"Hold on!" The woman shouted at me as I went to close the door behind me. Oh yes, I forgot I require a full-time audience now. She trundled her way over to the door and put her foot in front of it to prevent it from closing completely.

Unlike Sarah the day before, this woman seemed to be more willing to allow for some semblance of privacy for me and didn't feel the need to stand directly next to me whilst I'm doing my business. Mark didn't seem to say anything to her about not being in the room with me either and I certainly wasn't going to complain. I wonder if they changed the rules, or does this woman just like to follow her own.

I splashed some cold water on my face and sat down onto the toilet. As I began to pee, I realised that there wasn't actually any toilet roll in here that I could see. In fact, there wasn't anything. No soaps other than the dispenser on the wall, no towels, no toothbrush.

"Erm, excuse me" I addressed the foot in the doorway, somewhat embarrassed, "I can't seem to see where the toilet roll is."

I heard a loud huff before the response came. "Why didn't you ask for some before going in?"

"Because I didn't realise there wasn't any in here." I retorted, taken aback by this woman's abrupt attitude.

"You know you have to ask for any toiletries and personal items before you go in." She snapped. "Why do you always have to make things difficult!"

"Tom is getting her toiletries now" I heard Mark inform her, to which she huffed again.

I waited a few minutes, essentially drip drying at this point, before two squares of toilet paper were thrust through the gap in the door towards me. I quickly sorted myself out and washed my hands. It hadn't occurred to me yesterday when I had been in here with Sarah, that she had in fact, handed me the toilet roll at that time too. I had been so preoccupied with what was going on, and where I was, that I hadn't really noticed how sparse the bathroom was. I requested for some toiletries to wash my face and brush my teeth and was given items one at a time, through the small gap in the door. It was clear that any item I requested would not be handed over until the previous item had been returned. Once I was finished, I gave the door a small knock, unsure how to proceed with requesting my exit from the lavatory prison and the woman swiftly pulled the door open and moved to the side of the doorway to let me out.

"Let's go and get you some breakfast" Mark smiled at me, "you missed dinner last night, slept right through it, so you must be hungry."

I gave him a small nod and followed him out of the bedroom, through the small corridor and into the main lounge area. Little and Large were already up and eating breakfast at one of the tables together. Little seemed to be picking at a solitary piece of toast whilst Large was eating a giant bowl of cereal and dunking slices of toast from a plate beside it into the milk. I stifled the urge to gag at the sight and looked over to the hatch where I had been served lunch the day before, but it was shut.

Mark appeared to register my confusion and reassured me that another member of staff would bring something over to us once we sat down and asked me what I would like to eat.

"Just some toast please." I requested.

The three of us settled at a table and the woman, whose name I had still yet to learn, called over to a small looking guy wandering around the lounge, looking perplexed. "Oi, you there, get some toast for Chrissie, will ya."

The boy scurried over to the table, looking like a startled rabbit in the headlights. "Sorry Miss, where do I get the toast?"

The woman sighed and told him to sit with me instead and that she would get it. He sat down in the last remaining seat at the table, and she shot off into the kitchen behind the hatch, closing the door tightly behind her.

"Hello" the boy smiled shyly, "I'm Hugh."

I wasn't sure if he was addressing Mark or me, so I just smiled and said Hello back and Mark begun engaging the boy in conversation. Turns out, he was an agency member of staff who had never worked on this particular ward before so wasn't sure where everything was or what he was supposed to be doing when he wasn't on observations with a patient. Mark seemed exceptionally patient with him, pointing out some of the different doors that could be seen from where we were sat and what was behind them and letting him know to just ask if he is unsure about anything. Before long, the woman returned, almost throwing the plastic plate with two slices of barely buttered toast in front of me.

"Thank you, Miss," Hugh whimpered to her as she signaled for him to now leave. He got up from the table and almost bowed to her before shuffling off in the direction of the nursing office.

"These bloody agency staff will be the death of me, I swear" she groaned as soon as he was out of earshot. "They get paid more than us for doing half the job, and we have to pick up all the slack."

"They can't help what they don't know" Mark countered, "and anyway, without agency staff you would be on observations for your whole shift, and then you would be moaning about that."

She gave him a sharp glare back, clearly unamused at his defense of Hugh. I picked up a half slice of toast and begun to nibble at it. The bread was barely toasted, and the butter tasted like cheap margarine, but I forced it down me, not wanting to suffer the wrath of the battle axe beside me.

"You have a session with Dr. Short this morning, Chrissie." Mark said, whilst checking his watch. "It's actually in about 5 minutes time."

"Best you'd hurry up with that then" she stated as she watched me trying to force down the last few bites.

Once the toast was gone, we remained sat at the table, waiting for my session to begin. Mark had advised me that the nurses would receive a phone call to let them know when Dr. Short was ready to see me and then we would go to the therapy room, which was off the ward, in a different part of the hospital. Little and Large had now moved to the sofas, gazes both transfixed at the television screen again, which I now noticed had a giant crack across it. It wasn't clear from where I was sat as to whether or not it was the television or the Perspex screen in front of it that was cracked, but it certainly hadn't been like that yesterday.

"What happened to the television?" I asked.

"There was an incident last night with one of the other patients." Mark responded calmly.

I opened my mouth to start asking some more questions about it but was cut off before I could speak by Nurse Katie, poking her head out of the office door and shouting over that Dr. Short was ready for me.

We all got up from the table in quick succession and the woman began walking with purpose towards a door at the very end of the room. I followed after her, Mark close behind me. She pulled at the keys attached to her waistband, bringing up a small key fob that she waved in front of a sensor to the right-hand side of the door. Outside of the ward was a small square corridor, with two other doors leading off from it. I continued to follow the woman through a few other doors, all leading to more hallways with doors branching off of them, but every door required a key fob to get through and no door seemed to be opened until the previous door had been shut.

We soon arrived outside a door labelled 'Therapy Suite' and Mark knocked gently on the door. "Come in" rang from inside. Mark fobbed the door open and held it open, gesturing for me to go inside. I walked into a small room with two large armchairs separated by a small coffee table in between them. Much like the ward, the rest of the room was completely bare. Dr. Short was already seated in the armchair the other side of the table and smiled at me, waving towards the other seat for me to sit down. As I sat, I heard the door close behind me and I turned round to see that Mark and the woman had not followed me into the room.

"How are you feeling today, Chrissie?" Dr. Short asked.

"I'm OK" I replied, not really sure what else to say.

"Do you remember what we spoke about yesterday?"

I nodded but that didn't appear to be enough of an answer for her as she didn't seem to want to ask me anything else until I have proven to her that I did. "I remember you telling me that I'm in hospital under a Section and that I had been here for six months." I replied.

"Does it feel like six months to you, or does it still feel like you've only just arrived?"

"I'm not really sure." I paused, because I wasn't. I still didn't really recognise the ward or the staff on it, nor did I remember being in this hospital for such a length of time, but something felt off, almost like everything felt kind of familiar, even though it wasn't.

Dr. Short seemed to be aware of my internal struggles and just nodded reassuringly at me.

"As I explained to you yesterday, although you have been here for a while now, you've been very unwell whilst here so it's not unusual that you may not remember a lot of what has happened since you were admitted." She paused to allow me to take in what she was saying before continuing. "Up until yesterday morning, you hadn't spoken a word to anyone. You had been selectively mute, only communicating with the staff on the ward by pointing or screaming. But mostly your aggressive behaviours towards yourself, the staff and the ward environment have required necessary force and intervention to prevent harm and therefore you have been heavily medicated for most of your hospital stay so far."

I just stared at her, unsure of what to say, how to react. Yesterday I had felt so angry, like I was being tricked. But today, I just feel confused. Something feels true about what she is saying to me, even if I can't remember it.

"Can I speak to Tim?" I asked. There's not anyone here that I know I can trust at the moment. The only way I'm going to be able to figure out exactly what is going on, is if I speak to someone who knows me and wouldn't lie to me. And that person is my husband Tim.

"Why do you want to speak to Tim, Chrissie?"

Well, that seems like an odd question, why wouldn't I want to speak to him? Has something happened to him, and no-one has told me? Or has he found out about what I've done, and he doesn't want to be involved with me anymore? "Has he come to see me since I've been here" I asked, my voice shaking.

"No" she responded softly.

"Oh" I murmured, tears beginning to roll down my cheeks. So, he's probably left me then. I need to speak to him and try to explain everything. Try to get him to understand. I'm not a monster, he must know that surely. I'm his wife, the mother of his son, he must know that I did what I did for the greater good.

"Is Sam safe?" I whispered, struggling to get my words out. Petrified at what the answer may potentially be.

"Tim and Sam are both safe, Chrissie." Dr. Short responded. I brought my eyes up to meet hers and her expression took me off guard. I was expecting her to look empathetic, but she seemed more confused than I was currently. "Chrissie," she continued, "can you remember what happened? What brought you here in the first place?"

Oh god, I knew I was going to have to talk about this sooner or later, but I didn't expect it to be this soon. Is she trying to get a confession out of me so she can get me shipped off to prison? She said something yesterday about the Section I was on being instead of prison, so have I already been charged?

"What exactly do you want to talk about?" I asked hesitantly. I'm not entirely sure exactly how much she knows at this point or what I've even been charged for. Do they know about all the deaths?

"Well obviously there has been a few incidents that occurred before your arrest, so maybe we should start from the beginning and work our way from there." She reached down beside the chair and pulled out a notepad. She flicked open to a few pages in before looking up at me again. "Can you remember who you killed first and why?"

The question shocked me. The way she asked me so blunt and calm, almost as if she was asking me what the time was. She didn't take her eyes off me either. This woman sat across from me wasn't scared of me, nor did she seem to be trying to trip me up either. Perhaps she was just trying to help, and this was my opportunity to get my side of the story out. At this point, I couldn't put myself in a worse position that I'm already in.

I took a deep breath. Time to shit or get off the pot. If what she was telling me was true and I have in fact been in this hospital for the last six months, then nothing is going to change anytime soon unless I start co-operating. "I guess that would be Mr. Turner." I stated confidently. Although Mr. Turner hadn't been my first kill, I was still feeling fairly confident that no-one had connected Maeve's death to me, so I didn't want to incriminate myself any further than I was about to anyway.

Dr. Short looked back down at her notebook and then back at me again. "Hmmm" she murmured, "It's interesting that you refer to him as Mr. Turner. Have you always called him that?"

"I'm sorry?" I asked, puzzled as to why she was asking me that. What else would I have called him? I don't think I even knew his first name, and if I did, I certainly don't remember it now.

"It just seems a very formal way to refer to him that's all," she replied, "I appreciate it's likely hard for you to talk about him though. With everything that went on through your childhood."

"My childhood?" I demanded bemused, "What are you talking about? What has my childhood got to do with Mr. Turner?"

"Why did you kill him Chrissie?" her composed demeanour not wavering in the slightest.

I began to explain to her then, the story of how I had met Mr. Turner for the first time. Or I guess I should say saw rather than met. She sat across from me, her face blank, unreadable, as I explained about how he had cut me up whilst driving one day, how I had followed him and learnt of his extracurricular activities with one of his students. Not at any time did she attempt to interject whilst I described, in detail, how I had felt whilst watching him, how I had been unsure on the best way in which to kill him and then rounding up the story with how I had actually followed through with my plan. It actually felt quite liberating to speak it aloud, to be able to tell someone how and why I had done what I had done. I wonder if Dr. Short would have done the same thing had she been in my position.

"Chrissie," her serene voice interrupting my thought process, "Mr. Turner wasn't a secondary school teacher that you killed because he was a paedophile." I felt a pang in my chest, a sudden anxiousness take hold of me as I listened to the words coming out of her mouth. What was she talking about? How could she know who he was or why I killed him?

I went to respond, mouth agape, ready to start protesting. But she simply raised her hand slightly and looked me deep in the eyes before stating, "Mr. Turner was your father."

27

An intense, roaring laugh erupted out of me, shaking my whole body with its intensity. My father? What is she on about? Does she think that's some kind of funny joke? But Dr. Short wasn't laughing. She maintained constant eye contact with me, waiting for my laughter to end to discuss what she had just said further.

"I'm sorry" I spluttered through giggles, "that's just the most absurd thing I've ever heard."

Dr. Short continued to stare, her hands folding in her lap, waiting. I stopped laughing. "Chrissie, Mr. Turner was your father" she repeated.

I returned her stare for a moment, unsure how to approach this sudden revelation she was presenting me with. I felt tears begin to run down my face, streaming and landing with a splash onto my chest. When had my laughter turned into crying? Why did I suddenly get an intense feeling of shame?

Dr. Short allowed me to cry for some time. We both sat, without speaking a word to each other, whilst silent tears continued to pour. Sudden memories of my childhood began flooding back to me. I felt as if I was 6 years old again and hiding under my bed in the middle of the night, petrified that my father would find me. Flashbacks to my early teenage years, my dad whispering to me to never tell anyone what was happening, or he would kill me, all whilst trapping me in the bed and completing horrendous acts that no child should ever have to experience, especially not at the hands of their own father, the person supposed to protect them.

I looked up and met the doctors gaze, who was still looking at me intently, watching as I slowly began to process what I was remembering.

"Why did you kill him, Chrissie?" She asked me softly.

"He.... He hurt me." I spoke in barely a whisper, "all my life, he did things to me." I couldn't bring myself to say exactly what I had just remembered. I didn't want to relive those memories, or say out loud what had occurred, as if by speaking the words I would somehow have to go through all of it again.

"Tell me what happened the night he died Chrissie." Dr. Short continued to probe. I wasn't sure if she understood that I didn't want to discuss why I had done it further, or if she was just uninterested, but either way, a conversation about killing him seemed much easier and more comfortable than the reasons why.

"I hadn't been to see him for a while." I began, "I only ever stayed with him at the weekends, after he left my mum." I swallowed back further tears. "He had been having an affair with my aunt and left my mum for her. Mum never wanted to see either of them again afterwards, after he had run off with her sister, but she said I still had to. So, every weekend, she would make me go."

I looked over at Dr. Short, who nodded for me to continue. "I hadn't been for a while because when I turned eighteen, I told my Mum I wasn't going to go anymore. She needed me at home a lot and I had decided I didn't want anything more to do with him. But there was one weekend that I had to go, because it was just after my birthday, and he told me if I came to visit that he would buy me a car." My voice broke slightly, "I really needed a car."

Fresh tears began to spill and Dr. Short allowed a slight pause before asking me, "Why did your mum make you keep going to see him if he was hurting you?"

"I never told her." I admitted, "I was scared and ashamed, and she had already had so much heartache that I didn't want her to feel that way again."

"Sometimes you have to be able to protect yourself before you can protect others." Dr. Short stated wisely. "So, what happened when you got to the house?"

"I hadn't planned to do anything before I went. I had taken an insulin injection with me for protection, just in case, because I was so scared of him. I didn't think I would be able to hide a knife particularly well in my pocket like I could the syringe." I continued to recall the events, picturing it all in my mind as I described the scene to Dr. Short.

"How did you know that the insulin would hurt him?" She inquired.

"Mum has been diabetic for as long as I can remember. She has to inject herself twice a day and she always used to tell me when I was little about how dangerous it would be if I took any or played with the needles. So, I did a bit of research on it and learnt how much I would need to use" I paused, unsure how to finish the sentence, but Dr. Short interjected on my behalf so I didn't have to.

"How much you would need to kill someone." She stated, matter of factly, to which I just nodded.

"When I got to his house, there was a car in the driveway that I didn't recognise, a car I thought was going to be for me." I continued on, feeling more confident the more I spoke. "But Dad, he wasn't going to give the car up that easily. My aunt wasn't home, and it was just me and him. He told me that if I wanted the car, then I had to earn it, and I knew exactly what he meant by that."

I took a deep breath in, images flashing in my head of what had occurred at that moment, what I had done, the feelings of fear quickly followed by feelings of relief once he was dead. Dr. Short was still waiting for me to finish telling her what had happened, but she was patient, allowing me as much time as I needed to remember, relive and then recount.

"We were in his living room, and I told him that I wasn't going to do it. That I was an adult now and I didn't have to listen to him anymore. But he just smirked at me, almost like he found it funny that I was telling him no. He pushed me onto the sofa, and I remember him pulling down the zipper on his jeans and I just knew then that if I didn't act, he was going to hurt me again, and who knew how much worse it would have been this time considering I was older, and he hadn't seen me for so long."

Dr. Short leaned forward in her chair, "So, how did you stop him?"

"The injection was in my pocket. I had already put the needle on and turned the dial all the way round to the highest dosage. I pulled it out of my pocket and as he lowered himself on top of me, pushing his body against mine, pinning me to the sofa." I shuddered, suddenly feeling very cold. "I pulled it out and stabbed the needle into his leg."

Dr. Short nodded and settled back into her chair. "Did you know that by doing that, you would kill him?" She asked gently.

"I wasn't sure what would happen exactly." I admitted. "I wasn't even really sure if I had wanted to kill him or not. I just pushed him off me as he was caught off guard and ran out the house."

"And how did you feel when you realised that you had killed him?"

"Good" I stated bluntly. "It felt good. I was relieved. Relieved that I wouldn't have to be hurt by him again, relieved that he wouldn't be able to hurt anyone else." I paused before continuing further, "I also felt strong, like I had won the war after a long, grueling battle."

I felt that feeling of relief again as I finished recounting the events. The tears had stopped, and I was beginning to feel much happier, like a large weight had been lifted off my shoulders. I hadn't done anything wrong by killing him, he had deserved it, and I would do it again in a heartbeat. Dr.

Short hadn't offered an opinion on anything that I had said, but I could tell by the way that she had been looking at me and listening, so invested in what I was saying and what had happened, that she was clearly on my side. Maybe I will be able to get out of here after all. If Dr. Short can understand why I've done what I've done, then surely, they will have to let me go?

"So, what happens now?" I asked, watching as Dr. Short began scribbling notes down in her notepad again.

She looked up briefly and smiled warmly. "It looks like you may be on your way to recovery Chrissie. I think we've done enough for today, but we still have a lot to discuss and there is a lot more work to be done."

I wonder what she means by work to be done. Work to get my charges overturned, or to get me discharged from hospital. I guess from what she had said that she is going to want to discuss all the deaths with me. I hadn't thought about them yet though and suddenly more memories began flooding back, washing over me. I felt dizzy and sick. What was going on? Why was I suddenly remembering everything so differently? If Mr. Turner was actually my father, then who was the man I had been following? Is that someone else I had killed? Have I remembered any of the other deaths differently to what they had actually been?

"Dr. Short," I murmured, almost scared to open my mouth in case vomit escaped instead of words. "I don't understand."

She got up from her chair, walked around the coffee table and placed a hand on my shoulder reassuringly. Looking down at me from her now standing position, I felt a warmth of comfort emitting from her, like she was a guardian angel, here to make everything better.

"I know you don't understand right now Chrissie, but you will."

28

The rest of the day had seemed to go with a blur. I couldn't stop thinking about what I had disclosed to Dr. Short and all of the memories that had come flooding back to me. Dr. Short hadn't wanted to discuss anything further, she said she didn't want me to burn out, so I had been sent back to the ward, with my support staff in tow.

I felt lost in my own thoughts, going round and round in my head, everything that had happened previously, or what I had thought had happened. But no matter how hard I tried; I couldn't seem to remember anything particularly clearly at all. It was almost as if unlocking that memory of my childhood had completely altered my current reality, like I no longer knew who I was.

A loud scream echoed throughout the ward, interrupting my inner monologue of confusion. I was sat on one of the sofas, Little and Large sat opposite me and my support staff sat at one of the tables behind us. The scream was coming from the end of the bedroom corridor, but was getting louder with every second, heading in our direction. Suddenly Loopy Linda came bursting into view, screeching like a banshee and throwing herself around as she ran. The term bouncing off the walls had never made more sense, as she literally threw herself into the wall next to the nursing office. Her two support staff were running after her, one of which was Sarah, the other Hugh from this morning, both of them looking terrified of this screaming, bouncing woman in front of them.

"The spiders, the spiders!" Loopy Linda screamed, pointing directly at Hugh before lowering the volume of her voice and stating directly, "the spiders will be coming for you tonight." She let out a high-pitched giggle and then ripped her hospital gown from her body, throwing it to the floor, leaving her stood there in just her underwear, similar to what I was wearing under my own gown.

She unexpectedly lunged forward, grabbing hold of Sarah by her ponytail and pulling hard. Sarah screamed out in pain and clasped both of her hands on top of her head, across Loopy Linda's hand that was still fixed to her ponytail. Hugh didn't move, just continued to stand there looking at what was unfolding in front of him. Loopy Linda let go and put her finger gently on Sarah's nose before whispering something to her that I wasn't able to hear. Sarah's facial expression didn't give any indication of what was being said either. She remained calm in her composure, but her eyes looked scared.

Loopy Linda then began jumping up and down on the spot, her arms raised up above her head and began singing *"Spiderman, Spiderman, does whatever a spider can, spins a web, kill the staff, catches babies and steals their eyes, look out, here comes the Spiderman!"*

Hugh was just watching Loopy Linda in horror. Little and Large seemed to just be completely ignoring the spectacle before us and I hadn't heard any movement from the staff sat behind me. Sarah was attempting to speak to Loopy Linda whilst she was singing, I couldn't hear what she was saying over the bizarre chant but whatever it was, didn't seem to be having any effect. Loopy Linda then began advancing towards

Sarah again and as Sarah began to back away from her to avoid the flailing arms heading in her direction, she pulled down hard on a large black oval attached to her belt, next to her keys.

Beep Beep Beep Beep, rang through the ward, continuous and loud. Three members of staff came rushing out of the staff office, Mark included, and Loopy Linda was grabbed hold of quickly, Mark on one side of her and Katie on the other side. I wasn't sure what they were doing, but Loopy Linda was thrashing with considerable force against their holds. Sarah and Hugh both stood frozen in place, not offering to help or doing anything proactive, clearly petrified. A second nurse was attempted to speak to Loopy Linda as she continued to scream and fight against the staff holding her arms either side of her, but she clearly wasn't listening.

She looked over at Mark and spat at him, before laughing in a high-pitched cackle. Mark didn't flinch, nor did he yell. He just seemed to accept that this had happened. Either he was used to this kind of thing happening on the ward and was immune to it, or he was just extremely professional. Before I knew what was happening next though, Loopy Linda was on the floor with Mark and Katie on the floor next to her, the other nurse who had been speaking to her was lying across her legs.

The ward door burst open and in came three more staff, running over to assist the staff as Loopy Linda, now unable to move, continued to scream and spit. The nurse on her legs was quickly replaced by one of the new staff members who had just arrived, and I watched as she brushed herself off and continued to attempt to speak to Loopy Linda.

"Steph, we need you to calm down so we can talk about what's going on." The nurse's voice was calm and steady. You would never have guessed that she had just been laid down on the floor trying to fight this woman's legs. "Can we settle down a bit and have a conversation?"

Steph, so that was her name. I suppose I should stop referring to her as Loopy Linda now then.

"The spiders are coming; the spiders are here." She continued to scream, oblivious to what the nurse was saying to her.

"It's no use" the nurse said to the staff around her. Some further conversation was had which I couldn't hear and then the nurse ran into the medication room with another member of staff and closed the door behind them.

"Steph, we are going to help you to stand back up and take you to your room now." I heard Mark stating to her.

With what seemed like practiced precision, the team of staff around her assisted her to stand up smoothly and walked Steph back down the corridor in which she had previously come barreling down. Sarah and Hugh followed behind the team and Steph was still kicking and screaming until she was no longer in sight.

The two staff in the medication room emerged shortly after, and without saying a word to anyone else around, walked swiftly down the corridor together, towards Steph's bedroom. One of the staff carried a cardboard tray which looked to have a large syringe on it.

So, this is what happens when the patients aren't behaving. I wonder if that is what I had been like when I had needed to be medicated. Had I been trying to harm the staff or spitting? At least Dr. Short said I hadn't been speaking, so I wasn't spouting any gobbledygook about spiders or anything else equally insane. I turned round to look at my support staff behind me. I was currently being watched by an agency member of staff who hadn't bothered to introduce herself to me, and a lady called Mira who was a regular member of staff and had told me she had been working on the ward for a few years.

"Mira? Was I ever like that?" I asked, hoping for a positive response. Large snorted and Little gave a small giggle.

"There were a few incidents, yes" Mira responded, "But we always kept you safe."

"Kept me safe?" I asked incredulously, "If I was anything like that, I'd have been more worried about keeping you safe!"

Mira came over and sat next to me on the sofa, the other member of staff remained where she was seated at the table, not appearing to be overly interested in the conversation or getting involved in it.

"When you are very unwell, you don't know what you are doing or what is happening around you and that can sometimes lead to incidents like this, where staff can be shouted at or attacked." Mira informed me, her voice soft and gentle. "It's not something that can be helped, it's just something that can happen when someone is psychotic or manic."

"Don't you get mad when you are being targeted though?" I inquired.

"Not at all, it's the nature of the job and we understand that it's not you, it's your illness." She replied reassuringly.

"But why didn't you help Sarah when she was being attacked?" I confronted her.

"We can't, when we are on someone's constant observations we cannot leave them at any time, under any circumstances." Mira countered, "it's really hard for us to sit here and watch, but if anything had happened to you because we weren't with you when we should have been, we would get into a lot of trouble. There's plenty of other staff to manage these situations though."

"But I was just sat here, what could have happened to me?" I argued.

"It doesn't matter sadly, there have been issues before when people have left observations, so the hospital is very strict about it." She replied.

I felt waves of guilt overcome me. Had I been attacking staff and that was why they had been medicating me? None of the staff I had met so far had seemed worthy of attacking, maybe a couple of them had been a bit rude, but considering what they are having to put up with I suppose I couldn't be surprised if they felt a bit standoffish with the patients.

Before long, the screaming had stopped and all of the staff returned back down the corridor, apart from Mark and Katie who must have taken over on her observations. The staff returned to the nursing office. I tried to watch some television, but my concentration levels were shot. I felt restless and exhausted, wanting to do something to keep myself occupied, but not wanting to do anything at the same time. I heard the office door open and out came Hugh, carrying a backpack. He walked quickly across the room towards the exit door, head down, staring at the floor.

Once the door closed behind him and he had left the ward, the agency staff behind me stated coldly, "Another one bites the dust."

Mira looked round and shushed her, clearly not finding her comment amusing. Looks like Hugh had been sent home for the day, likely due to him not doing anything when Steph was trying to attack people and screaming. Or maybe it was something to do with the spiders.

29

"I think it might be time to have a chat about Kelly now." Dr. Short stated. She was sat across from me again, the coffee table between us, for another therapy session.

I had been petrified coming into the session today, unsure as to what new memories I was going to possibly unlock or what revelations would be coming my way. I hadn't even been sure if they had known about Kelly's death, but clearly, they do.

"What would you like to know?" I asked.

"Well, in our last session we determined that you hadn't been quite aware of who Mr. Turner was. How do you feel about that now?" Dr. Short queried, looking at me intently.

"I've not been able to stop thinking about it since you told me." I admitted. "I still can't remember a lot about what happened in my childhood, I've been having some fleeting memories come and go over the last day or so, little things that just seem to make more sense now." I breathed in deeply, further memories of what had happened to me as a child, flooding back, none of which were good.

Dr. Short allowed me some time to process, waiting patiently as I inhaled and exhaled, trying to calm myself, ready to start the next discussion, this time about Kelly.

"Before you start to tell me about what happened with Kelly" Dr. Short broke the silence after a few minutes, "I want you to have a good think about who she was and what her relationship was to your father."

"My father?" I faltered. Kelly hadn't had anything to do with Mr. Turner, or my father. Had she? She was the nepo-child of the hospital board of director, who had been promoted over my husband Tim at the hospital. She hadn't deserved the position, hadn't earned it, and certainly didn't have the skill set to do it. What could she have possibly had in connection with my father?

"Yes Chrissie, think back now, where was Kelly when everything was happening to you?" Dr. Short reinforced.

Further memories came flashing back to me, more images entering my mind of things that had happened to me previously, him entering my room of a nighttime, always putting me down and barely giving me any other consideration than that of the type of attention I should have never received from him. In the background of these memories was a woman. Standing, a silhouette hiding in the shadows. Never saying anything, never doing anything. Just stood there watching, why wasn't she doing anything?!

"She didn't help me." I whispered, as I begun to realise exactly who Kelly was. Or Auntie Kelly should I say.

"She didn't help you," repeated Dr. Short.

I could feel the tears begin to stream down my cheeks, silent sobs. How could she just let all this happen to me? To a child? Had she not cared about me? Did she hate me? What had I done to deserve this? I know she worked a lot; she was a medical secretary at the local hospital, but she was still around enough to be able to stop him or to do something.

"Can you remember what happened to Kelly?" Dr. Short asked quietly.

"You mean, what I did to her?" I choked through my tears, to which she nodded. It all started to come back, clear as day. I suddenly remembered exactly what had happened to her, exactly what I had done to her. Not only that, all of the memories I had been suppressing came flooding back, everything that I had thought had been fact, hadn't been at all. Everything that I had thought my life had been, was it all a lie? Some made up story I had completely fabricated in my mind.

"I remember," I stammered, unsure if I was referring to Auntie Kelly specifically, or if I had meant in general.

"What do you remember," Dr. Short probed, leaning forward in her chair.

"Everything" I mouthed, struggling to catch my breath as further tears cascaded down my face.

Dr. Short just nodded, waiting for me to continue, willing me to reveal to her what I was thinking. I needed time to process everything that was going on in my head. I felt like I had just suffered an incredible loss, like I was grieving the life I thought I had known.

"None of it was real, was it?" I asked, almost dreading the response to come.

"What part?" Dr. Short asked kindly.

"Everything I thought was real. Mr. Turner was my father; Kelly was my aunt...." I paused, I knew that these facts had already been confirmed, but I wasn't sure I was ready to receive confirmation for the rest of what I had just comprehended. "Tim.... Sam.... who are they?"

Dr. Short looked confused, which seemed to affirm my fears. "Who are they?" She parroted.

"Tim, my husband and Sam, my son." I gulped in a large breath, steeling myself for the response to come. "They weren't real?"

Dr. Short's face showed nothing but compassion as she watched me come to terms with the fact that the life, I had thought to be true was nothing but a farce, created in my mind to prevent me from fully having to deal with the acts of horror I had committed, or the abuse I had suffered. "Sometimes Chrissie, our minds have to help us in times of crisis. If we are not strong enough at the time to manage with what life has thrown our way, our brains can sometimes make up different versions or events, twist our memories, to protect us from what we have had to endure and to prevent any further harm."

"But" the words struggling to form as I attempted to understand what she was explaining to me, "It was all so real. I remember all of it, the way Tim smelt, how soft Sam's hair was and how it felt when he would run across the playground to give me a big hug after school." It didn't make any sense.

"Our minds are very powerful and the memories we have can become so distorted, so far from the truth, that it can be difficult to see how they couldn't possibly be real. But sadly, that doesn't mean that they are."

I just shook my head. Surely this couldn't be true. Everything that had happened, everything that had led me to being here, I remembered it all so vividly. I tried to explain this to Dr. Short, but the look she gave me now seemed to be one of pity.

"What do you remember before the killings, Chrissie?" She asked me softly. This caught me off guard. I hadn't thought of anything else recently, with everything that had happened, everything before had been so mundane, so boring, that it hadn't been worth thinking about. But now that she had asked me, I couldn't remember anything. "Can you tell me about your wedding day? The day you gave birth. Any of your wedding anniversaries or your sons' birthdays?" She implored further.

"No" I murmured. No, I couldn't. Such big events and I didn't remember a single detail about them. There were no memories forming whatsoever of where I had gotten married, who walked me down the aisle, what my wedding dress looked like. I couldn't remember the feeling of holding Sam in my arms for the first time, what his little baby head smelt like, or the feeling of his tiny fingers held in mine. I brought my hand and placed it against the flat of my stomach, the stomach I now knew to have never held a baby inside.

"So, if they weren't real? If Tim, wasn't my husband and Sam wasn't my son, then who were they?" I asked, trembling.

"I'm not sure, Chrissie." Dr. Short replied, "Perhaps they aren't anyone and they are just figments of your imagination, made up to help comfort you during what has been a very difficult time for you. Or maybe, we will discover who they are as we continue our therapy sessions."

I wasn't sure I was ready to know just yet. My heart felt like it was exploding out of my chest at the realisation that the two people who had meant the most to me, my entire world, weren't real and never had been. "Can we keep talking about Kelly?" I asked, in an attempt to redirect the conversation away from Tim and Sam.

Dr. Short nodded, appearing to have understood my reluctance to continue discussing them. "So, what do you remember now about Kelly? About what happened?"

"I blamed her," I began, "for not helping me. And for the pain that she caused my mum."

"Your mum?" Dr. Short interjected.

"Yes, she was my mum's sister." I explained, "her and my dad ran off together when I was young. My mum never got over it. She never remarried; I don't remember her ever dating. It was just me and her after dad left."

"I see." She nodded as she began scribbling on her notepad.

"I knew she was probably hurting after finding my dad the way she did. Well, I'm assuming she had found him, considering I had just left him there." I mused. "I couldn't stop thinking about her after it had happened. I wanted to make sure that she was suffering too, for everything that had happened to me."

I didn't even check to see if Dr. Short was still taking notes, I just continued on with my story. Wanting to get it out for my own sake more so than to tell her that had happened.

"I found a local widow's support group online and after a bit of research, I saw that she had become an active member on their forum. So, I joined up too."

"You joined the support group?" Dr. Short queried.

"Yes, but not as myself. I joined up with a fake name and picture. I called myself Ben." I responded. "I began talking to her online over the course of a few weeks. I made up a story similar to her experience, of having had a wife that passed away recently. We never discussed exactly what had happened, she never told me, and I never told her, which suited me because it meant I didn't have as many lies to keep remembering. We just spoke about how we were feeling and how we were coping day to day.

"Why?" Dr. Short interrupted me.

"Why what?"

"Why did you make a fake profile and talk to her about her grief? Were you trying to help her? Did you feel guilty? Or were you grieving the death of your father yourself and you wanted someone to speak to, someone you knew would understand?" Dr. Short asked, clearly looking for the good in me that I was beginning to think probably wasn't there.

I laughed. The same high-pitched laugh I had when she had told me who Mr. Turner was, and she looked confused.

"No, nothing like that." I giggled. "I had wanted her to trust me."

"Trust you?" She inquired.

"Yes. So that I could meet up with her and kill her." I stated casually.

"And that's what you did, isn't it." Dr. Short confirmed.

"That's exactly what I did." I agreed. I then went on to tell her everything that had happened. The restaurant we had agreed to meet up in, how I had hidden by the bar, keeping my face covered by a menu as much as possible and wearing a long red wig to hide my identity. Watching her sat at her table waiting for Ben to arrive, before heading to use the toilet and following after her. I didn't go into too much detail about what had happened next. I'm sure she probably already knew most of that from the police reports anyway. I looked over at her, she was still scribbling away furiously, clearly fascinated by the story I was telling her. It was like I was beginning to fill in the missing pieces of the puzzle that the coroners' details hadn't been able to.

I allowed her some time to finish writing up her notes and then waited for her next question. But it never came. She didn't seem to want to give any opinion on my actions either, so it was hard to know what she was thinking about me. Did she sympathise with me and understand why I had done what I had done? Surely, she could see why Kelly had needed to die too. She looked up at me then, her expression blank, not giving anything away.

"I think that's probably enough for one day, don't you." She stated, as she calmly began to close her notepad. "You've done really well today, Chrissie."

She stood up and gestured for me to walk over to the door with her, behind which were my support staff waiting for the therapy session to end. She placed her hand on the door handle, ready to open it, but then stopped and turned to look at me.

"This is going to get harder before it can get easier, Chrissie. But together, I believe we can get you on to the road to recovery."

30

As we walked back to the ward from the therapy session, it was as if all hell had broken loose. The alarms began ringing loudly, and staff members could be seen running towards the unit I had come from.

"What's going on?" I asked Sarah, who was the only member of staff on my observations at the time that I currently recognised. The other guy with her must have been another agency staff member and he looked pretty clueless.

"Your guess is as good as mine" Sarah replied, but she looked worried as we got closer to the door of the ward and loud screaming and banging could be heard from within.

The agency staff member with us opened the door to the ward before Sarah could tell him not to and Steph came running out, into the airlocked corridor with us. The staff member who had opened the door had been pushed to the floor as she had careened her way out and he looked a little disoriented. Her two supporting staff came running after her, one of which was Mark, another was a female I didn't recognise, another agency staff member again it would seem.

"The moon and the stars and the sun and the sky!" Steph was chanting over and over again, waving her arms above her head in some bizarre ritual.

"Come on then Steph, back onto the ward please." Mark commanded her calmly, which appeared to have no effect as she continued to chant.

My agency staff member had gotten up from the floor and him and the other female agency staff were both just standing by the wall, clearly unsure of what to do or how to act. Mark looked over at Sarah as they gave a small nod to each other. Steph began banging her fists on the ward door next to ours, a ward I wasn't familiar with, having not been on it myself. An elderly man came to the viewing panel window of the door and squished his face against the glass, licking it up and down and groaning as Steph proceeded to chant and punch the glass between the two of them.

Sarah leaned over to me and whispered, "I need you to stand with the two staff over there, can I trust you to help us out with this?"

I nodded in agreement and went and stood with the staff who both just looked at me, bewildered. Good thing I'm not in a bad mood currently and too busy thinking about my therapy session to want to act out myself, or these staff would have been in a whole world of trouble.

Once Sarah was happy that I wasn't going to attempt to run off or do anything to cause problems for them, her and Mark advanced towards Steph, ready to take control of the situation. She seemed to be full of a new found confidence I hadn't seen in her before.

Mark attempted to de-escalate her again, asking her to come with him nicely and return to the ward but Steph wasn't paying any attention to him whatsoever. Quick as a flash, Sarah and Mark grabbed hold of her, positioning themselves either side of her arms and marched her back onto the ward and to one of the sofas, where they all sat down together. We followed behind, I almost felt like I was in control of these agency staff rather than them being in control of me.

Steph continued her chant. She was clearly distressed and was becoming more and more agitated by the second. I could hear movement from behind the closed medication clinic door, so I had an idea of what was likely to come next. Poor Steph. I couldn't help but feel sorry for her. What must be going on in her mind.

Stamping noises suddenly came from the corridor, a very tall, stocky woman came stampeding into the main lounge area, clearly not in a good mood. She had three members of staff following behind her in quick succession, two regular members of staff that I recognised and yet another agency staff who looked absolutely petrified.

"You woke me the fuck up!" This dominating creature bellowed. I hadn't seen this woman before. Had she been admitted to the unit whilst I was in therapy?

Steph kept on chanting, paying no attention to the beast of a woman now towering over her. The woman's staff members looked ready to act, if necessary, but it seemed unclear as to what was about to happen next.

"You listening to me bitch?!" She screamed, still no response.

"Let's go back to your room away from the noise, shall we?" Katie advised, who was one of the staff members on her observations.

"I'm not going anywhere until this bitch shuts the fuck up." She yelled back. Steph continued her chanting.

Sarah was trying to get her to stop, trying to reason with her whilst holding her on the sofa, but it seemed to be falling on deaf ears.

On the floor, next to one of the sofas, was a metal drinking bottle. A ray of sunshine had just come in through the window that led to a small, enclosed back garden area that we would be able to spend time in when it wasn't raining, and the reflection hit the metal bottle like a beacon for all to see. As my gaze was guided to the bottle, so was this scary woman's in front of me. Katie had clearly seen it too as she lunged towards it, in an attempt to get it out of the way, but the goliath was quicker.

For such a large woman, she moved like a gazelle, diving towards the bottle and pushing Katie out of the way at the same time, who landed with a loud grunt onto the floor beside her. The two other members of staff on her observations tried to grab hold of her but it was no use, they couldn't gain control and before they could do anything further, she had grabbed the bottle from the floor and ran off down the corridor with it, slamming a door behind her.

David, the other regular member of staff with the woman began to run after her, however stopped in his tracks when he realised that he was the only member of staff to do so. Realising it probably wasn't the best idea to approach this woman who was now armed, on his own, he stopped and looked over to the agency staff member who was now helping Katie up from off the floor. Katie was rubbing her right arm, which she must have landed on when she hit the ground.

"I'm fine, really. We need to follow her." Katie stated quickly.

"She has the bottle and she's shut herself in her room." David replied, awaiting further instructions.

"Okay" Katie said, dusting herself off and taking a moment to assess the situation. "You two station yourselves outside of her door, but keep it closed. Don't be too close to the door either, you need to be able to get away quickly if you need to, but you also need to be able to make sure she's safe in there. We don't know what her intentions are with that bottle yet."

David nodded and signaled for the agency staff to follow him up the corridor. Steph was still chanting away, as if nothing else was happening around her. There were no other patients around the ward at this time, they were either in their own therapy sessions or hiding in their bedrooms away from the mayhem, which is exactly where I was intending to go, once I knew the corridor was safe to walk through.

Katie ran into the nursing office and out came the older not so nice support worker from the other day. She went over to where Mark and Sarah were sat with Steph, said something that I couldn't hear over the continued chanting about moons and suns and then she quickly changed position with Mark, who then ran up the corridor to join David and the other member of staff.

I looked over at my agency staff sat next to me, we had positioned ourselves at one of the dining tables as far away from the goings on as possible. They both looked pretty relieved that I wasn't getting involved or asking them to do anything.

A few moments later, Dr. Short came onto the ward, her heels tapping loudly on the linoleum flooring as she made her way into the nursing office. A few other members of staff came running in too, staff I didn't recognise, but didn't seem as oblivious as the agency staff I had been seeing so my guess was that they were regular staff that worked on other wards.

Two nurses then came out of the medication clinic, closing the door firmly behind them and holding the familiar cardboard tray with the syringe balanced on top. They walked with purpose up the corridor and Steph was then led off the sofa and up the corridor behind them by her supporting staff. I heard the door close behind them and the sound of the chanting became muffled.

"Well, that was fun." I giggled to myself, breaking the now silence that filled the room. My support staff just looked at me, confused, almost as if I was trying to explain the law of physics to them. Clearly, these aren't my audience.

I got up from the table and the support staff jumped up beside me. Now was my chance to go to my room before anything else happens. I began making my way through the lounge and towards the corridor, but I was intercepted by Dr. Short.

"Where are you off to Chrissie?" She inquired.

"I was just going to have a rest in my room, away from the noise of the ward." I replied.

"Unfortunately, that is not going to be possible for the moment." Dr. Short responded.

"Why?" I asked incredulously, I had had enough for one day and I just wanted to lie down.

"I'll explain to everyone in a moment." She replied shortly. "But how are you feeling at the moment?"

"Fine." I said curtly. Seemed like an odd question for her to be asking me considering what was going on currently on the ward and what we had not long been discussing in therapy.

"Do you feel like you are a harm to yourself or anyone else at this moment in time?" She asked matter of factly.

"No, I'm just tired and to be honest, I would just like to be left alone."

"Excellent" she replied, half looking at me and half looking at one of the nurses sat in the office behind her. "Change Chrissie's observations to 1:1."

The nurse came to the door of the office and thanked Dr. Short. She then proceeded to instruct the male member of staff that he no longer needed to stay with me. It was nice to know that I didn't have to be followed by two members of staff now, but I still would have liked a bit more privacy.

"Dr. Short, when can I come off the observations altogether?" I asked, hoping for a more positive response.

"We will review that again in good time, Chrissie." She then turned on her heel and proceeded to walk up the corridor. I watched her knock on all of the patients' doors one by one, instructing them to come into the lounge area and sit down. Everyone listened to her, without question. Even Steph whose medication must have started to kick in because she was no longer chanting or in restraint with her staff members. The only door she did not knock on was that of the bottle wielding beast. She gave a small nod to Mark and David who continued to be stationed outside of her door and advised them to maintain distance where possible. There was still silence coming from inside the room.

Once all of the patients were sat in the living room, Dr. Short seemed ready to address us.

"There has been a serious breach of security on the ward this afternoon which has left us in a position where there is a potential weapon on the unit." Dr. Short stated with authority. "With this being the case, we need to ensure we maintain the safety of all of you, as well as our staff at all times, and a full lockdown will therefore be put into effect."

"No, not another lockdown!" Shouted Little who had taken residence on her usual sofa next to Large.

"Unfortunately so, Ashley." Dr. Short replied. "The staff here have been instructed to take you up to the entertainment suite where you will remain until further notice. You will receive meals and medications up there as required until such a time that the ward is safe for you to return."

There were a large number of staff standing around that I hadn't noticed beforehand. All seemingly ready for action. On Dr. Shorts command, the staff began leading us out of the ward and through the corridors towards the entertainment suite, which sounded much more exciting than it actually was. As we passed near the reception area, a large gathering of riot police appeared to be readying themselves to enter the hospital.

"Ello lads!!!" Shouted Large, waving furiously at the police officers who paid her no attention. "Think they will come tell me off with their batons?" She giggled to Little, who laughed with her.

As we entered the entertainment suite, Little and Large found a new sofa to positions themselves in, Steph wandered over to one of the windows which had a good view out across to some hills and the other two normal looking women stationed themselves at a table and were talking amongst themselves. Unsure what to do with myself, I decided to take up residence on the table next to the other women's.

"How long do you think it will last this time?" Woman one asked.

"Who knows, do you know what was going on for us to go into lockdown again?" Woman two responded.

"Theres a weapon they said." Woman one stated.

"Probably something ridiculous again, remember last time they put us in lockdown because someone said they had brought something in but then they didn't find anything." Woman two retorted.

"It's a bottle." I chimed in, not sure how my eavesdropping would go down with the two women who were now staring at me in surprise.

"So, she can speak." Woman one chided.

"Apparently so," replied Woman two. "What bottle are you talking about?"

"There was a metal bottle left in the lounge and someone got hold of it." I replied, not wanting to bite at their remarks about my previous silence.

"Oh, for goodness' sake," sighed Woman two. "That will be Rebecca that has that then, seeing as she isn't here."

"I wonder what bright spark left that lying about on the ward" mumbled Woman one, clearly not wanting the staff to overhear her comment.

I looked at my supporting staff member sat with me; she had barely said a word to me since she had been swapped onto my observations when we were outside of the ward earlier. She looked worried, she was wringing her hands together in her lap and I could feel her legs bouncing up and down under the table next to me. "It was yours, wasn't it?" I whispered to her quietly.

She nodded, eyes full of guilt. "Everything happened so fast," she whispered back, looking around to make sure no-one else could hear. "I was with Steph but then she started to kick off, so I had to get up and follow her, I totally forgot it was there. There was just so much going on in the ward."

"Are you allowed bottles like that on the ward?" I asked.

"I don't think so." She replied quietly.

"I won't say anything." I responded quickly. I felt sorry for her really, she couldn't have known this would happen. But there's clearly strict rules on what the staff can and cannot have on the ward and this is the reason.

"Do you have anything you don't want finding in your room?" Woman one asked me.

"Like what?" I asked, thinking about how sparce my room was and the lack of belongings I was allowed to have at present.

"Just anything you aren't supposed to have. Hidden meds? Weapons? Contraband?" Woman one continued.

"I've not got anything in my room, I'm now allowed anything at all yet." I replied. "Why?"

"They will be searching the whole ward now." Said Woman two.

"But they know where the bottle is, it's in her room with her." I retorted, "why would they need to search anywhere else?"

"It's just part of the lockdown process they do; they check everywhere for any other contraband items." Responded Woman two.

"That must take them ages." I thought aloud.

"It always does, we will be stuck up here for hours now. They will get the bottle off Rebecca, put her back in seclusion and then search the rest of the ward before they let us back in." Woman two agreed.

"So, Rebecca was the woman who was put in seclusion the other day for smashing the television?" I asked.

Woman one nodded. "She only got out of there this morning, and I bet you that she's right back in there now."

"That woman goes in and out of seclusion like a frigging yo-yo." Woman two laughed.

The two women turned back to continue their conversation without me, and I glanced around the room. If we were going to be stuck here for a while, I guess I had better try to find something to occupy the time, so I don't lose my mind. In the corner of the room was a small bookcase, with a selection of different paperbacks to choose from. I made my way over to it and scanned the different titles on offer. Picking out what looked like an easy to read, romance novel, I settled down in one of the chairs and made myself comfortable.

31

    I was only about three chapters away from finishing the book I had started when Nurse Katie entered the room. I glanced at the clock, which was situated high up on the wall, out of arms reach. We had been here for about 4 hours, but the time had gone quickly. It had been a while since I had gotten into a good book and the plot had gripped me. I was reluctant to put it down at this point but when Katie spoke, it was clear that she was demanding of our attention.

"Thank you for your patience this afternoon." She said loudly, to ensure everyone in various parts of the room could hear her. "We have finished conducting our searches and you can now return back to the ward."

Everyone begun to get up from their seats and headed towards the exit, ready to follow Katie back to the ward. My staff member stood up beside me and gestured for me to put the book back that I was reading. I clung onto it; I wasn't ready to put it back yet. I still had three more chapters to read.

"Can I take it down to the ward please?" I asked my support staff, hoping she would understand my need to finish it. I wouldn't sleep tonight if I didn't get to find out what happens at the end.

"I'm not sure to be honest." She replied quietly "maybe we should ask Nurse Katie."

I headed over to the direction of Katie, who was standing by the door, holding it open as the rest of the patients and their staff members filed out of the room and into the corridor, ready to head back to the ward.

"Katie." I said, getting a good look at her stood there. She looked stressed. Her bouncy curls that usually flowed free were tied up in a short ponytail and her patient smile was missing from her lips. She looked over at me as I stated her name. "Sorry to bother you, but would I be able to take this book back down to the ward please?"

Katie gave a small, tired smile. "It's never a bother Chrissie," she responded, taking note of my finger placement between the pages, able to see how little of the book left I had to complete. "If you give it to me for now, I will have to ask Dr. Short before I can give it to you on the ward, I'm afraid. Your care plan still states that you cannot have any personal items at the moment, so we will need to discuss it with the doctor before I can give you anything."

She took the book gently out of my hands and placed her index finger where mine had been previously, to mark my place. She then pulled a small piece of tissue out of her pocket which appeared to have some notes written on it and placed this in the book instead.

"Thank you, Katie" I smiled back at her, feeling sorry for this woman who was clearly working too hard and needed a break.

I then followed the rest of the staff and patients back down to the ward, with Katie following close behind us.

Once back on the unit, Dr. Short was waiting for us in the communal lounge. She gestured for us all to sit down. All the patients took their places on the sofas silently, no one wanting to upset Dr. Short whose facial expression was blank. The supporting staff all took positions either stood behind their patients on the sofas or sat at the tables and chairs. The ward didn't look any different than when we had left it earlier and Rebecca and her support staff were nowhere to be seen.

Dr. Short cleared her throat. "Unfortunately, we have found some contraband on the ward during our searches." She stated matter of fact. "And as a result, those of you who have been found with contraband will require a review of your care plans to determine what action will be taken moving forward."

There was some muttering heard between Little and Large and between woman one and woman two before Dr. Short cleared her throat again, commanding silence.

"I am going to sit in the side room next door to us and I would like to see each of you, one by one to discuss what has happened this afternoon. I suggest those of you who knew that they had contraband to be open and honest about it so we can discuss why you have it and what we are going to do about it. As you know, this is a high secure unit and therefore any contraband whether it is intended to be used or not, is considered exceptionally high risk." Dr. Short began making her way to a door just off to the side of the nursing office, one I hadn't been in before so had been unsure of its usage until now. She looked over at Nurse Katie who was stood by the nursing office, listening with intent to everything that Dr.

Short had been saying to us. "Katie, I would appreciate if you could bring the ladies in one at a time. Any order is fine." With that she let herself into the room, closing the door behind her.

Little jumped up from the sofa. "I want to go first Katie." She shouted hurriedly.

Katie looked around at the rest of the patients sat staring at her, awaiting further instructions. I was sat next to Steph who hadn't said a word since we had returned back to the ward. In fact, she was the calmest I had seen her in a while.

"Come on then." Katie nodded at Little, who then strode briskly into the room.

As soon as the door shut behind them, Large let out a big sigh. "I hope she doesn't get in too much trouble."

"Why? What did she have?" Woman one asked.

"She had made herself a shank that she had kept hidden in her room. She's had it a while but that's clearly what the staff have found during the searches." Large replied in a monotone voice.

"Why would she make herself a shank?!" I asked, fearing the worst.

"She had made it for protection" Large muttered, trying to keep her tone of voice down to prevent the staff from hearing so much of the conversation. "She was petrified of Rebecca. Rebecca is so big, and she is so small, she was scared that if Rebecca went for her that she wouldn't survive it."

"Rebecca is pretty scary" Woman two agreed, to which all the rest of the women nodded in agreement, me included. "I bet those armed police had a hard time getting her back into seclusion."

"Did anyone else have anything?" Woman one asked, bringing the subject back to the matter at hand.

Everyone stayed quiet, either that was the only thing that had been found by the staff, or no-one was wanting to own up to anything further.

A short time later, Little came out of the room with Katie. It was clear that she had been crying. Katie gave Little a small pat on her shoulder and whispered something to her before Little then came and sat down, back on the sofa next to Large.

"Steph" Katie said softly, "Would you like to come in and speak to Dr. Short next?"

Steph stood up and made her way into the room. Once the door was shut again, Large immediately gave Little a hug and asked her what had happened.

"I told them everything." She spluttered between tears. "They had found it; I knew they would."

"Are they doing anything about it?" Large asked and everyone craned forward to hear the outcome.

"Well, I've lost my leave now." Little sniffed. "I don't know when I will get it back. She asked me where I had gotten the items from to make it and I told her I had bought some of it from the shop round the corner so she said until I can be trusted in the community again, I won't be getting any leave."

"What about obs?" Woman two asked, wanting to know if she was now going to have staff with her constantly also.

"She's not putting me on obs thank god." She replied. "I told Dr. Short that I had only done it because I was scared. I would never have used it. I would never hurt anyone I swear." She began to cry harder and Large pulled her close, almost absorbing her into her large bosom.

Steph appeared to bounce out of the room. She must only have been in there for a few minutes. Like me, she wasn't allowed anything in her bedroom and had staff following her at all times, so it seemed unlikely that she would have had anything she shouldn't. She sat back down next to me and leant across to whisper, ensuring that only I would be able to hear. "Don't tell the doctor about the soup."

I nodded at her, confused but not wanting to engage her in any further conversation. The other three women waiting to be seen all went in one by one, varying in time for how long they were in there for but none of them looking particularly upset when coming back out.

I was called in last. I went into the room, followed by Katie. It was very similar to the therapy room upstairs that I had gotten used to speaking to Dr. Short in. I sat down in a chair opposite the doctor and Katie remained stood by the door.

"It's been an eventful day for you hasn't it." Dr. Short smiled at me.

"Not sure about eventful, but definitely long." I laughed.

"Is there anything you feel that you need to tell us?" She asked me.

"I don't think so." I looked over at Katie, who was giving nothing away. Was there something I was supposed to admit here? They couldn't have found anything in my room, there was nothing there. Have one of the other patients said something about me?

Dr. Short just nodded, seeming to be accepting of my response. "Is there anything you would like to discuss with me whilst we are here?"

"I'm not sure if Katie has already asked this, but I was wondering if I could have a book in my room, please?" I asked, almost pleadingly.

"She had asked me, and I don't see an issue with it. In fact, we had discussed briefly about maybe allowing you to have some other possessions in your room as well." She responded.

"Really?" I asked excitedly.

"Nothing too much" she replied, "but I don't see any reason as to why you couldn't start having your own clothing back and some personal items in your bedroom. I will leave it to Katie to organise with you, probably tomorrow now though as it's getting late, and no-one has had dinner yet."

"Thank you so much Dr. Short." I beamed.

"You've earned some trust Chrissie. You are working well with us now; you're opening up in your therapy sessions and you have done everything that staff has asked of you over the last few days. Continue in this manner and we will review your observations in the near future also."

With that, Dr. Short got up from the chair and headed towards the door. "I look forward to our session tomorrow." She called over her shoulder as she left.

Katie gave me a smile and handed me the book she had been hiding behind her back. "Thank you so much" I smiled back.

"Let's get some dinner now shall we" Katie replied, leading me out of the room and back into the communal area where the rest of the patients were already queuing up at the kitchen hatch.

"I am hungry" I agreed, "Although I really hope it's not soup."

"Why?" Katie asked, looking somewhat confused.

"Never mind" I chuckled to myself and headed over to join the back of the queue, where my support staff member was already waiting for me.

32

As I sat laid back in the chair opposite Dr. Short, ready to begin our next therapy session, I took a moment to look down and admire the clothing I was now able to wear. The attire of the day was a grey pair of jogging bottoms and a plain white t-shirt. It wasn't fancy, but it was comfortable, and it was mine, so I already felt like the day was starting well.

"I think it might be beneficial to talk about the shop keeper today, Chrissie." Dr. Short began.

"Craig" I responded with a small laugh. "Who is he going to turn out to be, I wonder."

"Well, that is what I am curious about, of all of the incidents that have happened, he is the one that has confused me the most." She mired.

"What do you mean?" I asked.

"Well, we have already discussed your reasons behind killing your father and Kelly, and we still have some others to discuss, but Craig is the one I don't see any connection to." She replied, looking at me with genuine curiosity.

"So, Craig is just a shop keeper?" I queried, somewhat unclear as to where this was going.

"I presume so." She replied calmly. "Did you know Craig other than being the man who helped run the local shop?"

"Not that I can remember." I tried to think hard about what I could remember about Craig. "I can remember what happened. He upset me, so I killed him." I said stonily.

"From the information I have, that seems to be the case yes." She nodded. "So, if you didn't know Craig well and there wasn't any underlying reason for why you killed him, why do you think you acted so impulsively?"

I closed my eyes and began to think back, to not just the incident in the shop, but about what had happened before it. I was silent for some time, ruminating over my thoughts, suddenly remembering what had upset me so much before I had gone to the shop.

"The police had come to see me." I stated into the silence.

"When?"

"The morning of the incident with Craig." I replied. "I had been visited at home by a police officer, to tell me about Kelly's death."

"And why had that upset you?" She asked. "You already knew she was dead and from what we've already discussed, you don't seem upset about it."

"It wasn't them telling me that upset me, it was how they told me." I mused. "They didn't seem to be telling me like you would expect the news to be broken to a family member."

"I don't understand..." Dr. Short questioned further.

"I didn't feel like they were telling me. When I had been told about my father's death, I was told with compassion and empathy. When they told me about Kelly, it was almost accusatory. Like they were trying to gauge my reaction to see if I already knew."

"Did they say anything to make you think that they were accusing you?" She implored.

"No, but I could just tell from the way they were looking at me and their tone of voice." I paused for a moment. "And it made me angry."

"So, what happened then?"

"They asked me a few questions about where I had been at the time of Kelly's death, if I had known anyone who may have had any grievances against her. Asked me a bit about my mum too, implying that maybe she had something to do with it." I let out a small chuckle. "Like she could do anything at all, never mind kill someone."

Dr. Short made a few quick notes into her notepad, keeping her eyes fixed on me as she wrote, enraptured by what I was saying.

"After they left" I continued, "I was so angry, but I needed to get some things from the shop, so I had to go out. All I could think about was how rude the police had been to imply what they had, so when Craig was also rude to me. I lost it."

"Why did you have the insulin on you though? Why go to the shop with a needle in your pocket?"

"I didn't take it for him. I had taken it for my second errand that I needed to complete after the shop." I hesitated for a moment before continuing, knowing that this statement was about to open up a whole other can of worms. "It just turned out to be useful to have on me already."

"So, Craig was an impulse kill?" She asked, to which I nodded. "So then, what was your second errand that you needed to complete after the shop, that needed you to take an insulin injection for?"

I looked down at the flat of my stomach and then back up at Dr. Short, making eye contact as tears welled up in my eyes. "I had to do the school run."

33

I was given some time to compose myself before I began to explain to Dr. Short what had happened to Coleen. Why I had killed her and who Tim and Sam actually were. I dabbed my eyes with a tissue and got myself ready to start going through one of the hardest conversations I knew I was going to have.

"I'm guessing you know about Coleen." I began.

"I know what happened to Coleen." She looked at me intently and I could see the cogs turning in her head as she begun to piece things together." "What I don't know, is why?"

I took a deep breath, ready to admit to myself, as well as Dr. Short, as to who Tim and Sam really were and why I had killed Coleen. The realisation that Tim wasn't my husband, and that Sam wasn't my biological child had been a hard pill to swallow, but they were still my family and I had needed to get rid of Coleen so that we could all be together.

"I know Tim wasn't my husband, but he should have been." I stated confidently as Dr. Short raised her eyebrows. "And Sam may not have been mine and Tim's together, but he was still my son, and we were still a family."

Dr. Short put her notebook down on her lap and gave me a look of pure compassion. She knew what I had lost because of Coleen, and she could understand why I had done it. It was the only way to make sure my family could be together.

"How did you know Coleen?" She asked intently.

"I didn't." I responded, "I knew Tim and Sam, I only knew Coleen from what Tim had told me about her."

"And what was that?"

"He had never wanted to be with her. He was in love with me, but she kept threatening him that she would take Sam away if he ever left her."

"So how did you meet Tim?" Dr. Short queried, her compassionate expression now becoming more concerned.

"Tim was a doctor at the hospital where Mum had some of her treatment. He had looked after her a few times when she had needed to be admitted. He was always so nice to me every time we went in. He would always ask me how I was doing and if I was okay. He really worried about me you know." I could feel my cheeks begin to flush at the thought of how we first met. I could picture him in his smart suit and white coat, a stethoscope hanging around his neck, the metal glinting in the stark lighting of my mother's hospital room, twinkling as beautifully as his eyes did.

"What happened after you met him?" She implored further.

"We started an affair. We fell in love so quickly. We were soul mates. He told me all about his awful wife and his wonderful son. We would discuss raising Sam and running away together as soon as he could think of a way of getting away from Coleen."

"Did you ever meet Sam?" She asked me, her brows furrowed.

"Not exactly." I paused, realising that this was likely to sound a bit strange, "I knew where he went to school and where they lived so I sometimes used to watch him coming out of school, so I could get used to his routine."

Dr. Short began making some notes again, furiously in the notepad on her lap. She was starting to make me feel like maybe she wasn't going to understand and agree with what I had done. "Did Tim tell you where they lived and what school Sam went to?"

"He didn't need to tell me. I already knew where they lived because I followed him home one day after he finished work. I wanted to thank him for looking after Mum so well. But when he got home, I saw him go into the house, I saw Coleen giving him a hug and a kiss and I saw Sam...." I paused to allow my irritation to settle before I continued. "He hadn't told me about Coleen and Sam at that point yet. So, the next time I saw him I confronted him about it and then he told me everything. About how controlling she was and how he wished I was his wife and Sam's mother instead."

"How many times did you meet up with Tim before Coleen died?"

"We didn't really get a chance to meet up. Tim was always so busy with work, and he didn't want Coleen to get wind of what was going on in case she took Sam away."

"So how did you have an affair if you weren't meeting up?" Dr. Short asked quietly.

"What do you mean?" I asked incredulously. Surely, she wasn't doubting what I was telling her.

"Well, to have an affair with someone, would imply secret meetings, sexual activity, hidden contact…." She trailed off from her sentence, likely in reaction to me clearly not being impressed with what she was saying.

"You don't have to fuck someone to have an affair. You can have affairs of the heart too, you know." I stated bluntly. "Tim wasn't a cheat, he wanted to do right by me. I wasn't just the other woman."

"Chrissie….. tell me what happened to Coleen."

"I was sick of waiting for Tim to figure out a way to leave her. So, I took matters into my own hands. I had been following her for weeks to make sure I knew hers and Sam's routines. I wanted to be the perfect wife for Tim. I wanted to make everything as easy for him as possible after she was gone. I was going to just slot into her life."

"Chrissie…… what happened to Coleen." She repeated.

"I knew when she would be at the school, and I also knew that she was always super early for the school pick-up. I've no idea why she was always so early, but she would always be there a good ten to fifteen minutes before anyone else arrived. So, I took my opportunity then, when I knew no-one would be around."

"Why there, why not at the house where you would have more privacy?" She asked.

"Because I didn't want to spoil my new home. No-one wants to live somewhere that someone has died, do they? I didn't want to upset Sam either, what if he had found her?"

"So, after you killed her, what was the plan then?" She inquired, still looking somewhat confused and somewhat surprised, but not at all compassionate anymore. "Did you think you would just move into the home with Tim and Sam, like Coleen had never existed?"

"Well, not straight away of course. I had to let the death die down first so that no-one would trace it back to me."

"Did you speak to Tim after you had done it?"

"No, I didn't want him to know it was me. Although I'm sure he would have had his suspicions, but just in case, I didn't want to incriminate him, in case I was caught. One of us needed to be able to look after Sam after all."

"Chrissie…. When did you last speak to Tim?" She asked me softly.

"I'm not sure." I tried to think. When was the last time I had spoken to him? Had I spoken to him since Coleen's death? Surely, I must have checked in with him to see how him and Sam were doing. He would have told me about her dying, we talked all the time. Nothing seemed to be coming to mind though. I couldn't remember any of our conversations about it.

"Tim was interviewed after Coleen was found. He was originally a suspect in her murder due to the nature in which she was killed, and his profession." Dr. Short stated.

I gasped. What had I done? Had he been arrested because of me? Do the authorities know it was me that killed her and not him? Where is Sam and who is looking after him. I could feel myself beginning to panic, and I began taking some deep breaths to try and calm myself down.

Dr. Short could sense my panic and continued, "Tim was not found responsible for Coleen's death." I felt my whole body begin to relax with these words. "But once it was determined as to what had happened to Coleen, and her murder was connected to others, he was interviewed again to determine his connection to you."

"What did he say?" I spluttered, panic beginning to settle in again. What if they thought he had gotten me to do it on his behalf?

"Chrissie, Tim didn't know who you were." Dr. Short answered.

I shook my head. Was he saying this to stay out of trouble? Have I just incriminated him by telling Dr. Short how we were connected and why I killed her?

"Dr. Short you have to believe me, Tim never had anything to do with Coleen's death." I spoke quickly, desperate for her to understand that he was in no way to blame. "I never told him what I was going to do, he would never have let me do it if he had known. He's innocent I swear, he had nothing to do with any of it."

"I don't think you're understanding what I am saying to you, Chrissie." She stated patiently. "The police have fully investigated Tim, to ensure that everything he has said when interviewed was correct. His and your phone records have been searched as part of the investigation, his work colleagues have been interviewed, even his home and work laptop have been examined."

"So, what are you saying?" I asked, a deep feeling of dread sinking through me.

"Tim wasn't lying to the police." She asserted. "He may have been your mother's doctor, but he did not know who you were and certainly did not think he was having an affair with you."

34

I'm really struggling to open my eyes and my back is hurting. There's a draft coming in from somewhere and I feel cold all of a sudden. I stretch my arms and legs out; I can't feel anything around me but being able to stretch has eased some of the tension in my back at least. I pry my eyes open and take in my current environment. Stark white walls surround me, with nothing on any of them other than a large metallic looking door on one side and a toilet and sink on the other. I rub my eyes and can feel a pounding in my head. Where am I?

I sit myself up and notice that I'm sat on a singular blue rubber mattress. There's no sheets, no bedding, no duvet. Just the cold mattress lying in the center of the otherwise empty room. The toilet and sink to the side of me are the only solitary furniture, both appearing to be built into the wall, no soap dispenser, no toilet rolls to be seen and no privacy either. It's just there, on the wall of the room, for anyone looking in to see. And there were people looking in. I looked upwards and spotted what looked to be two recessed cameras in the ceiling, in opposite corners of the room from each other. I wonder if anyone is watching me now on them?

I pushed myself up off the mattress, into a standing position and almost fell back to the ground. My head was spinning as well as pounding. They must have drugged me again. Why though? They said that they only did that when I was too much of a risk to myself and others and I had been good as gold. I had even just been given some of my stuff back and had my observations reduced to just one staff member, so what had happened?

Once I regained my footing, I padded barefoot over to the large metal door at the other side of the room. Inside of the door was a hatch panel with a glass viewing window. I looked through it. The other side of the door was another room, although this one was not as bare. There were three large sofas, all of which appeared to be occupied by a member of staff. Two of them I recognised as Mark and a familiar agency support worker, the other was a young lady I didn't know. Mark looked up and caught my eye, staring at him through the window, and gave me a wave. Perplexed, I gave a small wave back.

"What's going on?" I shouted through the window.

Mark got up from his seated position and came over to the window I was shouting through. There was a small vent near the top to allow us to hear each other, but this appeared my only opening other than the large metal door between us as a means of exit from this room.

"How are you feeling Chrissie?" Mark asked me through the vent.

"What's going on?" I repeated back at him. Unsure if he would have been able to hear me the first time I had shouted it.

"You've just woken up. You had to be sedated again I'm afraid." He responded calmly.

I looked around the room again, taking in my current situation, trying to assess what had caused me to be here and why. This must be the seclusion room, I concluded. It certainly wasn't my bedroom on the ward.

"Why am I here?" I responded back.

"Let me give Katie a call and she can come and speak to you." Mark stated before pulling his radio from his belt and making a call to Nurse Katie across it.

"Are you hungry or thirsty?" Mark asked me kindly, "Do you want me to ask her to bring you anything?"

I shook my head. The only thing I wanted at the moment was answers. I certainly didn't want to risk drinking anything if I was going to have to use that toilet with an audience of three either.

Mark returned to his spot back on the sofa and I plonked myself back down on the mattress on the floor. The nurse arrived about ten minutes later, or at least I'm guessing it was about that amount of time. It's hard to tell in a room with nothing to look at. I heard a knock at the window of the door and saw Katie's smiling face on the other side. I got myself back up slowly, still not feeling particularly well, and made my way back over to the vent.

"How are you feeling Chrissie?" She asked. I wish people would stop asking me that, seems like a redundant question considering my current circumstances.

"Why am I here Katie?" I asked bluntly.

I saw a flicker of concern across her face before responding. "Do you remember who you are and why you are in hospital, Chrissie?"

"Yes, yes, we've been over this before haven't we. That's what I'm working with Dr. Short on."

She seemed relieved. Perhaps they had been concerned that I would have been as confused as I had been the last time they sedated me. They had told me that I had been non-verbal and not knowing what was going on for the last six months until recently, so maybe they weren't sure how I was going to be when I woke up.

"What's the last thing that you can remember Chrissie?" She asked me.

"I was in a therapy session with Dr. Short." I paused, thinking back to what we had been discussing at that session. A wave of sadness and anger cascading over me, remembering what she had said to me about Tim. About his denial of ever knowing me. I could feel the tears beginning to flow, was it true? Had I made the whole relationship up in my head?

"You became quite upset in that therapy session; do you remember?" She prompted.

I shook my head and thought as hard as I could, but nothing was coming back to me other than what she had told me. What had I done after that? How had I reacted? Did I blackout?

Katie looked at me, eyes full of sympathy. "It was a difficult session for you Chrissie, and unfortunately, there was an incident that occurred as a result of it."

Oh no, what had I done. Had I hurt Dr. Short? Had I hurt anyone else? A cold feeling of dread enveloped me, none of the people I had been working with in the hospital deserved to be hurt. I had seen what other patients had done and vowed that I wouldn't do that myself, but had I lost control?

"Is everyone okay?" I spluttered, choking back my tears.

"Everyone is fine, Chrissie. You didn't attack anyone, don't worry." Katie reassured me.

"So, what happened?"

"I don't know exactly what happened for you to get so upset" she begun, "Dr. Short doesn't discuss the content of patients therapy sessions with us unless it has a direct impact on their care."

I nodded along, it was nice to know that not everyone was being made privy to my personal information, but if they didn't know why I had done what I had, then what did they know? What did people think I had done?

"When you became upset, you broke the coffee table in the therapy room and was threatening to hurt yourself with some of the wood that had broken off." The nurse continued.

I looked down at my body, had I hurt myself? Nothing was hurting, I just felt groggy from the medication. I was back to wearing a loose hospital gown though which was disappointing, but at least made it easier for me to see whether or not I had acted out on my threats.

Katie appeared to notice that I was inspecting myself, "You didn't do anything. We were able to intervene before you could."

"So, how did I end up in here?" I asked.

"Unfortunately, we were not able to calm you down. We tried everything we could think of, but you weren't there anymore. Not like you are now. You wouldn't respond to any of us or look at any of us and you wouldn't stop fighting back against the restraint you had been put in to prevent you from harming yourself. So, we had to use sedation after a while as nothing else was working and Dr. Short suggested that you be brought to the seclusion room afterwards to recover."

"Why here and not in my bedroom though?" I queried.

"You were in your bedroom last time because the seclusion rooms were occupied by other patients, and it wasn't safe for them to leave yet. As a seclusion room was available this time, we decided it would be best for you to recover in here until we knew how you would be once you woke up." She paused before continuing, clearly unsure how to word what she wanted to say next. "We've been in this situation many times with you before, and up until recently, you haven't woken up from sedation knowing who you are or where you are. So, we weren't sure if you would or not this time."

As much as I didn't like it, I could understand what she was saying and why I had been brought here, but it felt like I had taken such a large step back from how far I had come.

"When can I come back out?" I questioned, hoping now that they could see I was okay, that the answer would be a positive one.

"You can't come out of seclusion until you are reviewed by Dr. Short, and she has deemed you safe to be returned to the ward." Katie recounted.

"So, can I see her then?" I pleaded, desperate to get out of this sparse room and to a more private toilet.

"I'm really sorry, Chrissie." Katie responded glumly, "Dr. Short isn't in today, it's the weekend."

"So, I have to stay here and wait?" I asked incredulously.

"I'm afraid so."

"What am I supposed to do whilst I'm in here? I'll go mad with boredom." I retorted, appreciating the irony of thinking about going mad, when I had learnt recently that I was clearly insane.

"You have to try and keep yourself as calm as you can for when Dr. Short comes back on Monday. That's the best thing you can do. I know it's boring but try to rest as much as possible. I can give you some Diazepam to help if you feel agitated and your support staff are outside here if you need them." She informed me.

"Can I have something to eat please?" I replied, defeated. I knew there was nothing more that I could do at this stage, other than wait and try not to lose my mind further.

"Of course, I'll get you some food now." With that she moved away from the vent and was gone.

I sat back down on the mattress and waited until another support worker arrived with a small tray of food. Mark's face appeared at the window and gestured for me to come over to the vent so that he could speak to me.

"We have some food for you here, you're only allowed finger foods I'm afraid." Mark said to me.

"Can you open the door so I can have it please?"

"Stand back for me, we will open up now." Mark shouted back.

I took a step back and heard the sound of keys entering locks and turning metal. It sounded like a fair few locks had to be opened to be able to open this door. The window of the door then swung open, like a small hatch opening, rather than the whole door itself and I saw Mark's long arms extending through the hole in the door to pass through a small rubber plate with sandwiches and crisps on it.

I received the plate and thanked him and before I could say anything else, the hatch was shut back up quickly and the sound of locks turning again.

"Once you've finished eating, give me a wave and you can pass the plate back to me." Mark called through the vent, and I nodded back to him.

I sat back down on my rubber mattress and began nibbling at the tuna and sweetcorn sandwiches I had just been provided with. I wonder if they knew that tuna was my favourite. It seemed like the kind of gesture that Nurse Katie would have done to try and make things a little more bearable.

I finished my food, passed the plate back to Mark through the hatch again and then settled down on the mattress. I laid myself down, got myself comfortable and decided that the best way to get through the next day or two would be to try and sleep through as much of it as possible.

35

I've no idea how much time had passed, whether it was day or night, or who was sat the other side of the door for most of it. I just laid on the mattress, not daring to move unless I had to get up to use the toilet or get something to eat or drink from the hatch. I didn't know how long I had been in seclusion for in total, but the boredom was beginning to eat away at me and there was only so much I was willing to let myself think about in relation to what I had recently learnt in my therapy sessions. It was almost starting to seem more beneficial for me to be sedated than not at present, at least then I didn't have to think about everything I'd been through and everything I'd done.

There was a sharp rap on the hatch door window, and I looked up to see Dr. Short staring back at me. I got myself up as quickly as I could and made my way over to the vent.

"Dr. Short!" I exclaimed, never having felt so relieved to see someone before in my life. "I'm so sorry!"

"There's no need for you to be sorry Chrissie." She reassured. Nothing I could see from her facial expression gave me the impression that she was upset or angry with me, which was a reprieve.

"Can I come out now?" I asked, my voice full of hope.

"We need to have a bit more of a discussion before we can decide if it is safe for you to return to the ward or not." She responded calmly.

"I've been doing everything I've asked" I promised her, pleading with my eyes, "I've just been laying here, I've not shouted or screamed, or anything, I swear."

"Let's go somewhere a bit better for us to have a proper conversation, shall we?" Dr. Short cut me off and gestured behind her to my support staff. "The staff are going to come over and open the door to let you out. There are some sofas that we can sit on out here for us to chat."

I nodded furiously, more than happy to be able to move from the rubber mattress to a rubber sofa.

"There will need to be two staff that stay in the room with us whilst we are discussing though Chrissie" she continued, "for safety."

I nodded again, at this point I didn't care who was around or who listened to us, I just needed out of this room.

"Stand back please" she commanded.

As soon as I stepped back, the noise of the metal keys turning began, taking longer than it had for the hatch alone. I began counting, there must have been at least nine or ten different locks that they were having to open to let me out.

The door swung open, and Mark was standing beside it. Dr. Short was sat on one of the sofas one side of the room and Nurse Katie was sat on the other. The middle sofa was empty and Dr. Short gestured for me to sit down on it, which I did. Mark remained stood where he was, by the open door, which he made no attempt to close yet.

I took a quick glimpse around the other parts of the room that I had not been able to see from inside the seclusion room. Either side of the door were television screens behind Perspex, showing the viewpoints of both of the cameras inside the room. That must be how they were able to keep watch over me without constantly having to look through the window.

Other than the sofas we were sat on, there was no other furniture in the room. Behind the sofa that Dr. Short was sitting on however, a large mural appeared to have been painted. A large, beautiful abstract scene that instantly drew my attention to it.

"Can you remember what brought you into seclusion Chrissie?" Dr. Short asked me, interrupting my steady gaze on the artwork behind her.

"I remember our therapy session" I replied, before looking over at Katie who gave me a reassuring smile. "I don't remember the incident that happened, but Nurse Katie told me about it."

"I see" she acknowledged, "and can you remember everything we discussed in our last session?"

I nodded, feeling the tears beginning to burn my eyes again. I still didn't feel certain as to whether what Dr. Short was telling me was the truth or not. She didn't seem to be lying, but maybe Tim had managed to hide everything from the police to cover his tracks. He was such a clever man, and he needed to do what he could to protect Sam. I couldn't admit those thoughts to Dr. Short though, she clearly wanted me to be accepting of the information she had told me.

"How do you feel about that session?" She probed further.

"I'm sad about it." I admitted, unclear what the correct answer would be to give to her, but picking my words carefully to ensure that I didn't say anything that might prevent me from being able to go back to the ward. "I didn't want to believe it, I really didn't. But I know that not everything I remember is true, so I know that what you've said to me is probably right."

She gave pause and bowed her head slightly. "You have been through some significant trauma Chrissie, and you're mind has to deal with it, in any way that it can. Sometimes, that results in us forging false memories or blacking out things that have happened to us."

"Is that why I can't remember what happened when I became upset?" I asked.

"You experienced what we call an episode of dissociation." She stated rationally. "When you dissociate, you are not necessarily aware of your actions or what is happening around you. We can't say for sure what you were feeling or thinking at that time, but you were not able to communicate with us and didn't appear to be responding to anything we were saying to you."

"Have I done that before?"

"Many times." She nodded. "But the difference this time, is that you are starting to have more consciousness around what is causing them and your feelings leading up to these episodes, which shows marked improvement in your mental health."

"So, that's a good thing?" I inquired, not sure that it sounded particularly good.

"It is" she agreed.

"But then why did I end up in seclusion?"

"Because although the triggers are becoming identifiable, the dissociative episodes are still not being fully managed and until we can manage these in a safer manner, we may still need to resort to sedation and close monitoring."

"So, what's next?"

"Well, that is very much up to you. Do you feel safe enough to return to the ward?"

"I do, I really do." I implored.

"Then we will let you go back to the unit, with two supporting staff members." She agreed. "Your belongings are still in your room at the moment, and I don't see any need in removing them at present if you feel safe to be around them." I nodded in appreciation, desperate to get back to my room.

"Shall we head back then together?" Katie asked me, as she stood up from the sofa.

"Yes please"

"I will meet with you in a few days to continue with our therapy sessions." Dr. Short informed me as she also got up to leave.

I followed Katie and Mark out of the seclusion unit and down a series of corridors, back to the familiar surroundings of the ward. I never thought I would be so relieved to be back here. I could smell something delicious, wafting over from the kitchen hatch. Woman one and woman two were already sat at one of the tables eating together and Little, Large and Steph were stood lined up, waiting to get their food.

I joined the queue behind Steph, noticing my belly was rumbling. I hadn't been allowed any hot food so the sight of steak and kidney pie with boiled potatoes and gravy was a welcome sight. By the time I had received my food, which seemed to be exceptionally piled high on my plate, the only seat available was next to Steph, so I went to join her.

"How was seclusion" she asked me, sounding the most lucid I had ever heard her sound.

"Horrible" I replied through mouthfuls of pie.

She gave a knowing smile, "Rebecca is still there; she hasn't come back since she went before you went in." She informed me.

I noticed Steph appeared to only have one staff member with her, she must have been feeling better over the last couple of days. She appeared to notice me looking. "I'm down to one-to-one observations now" she confirmed.

"Well done, Steph" I applauded, "are you feeling better?"

"I'm not sure better is the right word" she laughed, "maybe more grounded."

"That's a good way to put it actually" I agreed.

We finished off our food and Steph informed me that she was off for a therapy session, so she left the ward with her member of staff. I sat down on one of the sofas where Little and Large had stationed themselves and decided to enjoy some television time after having such a long period of silence in the seclusion room.

"Steph seems better" I stated to Little and Large sat opposite me. Large gave me a smile and Little nodded.

"For now," Little stated bleakly.

"Why do you say it like that?" I asked curiously.

"Steph has been here a long time." Large confided, "she has a lot of ups and downs."

"She's better off when she's mental though". Little retorted and Large just gave her a telling look.

"What do you mean?" I questioned.

"I'm not sure this is the most appropriate topic of conversation" Mark interjected, who had sat down beside me as one of my support staff.

"I would rather be insane than be aware of what she has been through" Little continued, ignoring Mark completely.

Katie was sat on the other sofa. "Come on now ladies, you wouldn't want to be spoken about when you aren't here would you?" She reasoned, but again this was ignored by Little.

"Do you know what happened to her?" She asked me, and I shook my head.

"You shouldn't know either!" Katie retorted, clearly not impressed with the way in which the conversation was headed, but powerless at this point to stop it.

"My cousin told me when she came to visit. It was all over the news it was." Little continued and Large nodded along glumly.

"I really think we should change the subject" Mark interrupted, but again the flow of conversation continued. Katie tried to encourage me to go to my room with them, but I was entranced now, I needed to know.

"She burnt her whole house down." Little carried on, "Was having voices in her head telling her the devil was going to come for her and her family and the only way to stop it was to burn down the house, so she did it."

"Enough now!" Katie demanded, standing up from the sofa and approaching Little and Large. "Do you want me to tell Dr. Short what you have been discussing today?"

Large began to apologise, but Little wasn't finished yet. She peered round at me from behind Katies slender frame that was now blocking her view. "She wanted to save her family, thought that was what she had to do...." She paused for dramatic effect.

"Right to your room now before I stop your leave this afternoon." Katie shouted, becoming angered by the lack of respect she was currently being shown.

Little got up from the sofa, but Large stayed seated. She saluted at Katie before beginning to walk down the corridor towards her bedroom. She was almost out of view, before she turned around, looked back at me and stated, "Poor girl didn't know her husband and two kids were still in the house when she set it alight though."

36

"How have the last few days been for you?" Dr. Short asked me casually. We were back in the therapy room, sans coffee table, which stood out like a gaping void between us.

"Okay, I think." I replied honestly. "I've kept my head down, been thinking about things a lot, and just trying to keep myself grounded."

"Grounded?" Dr. Short let out a small chuckle. "You've been talking to some of the other patients haven't you."

"I have" I admitted, "but the term really resonated with me."

"It's good to be able to find phrases to how we are feeling and how we want to feel" she agreed. "So, I think it's time that we spoke about the day you came here."

I knew it was going to come up at some point, and sadly, I believed that over the last few weeks all of my memories had come trickling back to me, bit by bit. I could remember every detail of what I had done and why I had done it, and none of it had been what I had thought had occurred. It was amazing what tricks your own mind can play on you, but also it feels like a bit of a relief that there was unlikely to be any further surprises for me coming from Dr. Short.

"I think I'm ready to just lay all my cards out on the table now." I stated.

"Once we have fully discussed everything, and we know exactly what happened and why, the real work can begin in your mental health recovery." She replied, reassuringly. "Everything you have done so far has been the hardest part. The acceptance of what has happened, reliving awful memories. It is only once we can accept these things, that we can start to heal from them."

I knew she was right. She hadn't steered me wrong so far, but I also knew today's session was going to be a painful one. I just hoped I didn't have any more blackouts or dissociate again.

"Ok, so where do we start?" I queried, bracing myself for the conversation ahead.

"Maybe we should start with your mother." She stated gently.

Here we go. The death I was most dreading discussing. The one that had started it all off and the one out of all of them, that I most regretted. I took a deep breath, closed my eyes, so as not to have to see Dr. Shorts facial expressions as I explained to her what I had done, and began.

"Mum had been ill for a long time. She had end stage lung cancer. She was so unwell, and I was her main carer. She never wanted any carers to come and help her and she relied completely on me. I was looking after her day and night for years." I paused, taking a small peep out of the corner of my eye to gauge her reaction, but her face was expressionless.

"I never felt like I was able to have a life of my own. Most daughters get to grow up, go off to college or university, get a job, find love....." I stopped for a moment, realising that all the things I had wanted to do once she had gone, I had prevented even further by my own actions. "She couldn't do anything for herself. I had to wash her, cook for her, feed her, clean the house for her. It was more than a full-time job and it just didn't seem fair."

"Why didn't you ask anyone for help?" Dr. Short interrupted softly.

"Mum was very anti-social. She didn't want anyone else around or for anyone to know how ill she was. So, I just had to keep doing everything for her. Until one day, I just had enough."

"What happened?" She implored.

"We had an argument. She could barely breathe, could barely speak most of the time, but when she could, it was always to ask me to do things for her. I just snapped; I couldn't carry on any further, but not only that, I couldn't stand watching her living like that anymore. I thought I was helping her."

"Helping her?" Dr. Short questioned.

"By putting her out of her misery, and mine. When it came to medication time and she needed her insulin injection, instead of turning the dial to the correct number of units, I just turned it all the way to the end and gave her the whole lot."

I dared to peek at her reaction again, but she still appeared calm. As if I was having the most normal mundane conversation with her. Although, considering what Little had told me about what had happened to Steph, I bet she was used to hearing all sorts of confessions from people. I wonder if she ever had trouble sleeping at night.

"Did you know that would kill her?" She asked.

"I wasn't sure, but I thought that it might. She had always told me growing up about the dangers of playing with her needles, so I had an idea that an overdose could cause some damage."

"Then what did you do? After she had passed?" Dr. Short probed further.

"Nothing" I stated simply. "I didn't do anything. I just shut her bedroom door and never went back in the room again.

"Did you tell anyone what had happened?"

"No, I just kept trying to pretend like everything was normal and that worked for a few days, but then the smell started...." I trailed off, remembering vividly how awful the scent had been seeping through the bedroom door, the way there was no hiding from it, no candles or air fresheners helping to cover the smell. The small bungalow we lived in, quickly becoming infested by the odour.

"How long was her body there before she was found Chrissie?"

"I'm not sure exactly, so much happened during that time frame, but maybe a few weeks." I guessed, not really wanting to try and work out the answer.

"So, how was she found then? Who found her body?" She continued to question.

Knowing this was the final piece of the puzzle, the final death to discuss, the last hurrah if you will. I looked up, her eyes staring deep into mine, and I told her. "It was Rachel."

37

"So, who was Rachel?" Dr. Short asked me, "and how did she find your mother?"

"Rachel was my mums' social worker." I continued, feeling like I was on a roll now, ready to get the last of the events off my chest, to begin healing. "She was a family social worker who used to check in on us to make sure that Mum was getting the right care, and that I was okay."

"How often was Rachel checking in?" Dr. Short queried.

"She mostly used to check in by phone, she would only visit the house if we needed her for something. As Mum got sicker, it got harder for her to speak to her on the phone so she would just speak to me."

"If she wasn't coming to the house regularly, then why did she come to visit at the time that she did?"

"I guess I had been avoiding her. After what I had done, I was so scared that she would know something was wrong just by the tone of my voice over the phone, so I just stopped answering her calls." I replied.

"And by not answering her calls, that alerted her to there being a problem and therefore resulting in her coming to visit the house." Dr. Short finished for me.

I nodded. "When she knocked on the front door, I immediately knew it wasn't going to be good. At that point, I wasn't sure if it was going to be the police at the door or not, I had become so paranoid that I was going to get caught that every time I heard a siren, a phone call or a knock at the door, I just panicked."

"Did you answer the door?" She asked.

"I crept up to the door as quietly as I could and had a look through the spyhole. When I saw that it was Rachel I was so relieved, I thought for sure that it was going to be the police coming to arrest me. I think my relief must have clouded my judgement because I just opened the door and let her in without thinking about it."

"And then what happened?"

"She knew something was wrong as soon as the door opened. In fact, I think she may have known before I even opened the door, because the bungalow was barely containing the smell anymore." I mused.

"Did she say anything to you?" Dr. Short appeared genuinely curious, she was leant forward in her seat, hanging on to my every word as I told her the story.

"She didn't have to. She asked to see Mum, said that she hadn't checked in for a while and just wanted to make sure we didn't need anything, but she was struggling with the smell I could tell. She looked like she was going to be sick. I led her into the living room, but I knew that I was going to have to kill her. I liked Rachel, she had always been so helpful, but there was just no other option at that point."

"Why did you feel there weren't any other options?" She interjected. "Did you not feel you could have come clean at that point? Maybe ask for help."

"How could I? I would have been locked up for the rest of my life." I exclaimed. I took a moment to reflect on the outcome after all, realising that I probably was going to be locked up for a long time now and that realistically, Rachel didn't have to die, and the outcome would still have been the same.

I could feel the tears arriving again, why had I done all of this? I've hurt so many people, not just the people that I've killed, but all of their loved ones also. I have ruined so many lives by my actions. I felt like I was choking on silent tears. My body wracked with emotion, as I slowly started to come to terms with everything I had done and how no matter how much I tried to justify it, none of it was for the greater good in the end. Every situation could have been handled differently; every outcome could have been better.

Dr. Short watched me intently. As if she could read my thoughts and knew exactly what I was thinking as the guilt swept over me.

"Do you know what happened to Rachel?" she asked me after a period of time.

I looked up at her, still feeling consumed by my grief and guilt. "She died, didn't she?" I spluttered through my tears.

"Did you see her die Chrissie?" She questioned.

"I didn't get the chance, everything happened to fast." I replied stoically. "Within seconds of me plunging that needle into her, the sirens came. I don't know how they knew she was there, or what had happened to get them there so quickly, but I just remember being pulled off of her body by two police officers and being thrown into the back of a police van."

Dr. Short had begun scribbling in her notepad again, waiting for me to finish speaking before she spoke again. "You never knew what happened after you were arrested then?"

"What do you mean?" I asked confused.

"Rachel didn't die Chrissie. She was very unwell for quite a while, was in ITU in a coma for two months. But she received treatment in time, and she is now alive and well and back home with her family."

I felt some relief at this information. At least that was one less death I was responsible for, despite all the hardship I had caused Rachel, at least I hadn't ended her life.

"Rachel had called the police for back-up before she knocked on the door. You were right, she probably could tell from the smell." Dr. Short continued on, watching me intently as she filled me in on the last details of what had turned out to be my own personal horror story, in which I was the monster. "The police had already had some connections with you for other deaths, so a call like that would raise the alarm. They sent a unit out immediately, sadly Rachel didn't follow their advice to wait for their arrival before knocking on the door. She told the officers afterwards that she was worried that the police would scare you and she thought she would be able to speak to you because you knew each other."

I felt a lump stick in my throat. She had risked her own life and gone against the police advice, because she knew me. She didn't think I was capable of what I was doing, she must not have thought that I would have hurt her, and I let her down.

"Do I go to prison now?" I whispered hoarsely through my tears. "Now that I have confessed everything to you?"

Dr. Short looked at me, eyes wide, her face an expression of empathy and compassion.

"Chrissie, everything that you have done, has been because you have not been of sound mind. Everything you have suffered in your childhood, all the trauma you experienced from the abuse from your father, to having to care for your mother and how isolating that had become for you, has shaped your mental health and led to your current diagnosis."

"But I still did these things, regardless of whether or not I was well." I shouted, "I still deserve to suffer! I still have to pay!"

"You may not be in prison Chrissie, but that doesn't mean that you have gotten away with anything. The courts ruled that you were mentally unwell at the time of your crimes, to which I concur. That is why you are now under Section indefinitely, in this hospital, under my care."

"Indefinitely? So, I can never leave?" I asked, not sure if I felt that I would ever deserve to leave.

"Not necessarily, when and if you are free to leave, will depend on your mental health. We have a long way to go on your journey of recovery and we have only just begun to scratch the surface. You will be remaining here, likely for the foreseeable future, where you will have extensive therapies and treatments, until you are well and able enough to return to society." She explained. "And if we do reach that point, there are still a lot of other legal hoops to jump through, which could result in some time needing to be spent in prison or you may be able to return to the community, but whichever way, this is not something that we are anywhere near ready to discuss. The work begins now."

"The work begins now." I parroted, not surprised by the outcome, but also feeling grateful that at least someone was willing to take a bet on me, to try and help me to get better, to become a better person.

"Dr. Short?" She looked at up at me again from her notepad. "Thank you for helping me and for believing in me, I really do want to get better."

"I know you do Chrissie, and I hope that in time, we will get you there. But whilst we are working towards that goal, maybe you should start calling me by my first name."

I felt like I had finally found some sense of comfort. Like I was getting ready to start a new chapter in my life, get used to the new norm and really begin to work towards mental health recovery and maybe someday in the future, doing something to help right some of the wrongs I had done. The session appeared to be ending for now and I got up from the chair, ready to return back to the ward, to the mundane routines I had begun to establish there and as I walked out the door, I turned back briefly just to say,

"Thank you, Alison."

The End.

Printed in Great Britain
by Amazon